UNRAVELED

MIA KAYLA

MAM BOOKS LLC

UNRAVELED

Visit my website at www.authormiakayla.com

Cover Designer: Sommer Stein, Perfect Pair Creative

www.perfectpearcreative.com

Cover Photography: © 2017 Wander Aguilar

Developmental Editor: Gwen Hayes, Fresh Eyes Critique

http://www.fresheyescritique.com/

Copy Editor: Megan Hand www.meganhandwrites.com

Proofreader: Mitzi Carroll https://www.facebook.com/MitziCarrollEditor

Proofreader: Marisa Nichols https://www.facebook.com/alatedbibliophile

ISBN: 978-0-9996757-0-0

To my Mommy. Now as a mom myself, I understand how self sacrificing but self fulfilling motherhood is. So thank you for all that you did and continue to do and thank you for spoiling my kids every single day.

Love you Mama.

CHAPTER 1

THE CLOCK FLASHED ten p.m. on the stand beside me.

One tequila. Two tequila. Three.

One wiener. Two wiener. Three.

10:01 and all I could think of at that moment was ... six more minutes. Six more minutes until he came inside me, and we were done. Done until the next time. Well, next Saturday night, just like clockwork.

Darkness surrounded us in our two-bedroom penthouse in the poshest area of downtown Rosendell, Michigan. The only light coming in through the window was from the city skyscrapers outside, the gleam highlighting the movement of his body against mine.

The sweat of his skin was slick against mine. The scent of sex permeated the air.

Sex was always the same—missionary style on our 1200-thread count sateen sheets, with him pumping into me. I closed my eyes and tried to let the sensations wash over my body. For once, I wished he'd call me sexy, talk dirty ... do anything to make me feel as though this wasn't a job that I was expected to perform.

I wanted to feel that connection—like we used to have—and not feel like we'd turned into an old married couple when we were only in our early twenties. Eight years together wasn't a lifetime. Being in a relationship shouldn't seem like a death sentence.

Sadness engulfed me while we were sharing the most intimate moment between two people. I forced down the loneliness before tears could slip down my cheeks.

I knew sex was coming tonight. After dinner, he'd made me a dirty martini. And it was Saturday. For as long as I could remember, he was the horniest at the end of the work week. Like a gourmet meal at a fancy restaurant, Saturday night seduction started with a martini, then small talk, ending with sex as dessert. I yearned for him to bend me over the couch first and then hand me a martini.

At 10:04, his movements turned erratic. He pumped into me faster. His chest heaved in exhaustion. A thin sheen of sweat covered his brow. My leg was cramping, yet I didn't care because I told myself for the millionth time—trying to convince myself—that he loved me. He still loved me. This was what couples in love did. And we were in love. This was making love.

So, why did I feel nothing?

My cheek fell to the side, and I stared at the city through our floor-to-ceiling windows because we had stopped looking at each other during sex a long time ago. Stopped talking after sex. Stopped cuddling after sex. Just stopped.

He didn't whisper sweet nothings in my ear that would send a wave of shivers up my neck, nor did he make me feel wanted for anything other than someone to get him off. The lump in the back of my throat became the size of a golf ball, the same way it had yesterday, and the days and months before when I'd thought of how we'd morphed into some fifties sitcom couple. We might as well have two twin beds in our bedroom.

"I love you," I whispered, all my pent-up emotion pouring out into those three powerful words.

Because I did. *I do.*

I loved him.

He was the only man I'd ever been with. The only man I'd ever known.

He didn't hear me, caught up in his own moment of getting off, so I said it again, louder this time. "I love you so much."

"Oh, baby, I love you, too." His words had once meant so much, but the meaning had dwindled over time.

He groaned, then he flipped me over, propping me on top of him. My dark brown hair cascaded over my slender shoulders. He'd said the words I wanted to hear, but I questioned whether he'd meant them. Why did I feel such distance between us even when we were in the same room?

His eyes were clenched shut. I wanted to see the spark of fire in his blue irises. Lock my brown ones with his. Feel the connection between us.

Trying something different, I reached for the ends of his light locks, tugging hard, but he pulled my hands down and moved my hips along his shaft.

I shifted until a sensation rubbed against my sensitive nub. I threw back my head as my hands pressed into his chest and I moved against him, my body beginning to let go.

"Oh, yeah. Baby, you feel so good. Does it feel good?"

"Yes," I sighed. I lifted my head, wishing, wanting, waiting for ecstasy, then finally a sliver of sensation spread down my legs.

When he gripped my hips tighter and shifted me, that slightest connection to an orgasm disappeared.

"Wait," I begged as I readjusted myself. The deep-rooted pinch under my belly tingled. Something I hadn't felt in a very long time. "Please." I took his hands in mine and urged him to let me lead the way for once.

And before I knew it, he stilled inside me and a loud moan escaped his mouth.

Done. Jilted. Robbed.

My body rolled off his. I turned my head, so he couldn't read my face, and the first tear pushed down my cheek.

He discarded the condom in a tissue on the side table then kissed the back of my neck.

I glanced at the clock.

10:07.

My whole body tensed, and I exhaled, half-frustration and half-relief that it was over. I had a week until we'd do it again.

"That was amazing, baby."

"Yes." *Amazing for you.*

10:08, just like a clock, he flipped over, conked out, and I stared at the ceiling, feeling empty inside as the thought pushed to the surface ... *There has to be more to my life than this.*

━━

Careful not to wake him, I slipped out of bed, threw on my robe, and darted toward the kitchen. I knew he had to go into the office today. Being a top investment banker for the largest private equity firm in the nation, he worked almost every weekend.

He said he'd take the weekends off, but so far, he hadn't.

What had gotten Roland to greatness was his drive for work and his need to always have the best and be the best.

I had been getting up earlier for the past few years, cooking him a full breakfast almost every day. Growing up in a family where my mother cooked constantly, I found myself believing that a good breakfast had the power to push the day in the right direction.

Reaching in the overhead cabinet, I pulled down the pancake mix, bowls, and sugar. When I heard the shower running, I moved faster, darting to the fridge to get out the eggs and milk.

I was about done—our plates and meal set on the table—when Roland strolled into the kitchen.

"Good morning," I said in my singsong voice.

Today was a new day. He had promised we'd go to that new Italian restaurant tonight, and I was more than a little excited for date night. We were double dating with my sister. I couldn't remember the last time we'd gone on a date that didn't consist of a business meeting with other investment partners and me on Roland's arm as his eye candy.

"Good morning," he replied, methodical and robotic, proceeding to the door as usual to pick up the newspaper.

He never looks at me anymore.

Roland strutted to the table in an Armani suit, handsome and professional in a 6'1" lean package.

In high school, where we'd met, he'd been a scrawny teenager with the best hair. And I had always been petite and dainty with stick straight dark brown hair.

But by our freshman year in college, he had grown into his skin nicely, working out constantly and running marathons. He was handsome, beautiful, and kind, and any girl would be lucky to have him.

I placed his favorite mug on the table and sat right next

to him. After he opened his *Wall Street Journal,* he picked up his mug. His coffee was made just how he liked it. Black. No cream. Two sugars.

I cooked for him and, in return, he folded and put my laundry away. Our relationship was oddly even regarding house chores, and from the outside looking in, we were the perfect couple.

I stilled. *No, we* are *the perfect couple.*

I poured the syrup over his pancakes and watched him eat and read his paper like he did every morning. We hadn't said anything to each other except, "Good morning," and my stomach dropped because I realized, lately, that had been the norm between us. Our everyday routine included pancakes, me watching him read his paper and not talking. I blinked, letting my reality seep in.

After five minutes of his head in the paper, I pushed out of my chair, sat on his lap, and wrapped my slim but strong arms around his neck. I needed to break the cycle. "I can't wait for tonight. I've only heard good things about Italia Clement. Your work schedule has been crazier than ever."

I leaned in closer, getting a whiff of his Creed cologne, a bottle of heaven for the insignificant price of five hundred dollars.

He leaned back against the chair, his features tightening, the stress of work evident on his face. "I know. I'm just trying to establish myself securely at the firm. I've been stressed out, and you know this is important to me."

I nodded because I knew. Inside, I truly knew he needed to succeed, do well in his job. But where did that leave me? Or, more importantly, us?

"Yes," I sighed. "I know."

Still, I couldn't help how I felt about our relationship

lately. That we were drifting apart, and I didn't know how to salvage us because it seemed as though our relationship had been in this lull for a while. A long while.

"You love me, right?" I asked sweetly, peering down at him, needing him to say it, mean it, needing to believe it. "Yes, Angie. Of course." His tone was dismissive.

"Say it, then." I needed him to say it in full light, not in the heat of the moment.

"I love you, Angelica Armstrong." He took one brief second to look at me, but then his eyes flicker to his paper.

He's distracted.

I tried to let those words wash over me, like a tidal wave, but there was no passion behind his voice, no light in his eyes. I swallowed back the lump in my throat and closed the gap between us, capturing his lips with mine. God, I needed more. We used to have electricity.

I moved to straddle him, trying something new as my kisses intensified. My robe exposed my bare breasts, and I didn't readjust myself. I wanted him now, to live in this moment.

A pure desperation tore through my soul. I wanted him to take full advantage of me. I wanted to have hot, wild sex in the open, in the daylight, not on our bed on a Saturday night.

When his breathing was labored, my hands moved to his waist to undo his belt.

Then he stilled, pulling back, and held my hands. "I'm going to be late for work if you start that."

"That was the point," I said in a silky tone.

"We can't. I need to be focused today." His tone leaked annoyance. He pecked me one last time and disentangled my fingers from his.

His words doused the flame inside of me with cold water, and all my muscles tensed. My jaw tightened, and I tried to hide the hurt behind my composed demeanor. "Sometimes I wish you'd focus on me," I said, surprised that I let those words slip out.

His look was that of my mother, serious, meaning business, and I didn't appreciate it. "I'll focus on you tonight at Italia."

"But I want you." I didn't mean for my voice to sound whiny, but it did.

He forced my robe shut and moved me off him. "And you have me." He nodded toward my food before ducking his head back into the *Wall Street Journal*. "Eat your breakfast, Angie, it's getting cold."

I bit my tongue before something crazy flew out and caused a full-blown argument. Picking up my plate and my mug, I proceeded to our bedroom. He wasn't going to talk to me anyway, not when he had his boring business news in front of him.

"Are you eating in the bedroom?"

"Yes," I said curtly, but you could still hear the hurt behind that one word.

He didn't seem fazed, only saying, "Uh ... Don't get crumbs on the bed, Angelica. I read an article on bed bugs the other day."

I gritted my teeth before I said something I'd regret. I never lost my temper, and I wasn't going to start now. That was something I prided myself in, something my own mother had instilled in me—composure.

At our bedroom doorway, I reminded him, "Our reservations with Christene are at eight. Please don't be late, Roland." Then I shut the door behind me, jumped into bed and grabbed my half-eaten pancake. As if flipping him the middle finger, I ate it with my hands, getting crumbs on the bed on purpose.

My hair dryer blew on high as I held my round brush above my head in our oversized bathroom. I took in my heart-shaped face in the mirror. My smooth, pale skin glowed with a rose flush on my cheek bones.

The noise from the hair dryer almost drowned out my phone ringing on the counter. One look at Christene's goofy face—cross-eyed and sticking out her tongue—had me smiling. Though I was the younger sister by only a few years, I acted like the older one.

After I switched off my dryer and placed it on the marble countertop, I reached for my cell.

"Angieeeeeee," she squealed in her typical greeting. "What time is dinner again?"

I wondered how Tene could remember every workday appointment but failed to keep her social calendar organized. All she had to do was scroll up on our texts on her phone to see what time I'd made the reservations.

"Eight." I pulled a strand of hair out of my eyes, staring at my brown-eyed reflection in the mirror, my dark locks cascading down my back. "Brad's still going tonight, right? I included him in the head count."

"Uh, well, it's Tim now."

"Who's Tim?"

"This guy I met at a bar last night." She laughed.

"Tene." I heard the scolding tone of my mother in my voice, and I bit it back. "Okay, sorry. As long as you're being safe, I shouldn't even care. You are, right? Being safe, I mean."

"Safe and sound. Nothing is popping out down there anytime soon."

My sister, though she was a party animal, was a business woman at her core. That's why my father trusted her with his company: Armstrong Real Estate Corporation. Our family owned more than half the real estate in Rosendell and the neighboring towns.

My sister had taken a more active role a year ago when our father had become ill. She was cutthroat and a no bullshit type of business woman. Our tenants knew she wasn't a pushover, and my father knew she could handle the business just fine. Now it was my turn to step up to the plate, and since I was finally done with my master's degree, I was more than ready to contribute to the family—finally.

"That's good." I pulled the cell closer to my ear, gripping it tightly. "I can't wait to see you tonight. It's been tense with Roland lately, and I think a double date would be good. I purposely invited you, so he wouldn't cancel."

"Okay, I won't cancel, then." Christene's voice tinged with humor. "I was going to ask you to go to Allswell tonight after dinner."

"Allswell?"

"Yes, hello! The former Clyde's Bar and Restaurant. I filled that space a couple months ago."

I furrowed my brow. "I thought our new tenant owned a restaurant."

"Restaurant by day, hopping club by the weekend. There's a ton of press on these owners and their clubs and restaurants nationwide. They opened last week, and it's the hottest spot in Rosendell right now."

My eyebrows pulled together. No wonder she was able

to jack up the rent, and the tenant was able to afford it. My father had been singing her praises for weeks at filling that space. I hoped someday I'd be able to contribute to my family in the same way.

Glancing at my half-done hair in the mirror brought me back to the present. "Roland's not the clubbing type. Please, Christene. We need this." Roland had been so focused on work, he needed a break. He needed a night out, other than dinner with his clients. And selfishly, I wished for a real date with my boyfriend.

"Okay, sounds good." Her tone was tinged with disappointment. "But maybe you and Roland would want to head to Allswell right after?"

I laughed. "I doubt it." My Roland at a club? If the place wasn't serving caviar and champagne, he wasn't a fan.

I glanced back at my reflection in the mirror, seeing a hopefulness in my eyes. A dinner date with two of my favorite people. Maybe tonight was the night he'd try something different. "I'll ask him."

After getting ready, I plopped down on our leather couch in the living room and watched TV. When a couple of hours had passed, I tapped my finger on my chin, staring at the phone resting in the middle of our circular glass coffee table. My feet pushed against the hand-knotted Persian Rug that Roland had ordered from Iran.

I had called him, yet nothing. I'd left a voicemail twice, but nothing.

He was late.

Patience was a virtue, but my patience for Roland's tardiness flew out the door about thirty minutes ago. Minutes ticked by and I wrung my hands together, wishing his neck was in between them.

It was seven-thirty. Our reservations were for eight, and

Roland had said he'd be back home at seven, so we'd make it to the restaurant in time. It had taken months to get this reservation. Italia Clement's management didn't care what my last name was. They occupied one of the few properties that we *didn't* own, so I didn't have any clout.

"Damn it, Roland." I stood and picked up the phone again, waiting for his voicemail to beep. "Roland, this is my third message. Please call your girlfriend back." My tone was calm, cool, and collected, opposite the burning ball of anger inside of me.

I ended the call quickly as my face burned bright and glanced at the clock again as I'd done just seconds ago.

In ten minutes, I was leaving with or without him.

Suddenly, my phone pinged with a text. Hope bloomed in my chest, but then I read his text, and that hope was obliterated like a bomb blowing up in my face.

I should've known better.

Sorry, I'm tied up at work.
Don't be mad.
Please, I'll make it up to you.

I'd heard that excuse before. Many times before. Like a broken record.

I squeezed the phone hard enough that the edges caused an indentation on my skin.

Anger was a crazy emotion. It could consume me and cripple me into someone I didn't like to be. As I slumped against the wall and read his text again, the thought of bleaching all his ties crossed my mind. Or even better yet ... throwing out his very expensive Edward Green leather shoes that had cost thousands. Though I'd never do it, the thought did float to the surface.

I huffed. It didn't matter anyway; I bet he'd just buy himself three more pairs.

If I didn't know him as well as I did, I would have thought that he was having late-night affairs. But since I'd met Roland sophomore year in high school, I knew that he was forever married to excelling in school and work and winning. It was his gasoline. His drive to be the best was what kept him alive, ticking, and well.

So why did I feel so much resentment?

I didn't respond as I stared at my phone, and then I did something unlike me. I texted Tene and did the unthinkable.

Guess who canceled?
I'm eating a quick dinner here.
Meet you at Allswell?

It didn't take long for her to text me right back.

Oh Angie, you just made my night!
I'm canceling with Tim. Meet me at the restaurant.
We're having dinner, baby. You're my date, and dinner is
on me.

My insides lightened, and a smile surfaced on my face. I bit at my thumbnail and peered down at my black tapered pants and cream, button-down silk shirt. I didn't have anything even remotely club appropriate, so I texted her again, and she promised to bring me something.

Most likely, my night would end up with me taking care of her or catching a cab home while she made out with some random dude, but I shrugged. Because that was more exciting than waiting around for Roland to come home and risk the possibility of me going crazy and destroying his wardrobe.

I glanced at my phone again, debating on texting him back, but thought better of it.

He wouldn't be thinking of me tonight, anyway, and I would try my hardest not to think about him.

CHAPTER 2

TENE THREW her arm around my shoulder and pulled me down the sidewalk to the bar. As we got closer, I realized a crowd had formed all the way down the block. There had never been a line when this place had been Clyde's. The new sign said Allswell.

My eyebrows pulled together, taking in the scene. Just a month ago, I'd been here to do an inspection as I was shadowing Tene. She had given Taylor, the last tenant, his deposit back, and she was showing me the ropes.

The building in front of me now—our building—had been transformed. The brown awning had been replaced with a classy lit-up sign in curvy letters against the building. Clyde's had been a jeans and T-shirt type of establishment, Allswell was not. Women in skimpy outfits, designer clothing that I was familiar with, and men in button-downs all waited their turn to get their IDs checked.

"Seriously Ang, you look smoking hot. I wonder how many guys will be hitting on you tonight." She flipped her highlighted locks over her shoulder. The color of our hair was identical, dark mahogany brown, but hers was lifted with the lighter burgundy tones of her smooth salon hair. Where my skin was naturally pale, hers was weekly-tanned. But no one could deny we were sisters. It was in our jawline and high cheek bones, which were our mother's, and the shape of our face and the big brown eyes that all belonged to Daddy.

"It's too bad Roland's not here to keep the men away." She playfully bumped her hip against mine. "When Roland's away, Angie will play."

Her chipper attitude broke through my sour mood, and a grin broke free on my face. Oh, how I needed a tall glass of wine inside the club. "Oh, I never asked you. What happened to Tim?"

During dinner, I'd vented about Roland while she listened, so I forgot to ask her about the guy who was supposed to be her date for the night.

She smirked and shrugged her shoulder. "I caught a bug. You know, the 'if I take you, you're going to ruin my game' bug."

I let out a carefree laugh.

The loud bass of the music boomed from inside as the crowd congregated, smoking and waiting by bouncers standing by the velvet rope.

Tene reached for my hand and ushered us all the way to the front. "I called the owner, but he didn't answer his phone." She shook her head, annoyed. "We own this joint. I'm serious. I'm not about to wait an hour to get in."

That was how she always felt—entitled. When we were younger, she exhibited the need to boss me around, take my toys, and be the first in line at every amusement ride at Disney. All because she'd been born first.

But ... she had also been the one to beat up the bully who used to pick on me because I had braces, lie to Mrs.

Conner about why I hadn't finished my project, and interview every guy I ever dated ... because she had been born first.

She had her quirks and faults, but she was my sister. And through the years, because of my family name and the money that went with it, I'd learned that, sometimes, family was all you could count on.

Tene reached for the tie holding her ponytail together and shook her long locks until they cascaded over her shoulders. Her hair lay right below her breasts, accenting her evenly spray-tanned skin.

A six-foot, dark-haired male eyed me, and then his sights flipped to her. She gave him her winning smile that made him smile back in response. He was a good-looking guy, lean with muscles that seemed like they wanted to break free of his fitted, too-tight T-shirt.

She leaned in, bending forward, showing off her perfect breasts, not at all adjusting herself when her tube top dipped a little.

"Hi, handsome," she cooed.

Oh, boy. This guy doesn't have a chance.

Her voice oozed everything sensual about a woman, sultry and sexy with an underlying ounce of sweetness. "My sister and I are on the guest list. Angelica and Christene Armstrong." She peeked at the clipboard in his hand. Of course, we weren't on the guest list. I doubted that Tene even knew there was a guest list, given that there had never been a guest list at the former bar. She could make anyone believe practically anything—the sky is brown and the earth is flat and brussel sprouts tasted like candy. Besides being born beautiful, she had been born a liar.

With his pointer finger, he scanned the list. When he peered up again, he shook his head. "Sorry, babe."

Her eyebrows shot up to the sky. "Let me take a peek," she said breathlessly. Close to him, she tiptoed and scanned the list.

His eyes drank her in. All of her. And I'd bet my next paycheck that he had a major hard-on. Men probably saluted with their dicks when she passed by.

I pushed down the jealousy that coursed through my veins as I wondered how it would be to always feel wanted. Every-damn-where you went. How crazy wonderful that would feel, to just walk into a room and be the envy of every girl and the object of every guy's affection.

I'd even take one guy's affection. My guy's affection.

I couldn't get the same reaction—naked, in front of my own boyfriend. I used to feel wanted and loved. That seemed like forever ago.

She perked up, her lip pouting as forced disappointment seeped out of her every pore. "I swore I called us in." She placed her hand on his bicep, lightly squeezing it. "Is there anything you can do?"

And then—she fluttered her eyelashes, which was almost the equivalent to dropping her panties, seeing as they produced the same effect.

Just as I expected, he peered at his counterpart wearing an earpiece. Tene took that opportunity to snuggle against him. "Why don't I buy you a drink inside? And if we can't get inside, I can't buy you that drink that you deserve." The sweetness in her voice was like molten chocolate.

She could've been an actress in her former life. I stared at the concrete to prevent a smile. He'd give in. They always did.

And as if on command, he uttered one low, "Yes." He reached to unclasp the velvet rope to let us slide in. "Sure, why not? I wouldn't want you pretty ladies waiting forever." Angling toward her, he said, "I get off at midnight. I'm Dax."

Tene smiled, but it was one that meant this guy had no chance in hell. "My name is Christene." She placed her hand in his and shook it lightly before reaching for mine and pulling me into the club. "Find me later," she called back.

Later?

She'd be with another guy by then.

The speakers were blaring some sort of techno music, just beats where I couldn't sing along, but the bass of the tune had my body shaking and not by choice. I preferred places where I could bounce on my seat and sing along to the lyrics. Allswell was not that place.

What had once been booths and circular tables was now reinvented with dark gray velvet booths that lined the perimeter of the room. Strobe lights illuminated the dark wood dance floor in the middle of the restaurant, high-lighting the people swaying seductively to the beat.

"Oh, my god. This place is totally amazing. It's crazy in here." I barely heard Tene and would've heard her less if she weren't already screaming into my ear. There was no way we could've held a conversation in the place.

A tall guy grabbed her from behind, and she exchanged words with him. I swore she knew everyone in our town. After she hugged him, she reached for my hand, forging us toward the bar, where everyone had congregated.

The place was jam packed with people, making my skin itch and me wishing for my couch, my PJs, and a tall glass of red wine.

I adjusted the spaghetti straps of my sister's teeny tiny tank top. I was a cup smaller than her full Cs, so I had no idea how she fit in the black sequined thing I had on as it pressed against my strapless bra.

The humidity caused a sheen of sweat to form behind my neck. I wasn't claustrophobic, but there were way too many people in here. Way more than what the approved legal capacity was.

I shook my head and told worry-wart-Angelica to stop.

The red fire Exits could be spotted at both ends of the room. I released a sigh of relief, thankful that Tene had the lights fixed when the tenant had moved in. I remembered my father mentioning something about the city inspection and our exit signs.

Once we were closer to the bar, she released me and pushed herself to the front to get us drinks. She raised her hand, and when the bartender turned around, I was shocked by an attraction so strong, I swore I stopped breathing. Stopped moving. Stopped thinking. Just stopped.

Wow. Just wow.

His eyes locked with mine. A deep, dark depthless color I couldn't distinguish drew me closer. His dark hair, almost jet black, shined against the strobe lights at the perfect angle.

His face was that of an angel, the planes of his cheekbones sharp but stunningly beautiful. His lips were full and luscious—and smirking.

He stopped making his drink mid-pour and drank me in. All of me. He scoured my face and then my body, as though in the dark room, there was a spotlight on me. And instantly, my body reacted. My nipples pebbled. My mouth went dry. And my insides heated to tamale-hot temperatures by just his one look alone. One look. If my body reacted to him with just one look, I wondered how I would react to his touch.

The moment the thought registered, I stiffened and forced the thought out of my head.

My sister snapped her fingers in front of his face and turned around to see that his focus was on me. Her smile was blinding, and she leaned in to whisper something in his ear. He peered up again and smiled a crooked smile. Not overly big, but just enough where the side of his mouth lifted.

When his gaze locked with mine again, his smile disappeared, and his face turned serious. An undeniable attraction surged between us, almost forcing me to take a step forward. His hands functioned with purpose, making drinks, but he would not tear his stare from my face. And I couldn't take mine off him, either. In those few seconds, it was as though we were the only two people in the room.

Through the darkness, he licked his lips. Heat pooled between my legs without my consent. I felt like he was picturing me naked in his bed, and he was having his way with me. I bit my bottom lip, feeling exposed and vulnerable at the idea of doing something forbidden.

I wiped my sweaty palms down Tene's tank top as his look turned dangerous, and all that yearning I'd been feeling for something more in my life rose to the surface.

For once in my life, I wanted to welcome this danger. I wanted to live on the edge.

After he handed Tene her drink, he whispered something to the other bartender and then surprised me by jumping over the bar.

I froze, wishing I hadn't welcomed danger mere seconds ago because danger was approaching. He stalked toward me, slow, seductive, and stealthy, like a cat. A really big one. He was almost predatory, and I felt frozen, yet I wanted to run in the other direction.

All thoughts, no talk and no action, I took a step away.

The closer he came, the more my palms began to sweat. His big-as-boulders shoulders blocked my view of Tene, so he was the only thing in my sight. I lifted my chin to take in the height of him, and something ignited deep in my belly—a feeling foreign, yet familiar. His face was ruggedly hot with sexy scruff forming on his cheeks, and a dimple deep in his chin.

But his eyes ... they were hypnotic. The color of steel, strength, and heat oozed out of them, and even if I wanted to, I couldn't take my gaze off him. His profile was strong and rigid, his skin a contrast to the darkness of his hair.

When he reached for my waist, I lost any sense of control, lost the sensation in my legs, my body, but mostly my mind. His grip was rough, but oddly it gave me a sense of protection.

He leaned into me, so close I could smell the mint on his lips, the masculine scent on his skin, and said, "Let's dance."

It was a command, not a question.

I blinked up at him. "I have a boyfriend."

His laugh was throaty and thick and oh-so-sexy. "Did I ask if you had a boyfriend?"

When he angled closer, I placed one hand lightly against his chest, given his proximity and how close we were, and given that I was already taken. He must have read the reluctance on my face because he uttered, "One dance."

With no other words spoken, he led us to the bass of the beats in the background. His hands moved to my slender hips, pulling me against him. Closer ... until he closed the gap between us and we were grinding on the dance floor.

My arms fell on his shoulders, and his hands tightened around my waist. Seconds turned into minutes. Minutes turned into ten, then fifteen. Songs changed, but we were still dancing, his hands on my body and our bodies in sync, and more intimately, our gaze never leaving each other's. I read lust, need, and want through his dark irises. And though we weren't talking, he might as well have been telling me what he wanted to do to me, to my body.

He felt amazing, he smelled amazing, and he looked ... edible. Too good to be this close.

When he turned me around and wrapped his hands around my stomach, pulling me into him, my body was on fire. This was bad. So bad. When his fingers fell right by my upper thigh, I stilled then moved away. This was no longer dancing. I'd let it go too far, and I wasn't letting it go any further.

I turned to walk away, but he grabbed my hand. Electricity surged at our connection. "Where are you going?"

My voice shook with guilt and grief and remorse. "Home."

He smiled his intoxicatingly beautiful smile. "I didn't catch your name," he yelled above the music.

I shook my head. He didn't need to know my name, and I didn't want to know his. It would've made our encounter more personal. I wanted my brief lapse in judgment to be between strangers.

"Well, I'm Cade." He waited for me to reply, but I didn't. "And you must be ..." he prompted. When I didn't say anything, he replied with his own answer, "Beautiful."

I blushed and averted my gaze. "I'm sorry. I have to go."

I searched for Tene in a panic, ready to get as far away from Allswell and the masculine bartender with the dark-as-night steel gray eyes.

CHAPTER 3

MORNING LIGHT HIT every corner of our kitchen, which only highlighted the grease stains and dust bunnies that I needed to clean later.

I stood by the stove, making breakfast, thinking about last night as guilt ran through my veins. I tried to reason with myself. I had stopped it before anything had gotten out of hand, hadn't I?

God, am I a mess. A total, utter mess.

Roland's footsteps into the kitchen broke me from my trance. He walked to the door as I continued to make *his* pancakes. I hadn't forgotten why I'd been at Allswell instead of Italia Clement in the first place. I should've boycotted making him breakfast, but, if anything, cooking made *me* feel better. I was consoled by the aroma of the food, and the scent lightened my mood.

"I'm sorry, Angie," he said, taking a seat at the table without looking at me.

It's not like I hadn't heard those three words before. They were etched in my brain from repetition, like a song on replay. But the truth was, if he valued our relationship, he would've shown up.

He had promised. He always promised.

He sighed as if he was tired and that was the best excuse he could offer. "I had a meeting with those investors. This new client could double my bonus."

Bonus? *His bonus?*

I had an urge to yell at the top of my lungs, but I barely bit it back. We had all the money in the world between our families. What we didn't have was time. You couldn't buy back time.

I pulled two plates from the overhead cupboard and placed our pancakes on them, followed by the omelet in the other pan.

When I sat down at the table, my gaze fell on him reading the paper. My hand briefly clenched then released.

I only had wanted to spend time with him so we could strengthen our relationship, rekindle anything we had left.

The guilt within me diminished and was replaced with a silent annoyance.

"Angie, I'll make a reservation for Italia for next week. I just needed to make that meeting." His head didn't lift from the *Wall Street Journal.*

"I don't want or need your money," I said softly. "We both know our families will be fine for generations to come. What I want is *you.* Your *time.* I want the man that used to take me out to dinner, surprise me on weekend getaways. I want the man that loved me above everything and anything." I pressed my hands to my chest and tried to control the quiver in my voice. "I miss us, the relationship that we used to have before you worked for Baird Equity Corp."

Now I was beginning to sound like a broken record.

How many times had we had this conversation, and after I'd complain, we would be fine. But that moment was brief—fleeting—until we both sounded like a bad sitcom rerun.

"Try to understand," he said, exasperated.

I stood, not wanting to hear the two words again he always uttered on repeat. I turned to face him, frowning, hurt seeping out of me. "I always try to understand, and what I don't understand is why you put everything above me."

Once again, I took my plate to the bedroom, closed the door, and ate breakfast by myself.

Sometimes, I could picture us during high school or at the beginning of college. Roland picking me up from school, holding hands as we took a walk by the lake. But the picture in my head was fuzzy—blurry—as though it was fading. Sometimes I wondered if it even happened.

When I heard the door shut, indicating that Roland had left for work, my heart hurt. I wished he would fight a little harder for us. There would be times that I would wait for him to burst into our room, get on his knees and apologize and mean it. In my scenario, he would kiss me hard and say it would never happen again. Then we'd have make-up sex, and he'd prove to me that I was loved, and for once, he was truly sorry. And this time I'd believe him.

I rubbed the center of my chest, the pang of rejection strong and steady. I stared blankly at the plate in my lap, focusing on the broken pieces of the pancake, broken just like our relationship.

Wallowing wouldn't lighten my spirit, so I lifted my chin, deciding that was enough of self-pity.

I emerged from the bedroom to get ready for work and picked up the phone and immediately dialed Tene. Speaking to my family always lifted my mood.

"Hey, Angie. One sec, I'm in the Starbucks line." She blurted out her order of a venti caramel macchiato with two extra shots of espresso before she got back on the line.

"Sorry, babe. I can't start my morning without my coffee, especially since I was partying all night long."

I had left the bar at one in the morning, while Tene had met up with a couple of girlfriends. Where the hell did she get all her energy?

"I still don't know how you do it." Where I was in bed daily at ten p.m., Tene was able to go out until three in the morning and still function the next day.

"I do it because I have to, and I still want to maintain a life and run Armstrong. Listen, I'm running to my flight, coffee in hand, so I have to hang up in about two seconds. It's the last call, and everyone has boarded the plane. Thanks again for handling downtown this morning. Training by fire. Good luck." She was flying to Corrington today, a few towns over, about three hours away, to sign a contract with a strip mall we owned down there, so I had to assist her in some business in downtown Rosendell.

I sucked in a breath and nodded. "No problem, sis. I've got this." Since I graduated with my master's a mere few months ago, I'd been handling the smaller properties on the south side of Rosendell and our suburban locations. I tended to the more stable tenants who'd been occupying our properties for years.

Downtown Rosendell was a different beast, high-end shopping and five-star restaurants and bars. Tene was used to dealing with the high-end retail space and high-maintenance tenants; I wasn't. She knew how to talk to them, how to please them, how to raise rent and make our tenants believe that it was their idea.

"You'll handle it just fine," she said firmly and with

confidence. "Okay, I'll see you tonight at Dad's birthday dinner. Love you. Oh, and stop by Allswell. The owner had a list of repairs that needed to be done."

"Uh ..." I stammered, looking for an excuse to say no.

And then she hung up.

I blinked. All I could think about was the too-hot-to-handle bartender, his hands ... his scent ... his lips. I rested against my down pillows, remembering the way he drank me in, making me feel wanton, lusted for. I remembered the way his thick, calloused hands gripped my thighs and held my stomach.

I wiped my sweaty palms down the front of my shirt and shook myself out of this daydream. Besides, I doubted he'd be there. But just in case, I'd go before the restaurant opened to talk to the owner alone. That bartender was danger and most definitely off-limits.

———

Training by fire, Tene had said?

No crap.

Bob, owner of Bob's Donuts, steepled his hand by his lips as he sat behind his desk, opposite me.

A light sheen of sweat formed at my brow and my knees bobbed with anxiety. Men who built an empire of donuts were successful for a reason, and it wasn't just in the recipe. Though he was in a teal signature apron, he was a businessman through and through. I'd heard stories.

"Did you have time to review the lease that Christene emailed?" I asked, forcing my voice to be steady.

"I did. I see you're raising my rent on a yearly basis." His tone was sharp, and there was visible tension in his neck and shoulders.

I shifted in my seat.

Christene mentioned he'd complain about the increases. He'd been complaining about the past few renewals.

"Bob, this is not something new," I tried to reason with him. "We have to keep up with the rise in maintenance and taxes. This was built into your lease when you signed with us ten years ago."

He sighed heavily with exaggeration. "I know, but you would think with a name like mine, and the fact that I've been in business for over two decades, you would cut me a break."

My hands twitched in my lap. One day I would be running Armstrong Real Estate with Christene, and I would need to learn how to deal with hard tenants. Today was that day.

Breathe. Show no mercy.

My stomach churned, and I wanted to throw up.

I forced a polite smile. "Bob, I assure you, we value your business and your loyalty. Bob's Donuts is indeed a well-known franchise—a household name, in fact. And because of that, we have kept your increases at a steady rate of three percent per year, which is less than the inflation rate and the rise of costs to maintain this building. And this is a prime location. You are on Elgin Avenue, where there is always traffic." Elgin Avenue in Rosendell was comparable to Michigan Avenue in Chicago. All the hip bars and restaurants were located on Elgin Avenue. Not to mention the high-end shops just a few blocks away.

He shook his head, and his jaw tightened. "I believe I'll be taking my business somewhere else, then."

Shit.

My stomach dropped, but I didn't give anything away. I

came here to have him sign the papers, not lose a well-known tenant. There was no way I could bear to tell my favorite person in the whole world—my father—that I'd lost one of his biggest tenants. A dizzying current spread through my body, making me feel as though I was on a rocky boat.

I lifted my chin, trying to get some semblance of control. "We'd hate to lose you, but this is a prime location, and unfortunately, we wouldn't have a problem filling this spot and asking for the normal increase of five percent."

His eyes hardened, and I smiled back to counter his harsh face. I had the desire to flee or cry to make him stay, but I kept my feet steadily planted on the floor, my hands lightly on my lap, my face even.

The silence seemed to drag on, and our staring contest went on for some time until, finally, he let out a low belly laugh, one that brightened his whole demeanor, but confused the hell out of me. His mood change gave me whiplash.

He shook his head and signed the papers in front of him. "You drive a hard bargain, Angelica. I'll tell your father you did well."

My father?

As though he'd read my thoughts, he said, "Your father told me to give you a hard time, and I happily told him I'd oblige. Freshman initiation."

I laughed, though I didn't find it as funny as he clearly did. "I'll have to give my father my own personal thank you when I get home," I said. I glanced around for show. "You don't happen to have old donuts lying around? Preferably the hard ones that'll take out some of his teeth?"

"He still has his?" Bob pushed out his false teeth with his tongue, then popped it back in. I almost dropped my purse in shock. "Too many donuts over the years." He laughed again, stood, and I followed his lead out to the kitchen. "How is your old man, anyway?"

"He's okay. Still recovering from his heart attack."

Over a year ago, the doctor had told us there was seventy percent blockage in Daddy's arteries. That day, my world had bottomed out. After his heart attack, a stent was placed in his chest, and my family had been careful with him since, making sure that work and stress were avoided. "He's getting better. I'm sure he thinks we're babying him, and my mother is driving him crazy because they're around each other all the time, but we just want to make sure he stays well. "

"I know," Bob said, patting my shoulder. "Smile, pretty lady. I'm sure he'll be just fine. I've known your dad a long time, and I'm sure he wanted to get back to work yesterday." Bob walked to the counter, shoved donuts into a bag and placed the bag in my hands. He raised an eyebrow, making a point. "Make sure you share, okay?"

"Yes, sir." I nodded. "And thanks again. Later, Bob."

I pressed a palm to my chest, let out a huge breath and swung the bag of donuts back and forth as I headed to my next destination, Allswell, which was conveniently the space next door.

After eating a powdered donut, I entered the club, now restaurant. The area was silent. There were no employees around, and thankfully, no bartender from last night.

The place had transformed once again. It was almost unrecognizable aside from the signature bar that spanned both sides of the room. Circular tables were set with silverware and plates, in the middle of what had been the dance floor. Booths adorned the perimeter wall.

I straightened my stance when the kitchen door flew

open, and a woman walked in, carrying a crate of wine glasses. Her dark brown hair was chin short, swishing against her cheeks. She had a piercing on her eyebrow that twitched when she met my gaze.

I approached her, cradling my bag of donuts in my other arm to offer my hand. "Hi. I'm Angelica Armstrong, from Armstrong Realty. I'm here to meet Ryder."

She dropped the crate on one of the center tables, and the wineglasses clinked together. She wiped her hands down her black apron before she took my hand. "Ryder?" She quirked an eyebrow. "I'm Kristy, I'm the manager here. Cade is in the back." She turned her head to call him out, "Cade!"

Cade?

I registered the name, confused at first, then panic set in. When he stepped out of the kitchen right behind the bar, my heart stammered loudly, so loud I wouldn't doubt if he heard it. He was the same bartender from last night. The same bartender that had me breathing hard and set my body on fire.

CHAPTER 4

CADE'S FACE showed confusion first before he proceeded to the center of the floor. "Hey." His semi-smile widened, and I lost any ability to speak as I took in one hundred percent pure masculinity right in front of me. My lips parted automatically, and I felt light-headed.

The electricity, the shock, the crazy intensity that surged between us at the club was only heightened by seeing this man in full light. His hair was a dark brown, almost black, while his eyes were the deepest set of steel gray. They had been dark as night at the club, but now they shined powerfully, softening at the edges, and hypnotic, similar to a gray sky right before a storm hits.

Intricate tattoos ran up both arms and looked as though they were part of his black fitted T-shirt. My cheeks warmed as I wondered where his tattoos ended or where they began. I had noticed them last night, but now they were more prominent, popping out of his skin like black ink on a white canvas.

"You're from Armstrong?"

His words brought me back to the present, and I

blinked, trying to find my bearings. "Uh, yes," was all I could muster. I breathed in heavily like I was in the middle of a heat wave, though I could hear the air blasting on high in the background.

He smirked, then ducked his head, speaking slowly as if I didn't understand English. "I'm Cade Ryder."

Kristy barked out a low laugh in the background.

"I'm Angelica. They call me ... " My brain couldn't catch up fast enough to my crazy racing heart. *What do they call me?* "Angie," I finally replied.

His eyes intensified. "You didn't give me your name last night." Warmth radiated from his body, and his every pore screamed danger. He inched closer, making me feel lost and found all at the same time. "Your name's Angie? Angel seems more fitting."

I swallowed. Hard.

He stuck out his hand. "Nice to formally meet you, Angel."

I reached to meet his hand, and the mere brush of his fingers sent my body aflame, causing me to drop my purse and bag of donuts on the floor. We bent down to pick them up at the same time, then bumped heads. I fell back on my ass, my skirt creeping up to my thighs.

His laughter was rich and throaty, breaking through our awkward greeting, and vibrating against my skin.

"Well, that was clumsy of me," I said breathlessly, laughing to cover my unease. When I pushed myself to my knees, he extended his hand. His eyebrows pulled in and his gaze locked with mine again, as though he was studying me, drinking and eating and devouring me at the same time.

My sweaty palm met his. When I stood, my breath quickened, and my pulse raced. The way my body reacted to his touch was unfamiliar, unreal, unprecedented. Explosive.

His soft tone broke through my daze. "Has anyone told you your voice sounds very lyrical?" Then he spoke so softly I barely heard him say, "You sound like her."

I shied away and turned toward Kristy who was staring in our direction. With one shake of her head, she took the now empty crates and headed toward the back.

"Lyrical? No," I croaked out. My voice sounded breathy, as though the words had come from someone else. I didn't do breathy. My had flew to my throat where I could feel the acceleration of my pulse.

"Come, follow me," he said.

I bit back the urge to reach for him again. I had a boyfriend. He was the only one allowed to turn me on. Even if he never took advantage.

Picking up my bag and folder, I trailed behind him, shaking my head into focus. "I'm here to discuss the repairs that need to be done."

"Where's Christene?" he asked.

I tried hard to shove away the instant sting of rejection. Of course, he wanted my sexy, voluptuous sister. Every man did. I never used to care, so why did it bite me so hard now?

"She had to fly out for business this morning, but she will still be managing this property going forward. She asked me to stop by today."

He flipped around and closed his eyes. "I had a leaky sink and a couple of electrical sockets that blew out."

I watched his deep inhale and the expansion of his chest, wondering why his eyes were shut as he spoke to me.

My lips parted as I took in the broadness of his shoulders and strength in his arms at his sides. "We have a list of contractors we use. I can get ahold of them and schedule a time for them to come here if you want."

I waited for a response from him, any response. When I didn't get one, I couldn't help but ask. "Is there a reason your eyes are closed? It's a little bit rude, not to mention awkward."

His eyes burst open, and he stalked toward me until he was inches from my face. "The inflection in your voice ... it reminds me of someone." Pain flashed over his face, but in the next moment, it was as if I had imagined it.

I peered up at him, taking in over six feet of potent masculinity. "Okay?" I wasn't expecting an answer, and I couldn't find my next words being this close to him. Instead of the cat, Cade got my tongue.

"No need to call those contractors. I decided and got it fixed myself. You can just take out the expenses from my rent. I have the invoices upstairs." With his finger, he swiped at my lip lightly. The movement was slow and sensual, and it shocked me with heat. When he brought his fingers to my lips, I stilled.

"Powdered sugar," he explained, then winked. He turned around and stalked toward the end of the bar. "Follow me," he said again.

Oh. My. Goodness.

"Where are we going?" My voice trembled, and a flush of adrenaline tingled through my body.

"My apartment."

I staggered and stopped mid-step, making him turn around.

"Don't worry, Angel." His tone lowered, husky, sexy, and soft, and I pressed my thighs tighter together to stop the ache. "I'm not going to take advantage of you. Well ..." He chuckled darkly. "... unless you want me to. Just say the word, and I'd be happy to oblige."

"No, no," I rushed out. "That wasn't what I was thinking." I blinked, catching my breath, and then followed him into the steel freight elevator in the back of the building.

The elevator could've fit a king-sized mattress, but with Cade and his broad immense frame near me, I felt claustrophobic. His presence was overwhelming, overpowering, over-the-top.

Never in my life had I met a man so beautiful, so masculine, so intimidating that I had difficulty even looking at him, yet I couldn't look away.

The air was charged, and I wrung my hands together in front of me, concentrating on anything but him, focusing on the sounds of metal scraping metal and the squeals and squeaks of the elevator rising to the top floor.

"You live here?" I finally asked, finding my voice.

I knew the prior tenant above the restaurant had been a legal firm.

"Yep. Moved in two weeks ago."

When he keyed in, I walked into the room and noted the floor that had formerly been carpeted was now dark mahogany wood.

In the middle of the space was a literal gym, complete with a treadmill, a power lifting station with weights, a workout bench, a rack of kettlebells, a weight tower with dumbbells, and a boxing bag. Backed up against the wall was a dresser and an awkwardly placed king-sized bed. A few of his personal belongings were scattered on the bed and on a single side nightstand.

"This is where you live? This isn't an apartment. This is a gym."

He pointed to the corner, a look of amusement on his face. "There's the bed. Would there be a bed at the gym?"

"No," I choked out and took a step back. The way he looked at me made my skin flush and my mind race with forbidden thoughts.

"It's a comfy bed," he added with a wry grin. "Try it."

Maybe I should've been frightened; handsome men could be serial killers, too.

But as I took in his crooked smile, I could tell he was only trying to get a reaction out of me. And he was succeeding in every possible way. He was probably used to women everywhere reacting to him like this, wanting him, dropping their panties, and begging him to take them.

I gulped. "No, I'm okay. Thanks."

He stepped toward me, and I jerked back, but he took another step, then another, and another until I was backed up against the wall. "I'm sorry. You said you had some invoices to give me." My voice squeaked like a teenage boy in the midst of puberty.

He angled toward me, his nose barely touching my nose and inhaled deeply. When he leaned in, I stilled, before he reached for something behind me and took a step back, leaving me feeling instantly cold and bereft.

"Yes, why else would you think I took you up here?" He let out a low laugh and pulled out my hand, pressing the receipts into my curled fingers. Sweat formed behind my neck as I peered up at him, hypnotized again by his over-the-top fineness.

When his cocky grin surfaced, I pulled my hands from his.

My assumptions were right, he was doing this on purpose, and the worst thing was, I was falling for it. My body was betraying me in more ways than I could count.

The thought made me want to get out his boxing gloves and teach him some manners.

"Those are your copies. I have the original receipts. You can just deduct it from next month's rent. I have one more lying around here somewhere." He glanced around toward the other end of the room at another set of drawers.

I unfolded the crumpled receipts and stuck them neatly in my folder. When he walked toward the drawers, my shoulders relaxed. I could finally think, finally breathe, finally function.

I bit the inside of my cheek, forcing myself to focus and not act like a thirteen-year-old girl with a crush. "The rent here must be killing you. Why don't you find a normal apartment?" I managed to say casually.

"The rent isn't the problem. I can afford the rent," he said, shuffling through another set of file cabinets. "Anyway, I'm not staying long."

My shoulders sagged as I watched him filter through his papers. I shouldn't have been disappointed by his words, but I was, which made absolutely no sense because I hardly knew this man.

"I moved here two weeks ago to make sure Allswell was up and running by opening night. I'll make sure that everything is running smoothly before I hand over the reins to my manager on-site—Kristy."

I cleared my throat, trying to act like I didn't care. "Then where will you go?"

He picked up the pile of paper receipts. "The next place. Wherever I decide to set up. Probably Toline in Texas. It's up and coming. My two brothers, who are my investment partners, and I are looking to expand. I move wherever we decide to set up our next restaurant or club."

Brothers? There are more like him out there?

It was difficult just being around him. I couldn't imagine three more Cades walking around.

"Is your family from around here?"

Suddenly, he lifted his head, and his face shut down. I thought our conversation was over until he spoke again. "My brothers are all over the place. My mother, she's back in Kritell in Ohio, about five hours away."

By the tone in his voice, I knew his family was off limits, so I asked the next question that popped into my mind. "Don't you get lonely?" I imagined his life, hopping from city to city without any family. Besides moving away to college, I'd lived and grown up in Rosendell, with my family just minutes away from me.

"No. Plus I go home often to visit my mom. So, no, not lonely."

"Really?" I raised my eyebrow, being nosy and knowing it.

He took a step toward me, and my stomach flip-flopped. "Trust me. I don't get lonely."

"Okay," I said, backing off because I was afraid he'd start giving me the gory details. I tapped my heel against the hardwood floor and fidgeted with the edge of my shirt.

"You're nothing like your sister." He eyed me with curiosity, his tone low as though he hadn't meant those words to slip.

He didn't have to state the obvious.

I held my chin higher, wanting to tell him I had qualities that outweighed hers that couldn't be seen. I was loyal to a fault, compassionate to all those around me, and had graduated summa cum laude at Yale.

He reached out his hand, and I froze. Then, with his fingertips, he smoothed out the wrinkles on my forehead and our eyes locked, the magnetic pull between us was undeniable. His eyes brimmed with curiosity, and I could feel the sexual magnetism bounce off him. "That's a good thing," he added, his voice seductively low, "that you're not like her."

His words snapped me back to focus. "Hey," I said. "That's not very nice." Another quality of mine was that I loved my family to a fault. Sometimes putting their happiness ahead of my own. "That's my sister."

"I didn't mean it as an insult to her. I'm just noting the difference."

"Yeah," I muttered. "Plain to beautiful. I've heard it before."

He leaned in and brushed an escaping strand of hair from my face. The touch was so intimate that a dizzying current raced through me.

"You don't see yourself very clearly, do you?" His voice was low and intense.

I took a steadying breath. "No, I do." I've always been sure of myself. That's what I prided myself in. I was the dependable one. Not the most beautiful, but I was comfortable in my own skin.

"I don't think so." He angled closer, so close that I could smell the mint of his toothpaste on his lips. "But I see you very clearly. I haven't seen a sexier little thing in a long-ass time."

I gazed up at him, shocked by his words. His focus flickered to my lips, and I breathed in his scent, a mix of cologne and masculinity, and my body zinged with arousal.

My eyes fell at half mast, about to kiss him, when clarity and sanity pushed to the surface. "I have a boyfriend." My voice was barely above a whisper, as though I wanted to fully disclose my status, yet I didn't want him to hear it.

His response was immediate. "I don't care."

I blinked out of the haze, out of the cloud of Cade. It was exactly what I needed to hear to slap me out of my daze. "I do care. You can't touch what's not yours."

Amusement filled his face. "Why were you going to let me kiss you, then?" he challenged.

"Was not!" I retorted though I wasn't exactly sure. "Are you admitting you're a homewrecker?"

"Not at all, baby doll. I've never slept with a married woman."

"Well, that's good to know," I said without thinking.

He inched closer, those steel gray eyes intensifying. "But you're not a married woman, are you?"

I swallowed hard. "Even though I have a boyfriend, that wouldn't stop you from sleeping with me, would it?"

This man was danger personified.

"Angel," he began, his profile strong and serious, "everyone has a choice. Everyone. It's if you can live with those choices, that's what makes you or breaks you. Me? I live with my choices every single day. And hell, if I wouldn't choose to bed a sexy thing like you." He shrugged a shoulder, unaffected. "In this situation, I have everything to gain, and you have everything to lose, so here it's lady's choice."

I would've never guessed how those words, his words, would haunt my future.

His boldness caught me off guard, and I scoffed out one word, "Never."

"Angel, never say never. I've learned that can bite you in the ass." Then he winked, and my temperature rose. I wasn't sure if it was that I was irritated at him for thinking he could have me or that I was so aroused at the thought.

After a beat, he turned and headed for the door. "After you."

I walked in front of him, but the heat of his stare

scorched me the whole way back to the elevator. When I turned around, his eyes were focused on my ass. He didn't even try to hide that he was checking me out.

With a shrug of his shoulders, he said, "What? I can't touch, but baby, don't tell me I can't enjoy the view."

"You're horrible," I muttered, stepping into the elevator.

"You're beautiful," he said, catching me off guard yet again.

"Stop flirting," I said.

"Flirting is harmless." He turned the key and pressed the down button on the elevator. "And I think you like it when I flirt with you."

"I certainly do not." It was hard hiding a lie when my face was flaming red.

"I think you do." He leaned in, so close that I got a whiff of his intoxicating scent again. "You're so damn beautiful. And the hottest thing is, you don't even know it."

"Whatever. You're flirting again," I whispered without the bite in my voice.

"No. Just telling the truth." He angled toward me as I backed against the wall of the elevator. Caging me in, he placed his forearm right by my head. "Flirting would be like this."

I peered up at him, taking in over six feet of oh-all-man.

"Listen, sexy. Allswell is having a ladies' night next weekend. You get in free, and cocktails are half off from seven to nine. I want to see you there." He ducked his head, gazing at me with that stupid crooked smile on his face. "This is flirting, and dangerously, I might add."

I inhaled deeply, biting my lip, using the wall behind me to keep me upright, keep my weak knees from giving out.

Oh, goodness gracious, great wall of fineness.

"Now you can tell me to stop flirting," he murmured.

"Stop ... Stop flirting," I said weakly, not convincing even to my own ears.

He leaned in even closer and whispered softly in my ear. "All you have to do is say stop, Angel." He backed away as though it hurt him to do so, then the elevator pinged open, and he motioned for me to exit before him.

But I could still feel his eyes on me, watching me. And god, I hated to admit it, but it felt good for once to feel ... to feel ... what was the word? Wanted. That's it.

He made me feel wanted.

CHAPTER 5

THE DRIVE to Clarington took only thirty minutes, but riding with Roland in a silent car made it seem like an eternity.

"I got your father a bottle of Haut-Brion. Do you think he'd like that?" Roland's focus didn't stray from the traffic forming in front of us.

"Yes, it's his favorite."

He'd asked me a week ago what he should get my father. Did he remember that the Haut-Brion had been my idea?

The overhead moonlight highlighted Roland's features: the tall bridge of his nose, his clean shaven, strong jawline. He knew me more than anyone else on this planet, and we shared so much history, so many years together. Our parents were great friends, our families interconnected like puzzle pieces that formed a single, solid, happy picture.

But that was no reason for our relationship to be like this—routine, boring, predictable. I refused to live in an endless cycle of unhappiness.

Stepping into my parents' foyer, the scent of Grandma's sweet apple pie hit my nostrils as my heels clip-clopped against the imported black Italian marble floors. I heard the commotion in the kitchen and my sister's loud laughter echoing through the corridor, followed by my father's voice, most likely the guilty culprit making her giggle like a little schoolgirl.

"Honey, I'm home," I announced. "Where's the birthday boy?"

My father was sitting at the kitchen table, and I rushed to him and hugged him full on. I pulled at his Santa-like beard and planted one long kiss on his cheek until his belly shook with laughter.

"How's my old man?" I reached for his hand and jiggled it between both of mine.

"Still alive and healthy at the tender age of twenty-one." He winked.

Nana waited patiently in line behind him, needing and wanting some affection. She enveloped me in one of her infamous, tight hugs. At 5' 2", including her gray full bouffant, she had the strength of a bear. She gripped me to her chest, almost constricting my lungs of air. "My beautiful Angie. So pretty. Always prettier, every time I see you."

"Whatever, Nana." I laughed. "I just saw you last week."

"And look at you, Roland." She pulled back and snickered. "You look just like your daddy. We'll have to fix that." She walked up to him and tiptoed where the top of her bouffant hair met his chin.

Roland fidgeted while Nana undid his tie and tugged the side of his button-down shirt, untucking it. "See? Much better already."

Nana made him nervous, and it amused the heck out of the rest of our family. Well, everyone except my mother.

My mother approached, disdain on her serious face. "Agnes, please don't torment my future son-in-law."

Roland and my mother touched cheeks in their typical formal greeting. I held my tongue. Marriage between us was inevitable; it was the next step in our relationship. But I wanted to be elated when he popped the question, and until I was sure there were no more empty promises, I knew that I wouldn't be.

Tene was making her infamous dip at our marble kitchen counter underneath the dangling pots and pans from the hanging rack.

"Hey, I need to talk to you later." I raised an eyebrow and threw her a glassy stare.

She let out a short laugh. She had led me right into Cade's restaurant this morning, and she was going to get an earful from me.

When the doorbell rang, my mother flattened her unstained apron. "Roland, your parents are here."

Roland walked out of the kitchen, followed by my mother, who turned around and clicked her tongue.

"Angelica." Her tone said that I should come along.

Tene crossed her eyes and touched her nose with her tongue, making me laugh. I pointed my finger in her direction and squinted. "We're not done here, sissy."

"Oh, boy, I'm in trouble," Tene said, amused, "and you know how I love to get in trouble."

In the foyer, Kathleen Spencer stood tall, with her hair neatly pulled back in a sleek blonde ponytail. Not one hair on her head was out of place. She clutched her Louis Vuitton purse tight to her side as her floor-length white linen skirt laid at her ankles.

"Liz, lovely like always." She touched cheeks with my mother like the Europeans they weren't and approached me and my father. "Leo, dapper as always." After giving my father a slight hug, her arms wrapped fully around me, in an embrace to rival my grandmother's. "My sweet Angelica. How did my boy get so lucky?" She cupped my face, and her easy grin surfaced.

One of the things I loved about Roland was his mother. She always welcomed me with a motherly love that I sometimes lacked from my own mother.

"Roland." Her voice softened with such reverence for her golden boy. "Son, what happened to your tie?" Her hands flew to his neckline as she redid the tie that my grandmother had messed with. My father chuckled when Kathleen began to tuck in Roland's shirt.

"Mother, please." He backed away, stuffing his own shirt in his pants. Sometimes Tene would joke that she believed Roland's mother still nursed him. She asked me if he fell asleep at my breast, making suckling noises.

When I caught the humor on my father's face, I had to turn away or else I would've busted out laughing.

James Spencer stood tall behind his wife, peering down at his smartphone, most likely taking care of business. Also in the world of finance, James, along with his brother, owned one of the largest accounting firms in Rosendell.

"James." My mother's tone was low and authoritative, which forced James' head up from his phone.

He tucked his cell into his back pocket. "Liz, thanks for having us over."

"Of course," she said, taking his hand in a friendly greeting. "Quick, let's sit in the family room, while I get dinner served."

I assisted my father over to the love seat, taking his cane and resting it against the end of the couch. I leaned over and whispered, "I've got a surprise for you."

"I know what it is." His sly smile broadened.

Of course, he did. It wasn't a surprise if I gave it to him every year. "I'll be back. I've got to prepare *the* surprise." I gave him one last hand squeeze before escaping to the kitchen.

I walked in on Tene washing the dishes, singing some Ed Sheeran song and shaking her hips like she had last night. Surprising her, I approached and pinched the innermost part of her arm, the part that hurt.

"Hey!" She turned and flicked water in my direction.

"Why didn't you tell me the bartender was the owner of Allswell?"

A devious grin encompassed her face, making me pinch her again.

"Stop it!" She flicked more water in my direction. "Why does it matter, Angie?"

"It doesn't." I didn't bother to tell her that he propositioned me. She'd probably go over there and congratulate him. Possibly give him a trophy.

She raised her eyebrows. "If it doesn't matter, then why are you asking about him?"

I turned away as a flush touched my cheeks.

"Angelica," she said, hedging, "do you have a little crush on the bad boy?"

"I want to know what you told him last night at the bar."

She giggled, and I narrowed my eyes, meaning business.

"Tene, I'm serious." I placed my hand on my hip. "Come on!"

"That is between Cade and me."

My mother popped in her head, breaking up our conversation. "Christene, the appetizers."

"Oops, gotta go, sis." She winked and picked up the tray of vegetables and dip and sashayed out of the kitchen.

I wrinkled my nose, walked to the counter, and opened the tub of frosting I'd made at home. I had a sinking feeling that I'd never find out what they had talked about, and I'd be curious till the day I die.

CHAPTER 6

OUR FINE CHINA plates lined with gold were set in front of us on the table, while the full glasses of wine sat right beside our dishes.

"Angelica, why don't you say grace?" My mother always asked me to say grace, never Tene, and I wondered if Tene remembered why.

I lowered my head and pressed my hands together. Grace was a time of reflection, a time to be thankful for the things we were fortunate to have when so many didn't. I was thankful for so many things. Especially for my father. That he was able to spend another year with us.

When we almost lost him to the heart attack, over a year ago, my mother couldn't deal, and I'd been there for her emotionally.

Tene was the one who had kept the family going. She was the one who'd gotten up every day and taken charge. She'd hired property managers for those properties that weren't local and had made her rounds to all our local tenants to formally tell them that she would be handling all their needs in the interim.

My mother cleared her throat, reminding me of my duties. "Thank you, God," I started, "for allowing us to gather here in your presence to celebrate another birthday with my father. May you bless him with many more years to come. Keep him healthy, happy, and safe." And then I began with the standard prayer of grace. "Bless us, O Lord, and these, Thy gifts ..."

When I finished, Tene chimed in, "Rub-a-dub-dub. Thank you, Lord, for this grub, amen."

Everyone laughed. Everyone except my mother.

"So how was Corrington, Christene?" Mom asked, picking up her glass of wine.

Tene straightened in her seat, and her face pinched with annoyance. "You asked me this earlier, mother. It was great. Hobson wants to rent our other strip mall when the grocery store's lease is up at the end of the year."

My mother wanted Tene to repeat this story for the Spencers' benefit. I was sure my mother and father had heard this as soon as Tene had walked into the house.

Kathleen, Roland's mother, turned toward my father. "Leo, are you building out more properties?"

My dad leaned back against his chair and took a sip of wine. "Not at the moment." Words didn't need to be said to understand that the state of his health wasn't well and that we weren't even sure if he'd ever return to work or be retired forever. "We're concentrating on acquiring developed properties in Rosendell and the cities we're currently in; then we'll look to branching out in cities out of state." Christene talked with an air of authority and confidence, one that I was jealous of. "With all the changes in management, we're working on maintaining our relationships with our current tenants and adding new ones. The latest big win for us was landing CJW Investments LLC at our downtown

Rosendell location. It's that new restaurant and bar on Elgin Avenue."

I perked up straighter on my seat, wanting to know more about Allswell.

"Who's CJW Investments?" Mother's head poked up, a forkful of pasta in her hand.

"Only one of the most well-known investment groups. They own half of the upscale restaurants and bars across the nation." Christene lifted her chin and sported a satisfied smile. "Have you ever heard of Everest in the Bellagio or Cloke at the Caesars?"

My mouth dropped open, my fork pinging against my plate.

Tene shrugged one shoulder. "I have to know these things. It's all part of the business."

My father nodded as though he knew them as well, but it saddened me to see him take such a back-seat role to the company he'd built.

"Cade ... I mean, Mr. Ryder," I corrected, "is the owner of those restaurants in Vegas?"

My sister smiled teasingly at me. The kind of smile that made my ears warm and my cheeks flush bright red. I tore my gaze from hers and stuffed more pasta into my mouth.

"Yes, he's one of the investors and runs the businesses. I guess he has some silent partners. I asked about them, wanted to know if they were single," she said nonchalantly, but I wanted to shove a fistful of pasta in her mouth.

"Christene," my mother scolded.

"Mom, I'm kidding." She chuckled. "But really, I'm sure his silent partners have more than enough money to fund his business ventures. They paid a whole year's rent in cash."

I went to pick up my wineglass, noticing that my fingers

trembled against the stem. "Why are they picking Rosendell as their next conquest?" I took a sip of my wine.

"I've heard of them," Roland said, causing me to cough up my drink.

All heads turned my way. "Sorry. Wrong pipe." I waved a hand, playing it off.

Roland leaned back in his chair and tucked his hands in his armpits. "I mean, we're into investing in manufacturing companies, not restaurants, but yes, CJW is pretty big." There was a certain gleam in his eye, the same look he got when he talked about work.

My father spoke up, answering my question while everyone else ignored it. "Rosendell has a lot of money, dear. High-end shops. It's the small-town New York City."

"Yeah, I guess, but Vegas compared to Rosendell?" I'd never been to Vegas, but I knew there was no comparison.

Tene poured more wine in her glass. "I asked Cade that same question, Ang. They've taken on the biggest cities in the nation—New York, Chicago, Los Angeles—and now they are branching out to the smaller, lucrative cities. And get this ..." She leaned in closer as if clueing us in to some little secret. "After they've conquered the US, they're hitting international. Ibiza is next."

"Wow," I said, like a kid surprised by a present. I was floored that the tattooed hottie was a total businessman.

"Good win, Christene," my father commented, patting her on her back. She smiled sweetly at him, and he pinched her cheek.

"Like daughter, like daddy." She held out her fist, and he bumped it with his own.

I bit my bottom lip, taking in their interaction. I'd always been jealous of their relationship. It was as if he had favored her to outweigh the expectations and tension between my mother and her.

"Christene, you're doing great. Armstrong Enterprises is going to be just fine," Roland said, before reaching for my hand and squeezing it. "Don't worry, babe. You can just raise our baby. I'll be taking care of the both of us." He was obviously teasing, but under his cheerful chuckle, there was some truth to his words.

I sucked in my surprise, carefully closing off my features. "I don't think my parents want to see all their hard-earned investment in my education go down the drain." I let out a forced laugh and took another sip of wine. Maybe more wine would calm the blood boiling beneath the surface.

The table turned silent and everyone's stare ping-ponged between us.

"There's nothing wrong with raising children. I haven't worked a day in my life," Kathleen said. Though she'd had her housekeepers to help her clean and raise Roland, Kathleen prided herself in keeping house, and I didn't think there was anything wrong with that. But that was her life, not mine. I didn't want the same things.

Roland seemed to sense my tension. "I didn't mean you couldn't work for a while before we ..." he began, but his mother placed her hand on top of his, stopping him from digging himself deeper into the hole with each and every word that sputtered out of his mouth.

"Actually," Christene said, pausing to swallow her drink, "when we take over, she'll technically be making more than you so you could be the one to watch your babies." She let out a boisterous laugh. So loud, so obnoxious, as though she thought she was the funniest thing in the world. And, in turn, my lips turned upward.

I glanced at my father, and when our eyes met, he started to laugh. Even Nana was laughing.

My mother was not. "Christene," she said through clenched teeth.

"Chill, mother," Tene said tiredly. "It's a joke. If Roland wants a baby that badly, Angie should go to the bathroom upstairs and push a little turd out for him right now."

My father, Nana, and I laughed harder.

"Christene!" my mother scolded, now red-faced and furious.

My father tapped his fork on the table, wisely changing the subject. "Anyway, I've been thinking about the future of Armstrong lately."

My mother turned toward him, her furious face fading, and being replaced with genuine concern. "No, you are not working until you are one hundred percent better and you have clearance from your doctor."

He leaned over and kissed her cheek to placate her. "Of course, dear, and until the wife clears me to work."

While Christene had a knack for making every awkward situation lighter, my father had a knack for switching my mother's mood in a nanosecond.

When her concern didn't ebb, he added soothingly, "Don't worry, I plan to get better. I wasn't thinking of going back anytime soon. Christene has done an amazing job. More than amazing." He winked over the table at her. "We were able to acquire new locations, fill tenancies to almost one hundred percent occupied."

"Uh, Dad, why does it seem like you're firing me?" Christene cocked her head.

"Of course not, honey. Let me finish. Plus, with the win of CJW Investments, I could not be prouder of you. But I think we should switch it up for a bit."

Christene brightened suddenly, grabbing her wineglass and doing a dance-y sway. "Switchity uppity up? Throw in some spice? Let's hear it. I like a little spice in my life."

His face became serious as he addressed us both. "Let's switch properties. Angie, you handle all of Rosendell's properties downtown, and Christene, you handle our suburban properties and all properties out of state. This will give you more free time to concentrate on expansion in the neighboring states."

"What?" my mother and I gasped in unison.

Christene nodded approvingly. "I think it's a perfect idea, Dad."

Christene smiled sweetly at me, and I'd bet my trust fund she was thinking the same thing I was thinking—Cade.

My mother shifted in her seat. "Honey, do you think that's a good idea? Angie is barely getting her feet wet with the business."

"It's fine." He gave me a look that showed his confidence in me, and I felt touched, although still unprepared. "She's doing an amazing job. I heard Bob tried to get out of the annual increases when she went over there to have him sign the lease extension." There was a glint of humor in his eyes. "But you held your ground, didn't you, Angie?" He tipped his chin, pride heavy in his eyes.

Everyone turned in my direction, and I averted my gaze, afraid they'd know the truth. That my father had put him up to test me, and Bob had never really been planning to leave.

"I guess," I said quietly.

"You'll do great." He pushed back his chair and lifted his plate. "I guess baby making will have to wait, Roland." He didn't smile when he uttered those words, his tone serious.

My father and mother had raised independent women,

and he wasn't too pleased about Roland's grand plan for my future.

Maybe someday, I'd want to stay home and raise children, but not at twenty-four. I wasn't thinking of babies yet.

My insides fluttered with the excitement about my new responsibility. Finally, my time had come to contribute to this family.

My father picked up my mother's plate as the others began to disperse.

"Let's blow out the candles in the kitchen," my mother called out, stacking the Spencers' plates and separating the silverware.

"Don't worry. You'll do great." Christene pinched my bottom, making me jump. She added discreetly, "Plus, I hear some of your tenants are pretty hot."

I wrinkled my nose at her, and she just laughed.

Cade was hot, there was no doubt. But nothing was going to get in my way. I was going to prove to my father that I was up for this challenge.

Business, not pleasure. Business, not pleasure.

That would be my mantra until Cade left to pursue his next restaurant. Which, hopefully, would be soon.

━━

Sometimes, I was the biggest kid out there, even in my early twenties. I bounced on my toes as excitement rushed through me. I peered over my father's shoulder to make sure his eyes were closed. "No peeking, Dad."

Everyone congregated around my father as I placed the three-layer chocolate cake in front of him. In curvy letters, it said "Happy 57th birthday, Dad." On top of the cake, a replica of the city of Rosendell had been sculpted from fondant, primarily the street where our main buildings were —Elgin Avenue. It took me hours to prepare the cake, from baking to preparing the buttercream, then decorating with fondant.

Christene and I had taken my mother for a cake decorating class once for one of her birthdays. However, I was the only one who continued to make cakes. Tene was the one who continued to eat them.

When I lit the candles, one by one, my father twisted in his seat. "Keep your eyes shut," I commanded.

My mother and Tene assisted in grabbing the candles on the cake and lighting the other candles.

"Darling, you have talent," Kathleen commented next to me, placing her hand on my shoulder.

Roland chuckled. "Yes, Mother, and I am the benefactor of her talent. Speaking of which, someone else's birthday is coming up soon." He poked at my side teasingly, and a cheesy smile crept up my face because my big day was next.

When all fifty-seven candles were lit, I clasped my hands together and stood right next to my father. "Okay, open them."

My father's whole face lit up and his eyes filled with pride. "It's your best work yet, Angie."

I swallowed hard, feeling emotional. We had stopped doing presents for him five years ago when he'd said he didn't need any more junk and he had everything he needed in his life—his family. But I always felt a joy swell inside me at seeing how pleased he was with my cakes.

And then I whispered the three words I personally waited for every year. It's what I wanted to do on my birthday, and I'd never missed a year since I was a little kid.

"Make a wish." Birthdays meant new beginnings. A new year, a new start, and that one wish—whatever you wanted to wish for on your special day—was epic. My father was only ever going to be fifty-six once, and this meant a new beginning at fifty-seven, as well as moving on from a difficult previous year with the high hopes that he didn't encounter health issues anymore.

As he closed his eyes, time stood still. I watched him blow out all fifty-seven candles. It was as though he was blowing out the old him and simultaneously wishing for something new.

My mother planted a sweet kiss on his lips. "Happy birthday, darling."

My father and mother were opposites, but their love had gotten him through his sickness. Despite either of their flaws, their love had persevered through years of marriage.

When I walked to the other side of the kitchen to the cabinets to get some plates, Roland came up behind me and tugged on my arm. "We need to leave."

"What? No." I ignored him and proceeded to get out the plates and cutlery.

"I just got a text from Conner. He sent me a contract, but it's too big to pull up on my phone. I need my computer." His face was expectant. "So, we need to leave right now."

When he gripped my elbow, I jerked away. "It's my dad's birthday."

"Be a little more considerate here, Angie," he said impatiently.

"Considerate?" I scoffed. "That's funny coming from you. It's my father's birthday. You should have driven here separately. Conner can wait a few hours."

He straightened and projected his voice so the whole

room could hear. "Liz, I'm sorry, but we'll have to get going soon. I have an early day tomorrow."

My mother smiled from the coffee machine. "Of course. Just stay for a few to give Angie enough time to eat her cake."

The vein in my temple twitched. "You didn't tell me we were leaving early, honey." I gritted my teeth, grinding my molars. Everyone's focus was on us, but it didn't dim the anger that flowed through me.

"Angie, we're just about done here," my mother insisted. "We wouldn't want you to go home too late, anyway." When she waved a hand and continued to pour coffee for our guests, I stormed past Roland who was in my way.

"Excuse me for a second. Bathroom break." I rushed through the kitchen doors, up the stairs and into my child-hood room, where I shut the door and plopped on the bed, clutching the pillow against my chest.

I needed a minute. One minute.

Deep breaths left my mouth, and I focused on the ceiling as memories of the past few days, weeks, and even years pushed to the surface.

Any other day I would've given in, but not today, not my father's birthday. And my mother? Couldn't she sense the distress in my tone? Why did she constantly take Roland's side?

I peered up at the pink and purple curtains that hadn't changed since I was a kid. The light colors had comforted me when I was younger, but not today.

A heavy sigh escaped, and I let all the frustrations of the day and our relationship pour out of me. The deep-rooted animosity that was growing within me directed at Roland could not be healthy.

I was unhappy.

That was the truth of the matter.

And things had to change.

─────

After ten minutes and in typical Angelica fashion, I put a smile on my face and headed downstairs like everything was right in my world, just as my mother had taught me. The house could be burning down, but my face would maintain its steady calm.

I ate my cake, while Roland stood, tapping his watch numerous times. But I'd decided I wouldn't let him ruin one of my favorite celebrations, so I simply ignored him.

Was this my life now? My insides twisted from fear of my future. It was only going to get worse down the road. He'd work more, expect more from me, be more controlling with my time. I couldn't allow this to happen. I wouldn't.

Not able to stand Roland's face any longer, I moved to the kitchen and helped Tene and Mother clean up the dinner dishes, while the Spencers sat with my father in the family room, enjoying cake and coffee.

You'd think Kathleen Spencer would've offered to assist, but no. Not when she thought that was purely the maid's job.

One thing I appreciated about my mother was that, though we could afford maids and butlers and chauffeurs, we never had them. My father had taught us the business side of Armstrong Realty, but my mother had instilled in us the value of a clean house and taught us to be self-sufficient.

I continued to empty the leftovers into the garbage while Tene filled up the dishwasher.

"Girls, I've booked us tickets to the Jones' charity function in a couple of months," Mother said.

The tension in the room was palpable. Tene had already told my mother that she had plans and couldn't attend, yet my mother seemed to ignore her. It was a never-ending battle between them. An emotional tug of war.

Tene's jaw locked as she crossed her arms across her chest. "Mother," she hissed, "I told you how many times that I couldn't go to the Jones' function? That I bought tickets to Ed Sheeran way before you even told me about this charity event."

My mother turned toward her nonchalantly, scooping the extra pasta into a Tupperware container. "Well, you know we have to show a united front. Especially at an event as big as this." She turned toward the fridge, opened it, and glided the container inside. "Cancel it." Her tone was clipped and short. She wasn't budging.

Tene's eyes shot in my direction, as though asking me to help her out. If looks could kill, my mother's head would be mounted on the wall like a deer's head. She motioned her hands in a choke hold as though she wanted to strangle my mother.

I pinched my thumb and pointer finger into an okay sign. "Calm down," I mouthed.

Tene was anything but calm. I knew the next thing out of her mouth would be bad.

"Mom, we don't need Tene there," I said quickly. "I'll be there, plus Roland will take her spot."

She flipped toward me. "Roland is already going with his family to show support for the Jones' loss of Abigail to cancer. They are showing their support, and we need to show ours. It's disrespectful if we don't."

My sister's nostrils flared, her face turning a shade darker. And I knew she was about to huff and puff and blow the house down. "We aren't even close to them. We only started going because your country club friends started going to the Jones' fundraisers."

I got between them, blocking Tene's view of my mother. "We've been going ten years in a row, and it's really not Tene's fault that they moved the date when they specifically had the first weekend in October every year before this year's event."

"Well, you just can't assume things, dear."

"Mom," I begged.

"Oh, my god," Tene sassed. "You're too much. Seriously?" She raised her hands, exasperated. "How the hell was I supposed to know they'd change their date? What did you want me to do? Wait for them to decide? Mother, that's ridiculous!"

I could see the train wreck coming and felt a panic, desperately wanting to stop it. You'd think since these blowups happened on a semi-monthly basis, that I'd get used to it. Still, I hated confrontation. It wasn't in my nature, and most definitely not when there was tension in the family.

"Tene ..." My wide eyes were begging her to chill out, but it was too late. All I saw was pure rage in her features.

"Lower your voice. We have company." My mother's features turned murderous as she moved her focus toward the door.

Tene's temper flared. "What? So everyone doesn't know how dysfunctional we are! How you like to control me or, more so, this family? That all you care about is what people see on the outside? You don't care that I'm unhappy, that this is more a dictatorship. This family. This life. That if we don't do what you say, you'll throw our trust fund in our face." Her voice was cold and lashing. "I made those plans more than six months ago. I'm not purposely doing this to spite you! What don't you understand? I'm sure the Jones' won't even know that I'm there."

"Enough!" My mother's shout silenced her.

Tene's chest rose and fell with each breath, as though she'd just run a mile and was not slowing down. Her face was flushed pink, and her hands were fisted tightly at her sides.

My mother pointed her manicured fingernail in Tene's direction. "You're canceling that concert."

That was the last straw. Tene's anger hardened her features. "Nope. Not going to happen. I'm going to that concert. And while you're at that charity function, I'll make it a point to get butt-ass wasted and laid—by multiple men."

My mother's jaw tightened, her disgust clear on her face. "That's all you're good for, anyway."

"Mom," I pleaded, "Stop. Please."

Tene flinched at her words. "I'm leaving this joint. Tell Dad, Roland, and the Spencers I said bye." Tene crossed the kitchen, gave me a hug, and stomped past my mother and called back, "You never know, I could be the one to give you your first bastard grandkid." She laughed without humor as she stormed out and the door slammed shut behind her.

My mother huffed through her nose, shaking it off as though it had never happened, then she turned to me, smiling. "Should we bring the cookies out?" She maintained composure, though her eyes showed the true torment reigning in her heart. That's how we were built the same. Everything around us could be burning down to the ground, but we'd maintain composure with a smile on our faces.

Concern crossed my features. I knew their relationship took a toll on her, but I didn't know why she pushed Tene so hard.

I approached her and put my hand on top of hers, to

stop hers from trembling. "You know she says those things to get a rise out of you. Just like you say those things to get a rise out of her." Silence ensued until I spoke again. "Are you okay?"

My sister dated, but she was no hooker. She didn't just sleep with anybody. If anything, she was far pickier than most of the girls in Rosendell.

My mother's trembling hand touched my face. "At least I have one daughter that cares for the well-being of her mother."

I smiled, just a small smile, but my insides churned. Her words spoke to the truth of the matter; I had always been the obedient one, the one who listened, the one they depended on. The one who never strayed.

As many times as I'd been jealous of my sister because of her beauty, I'd been equally jealous of her I-don't-give-a-shit attitude. Because there was freedom in doing what you wanted and not basing every decision on how your choices would affect others.

And I was certain there was happiness in that freedom.

━━━

I had a pounding headache during the ride home, so I rubbed at my temple and tried to tame the brewing migraine that heightened with the sound of Roland's voice.

"It's almost eleven o'clock." There was an eerie calm to his tone with a menacing undercurrent. "You know I have work tomorrow. You know that I will most likely be up all night. We should've left earlier."

I simply stayed silent and still, and the only indication of the anger brewing inside of me was my nails indenting my palms.

I tried to block him out, but he kept going and going like the Energizer Bunny, his mouth, his complaints, flowing nonstop.

When he pulled into our garage, he grumbled about work and having responsibility. By the time we walked into our condo, the meter on my mood box went from hot to boiling hella overflowing hot. The pounding in my head intensified as though a jackhammer was drilling holes in my brain.

On autopilot, my feet took me into our room and into our closet, and I pulled open the dresser to get my pajamas.

"And now I'll be up all night working on this proposal. If we only left when I told you to leave." He had followed me into our closet.

I jerked in his direction, unable to handle it anymore. "Can you please be quiet? I get it, okay!"

My pounding headache coupled with his dictating tone had been my undoing.

He glanced at me with indignation. "I don't think you get it. How important this job is to me ... how important this deal is."

My eyebrows shot to my hairline, and the pounding in my head now spread to my ears, my neck, my pulse.

Boom! Boom! Boom!

"Will you shut up? You know what I'm not dealing with? This!"

At my wit's end, I pulled out a suitcase and stuffed some work clothes and undergarments and toiletries for the next week into a duffel bag. Maybe I could sleep over at Tene's for a night. But if I didn't leave soon, all this pent-up animosity would turn into a hatred for the only man I'd ever been romantically involved with.

"Where are you going? Are you leaving me?" He barked out a laugh, his tone dismissive.

And then he proceeded to change into sweatpants and a T-shirt while my suitcase laid directly by my feet.

Something suddenly sparked inside of me, and I felt a fight forming within me.

He doesn't believe I can do it. Leave him.

Who is this man? Where is the man I fell in love with?

I couldn't take any more of this life, any more disappointments, any more heartbreak. I grabbed the extra keys to the condos I managed on the southside of Rosendell and slipped the oversized bag on my shoulder. When I stormed out of our walk-in closet, Roland was strolling out of the bathroom.

"Where the hell do you think you're going?"

I said the words to his face, so he'd know I was serious. "We're done. We've been done for a while now."

The words rang out true and loud, like a final bell in a Las Vegas fight.

I lifted my chin, though my pulse beat a million times a minute.

I can't believe I'm doing this. Actually leaving him.

But I was. I felt the decision solidify inside me, and I knew I was doing it. "It's over, Roland. We have a lot to talk through—the logistics of the apartment and our belongings —but since I know you'd rather work, and you have a *long* day tomorrow, I'm going to be considerate, and we can talk about this later." My voice dripped with icy sarcasm.

He gripped my wrist tightly, and his face paled with anger. "You're being ridiculous."

I tugged at the hand clutching my wrist, cutting off the circulation. "Let me go, Roland. You're hurting me."

When he didn't release me, I jerked my hand away from his grasp and turned toward the door.

"You're acting crazy." He followed me down the hall to our foyer where I slipped on my shoes and stuffed an extra pair of heels into the bag. "Get back here!" His tone hitched with a possessive desperation.

I stormed through the doors, and he followed me into the hallway, throwing his hands in the air. "Throw your tantrum, Angie. That's fine because you know you'll come right back here." Such confidence in his words, but for the first time in our relationship, I saw a spark of doubt in his eyes.

I stood there, hoping that he'd soften, fight for me, fight for us, something, anything.

But after a few seconds, I knew he wouldn't.

When the elevators pinged open, I stepped in. I watched the elevators close in front of me, shutting the door to my old life out and leaving me all alone with my new one.

But for the first time in years, hope bloomed. And my faith flared in promises of a better future.

———

Armstrong Realty owned condos on the south side of Rosendell. We rented them out as temporary housing, mostly to working professionals. Fully furnished with pots and pans and dishes, our condos were in move-in condition, and I was ready to move in.

Maybe this was reckless. Maybe I wasn't thinking things through for once. But one thing I knew was that I was done with empty promises, and I was emotionally and physically tired of being in a one-sided relationship. I threw my packed bag on the kitchen counter and surveyed the area. The one-bedroom condo was modest with a tan microfiber couch against the wall, kitty-corner to a 50" flat screen TV.

My phone pinged again with a text. I ignored it because it was most likely from Roland. He'd been texting since I'd left, but there was nothing that would get me to talk to him. I'd said my piece back at the apartment.

I grabbed the small suitcase and proceeded to the room. The motif that Tene had decided on fit the room perfectly. Everything seemed to match, from the purple trim on the curtains to the bedspread, to the throw pillows on the couch.

This was one of the properties that I knew well. There were seven units per floor, and we were ten stories high. Every room had exactly the same furniture in exactly the same spot. I dealt with the condos because those were, in my mother's words, "easier" to take care of. As though I couldn't handle any more than that.

Although this property and another set of condo units down the street were my responsibility, Tene did the decorating, like I couldn't handle making decisions for a property I was in charge of.

A thick cloud of bitterness surrounded me, almost shocking me because I'd had no idea it existed. Why hadn't I realized this before? Had my natural calm nature suppressed all this hidden animosity?

I pushed all the negativity aside and propelled myself facedown onto the bed. My body was surprisingly tired, and all my muscles went limp.

Eight years.

Eight long years with Roland.

Any other man would be begging for his girlfriend back by now, but Roland had too much pride.

I knew in my heart that I couldn't live like that anymore and fight for an already dead relationship. The realization hit me, directly in my chest—that my dream of forever had ended.

And this was not how I expected my life to turn out.

CHAPTER 7

TODAY WAS A NEW MORNING, a new day, a new start in life. My breakup with Roland weighed heavily on me, but I trekked forward. My father had entrusted me with the downtown locations, so, although my mind was mush, and I was tired from lack of sleep, I had pushed myself out of bed this morning and visited all my tenants downtown.

I'd woken up early to tell everyone that I'd be taking over Tene's territories. Now I was at my hardest stop of the day—Allswell.

The restaurant was jam-packed when I'd arrived, full of businesspeople and some families with kids in the outer booths.

Cade was behind the bar, tending to a woman who looked twice my age. By the way she sat, leaning into him, I could tell she was flirting and not hiding it. Had to give it to the aggressive cougars out there—they knew what they wanted and weren't afraid to pounce.

As if knowing I had just entered, Cade's head lifted, and when our gazes met, he smiled, accenting the dimple on his chin. His reaction to my entrance was noticeable as the woman in her tight, fitted skirt suit turned her whole body to see where his attention was focused.

I decided to sit at the edge of the bar and wait until he was finished. When he abandoned the woman and walked over to me, my pulse increased, thumping on the inside of my wrist.

"Angel." That one word falling from his lips had goose bumps forming on the back of my neck.

"C-Cade." My voice quivered with an embarrassingly husky desire.

Goodness, I need to get a grip.

A sexy smile played at the corners of his mouth. "How can I help you?"

I tucked an escaping strand of hair behind my ear and readjusted myself on my seat. "I came over to discuss a couple of things."

"I'm not usually one that can mix business with pleasure, but with you, I can. Name your poison."

You.

The thought was quick. Automatic. I jerked back and forced it down, all the way down to the pits of hell. I was glad I hadn't spoken that out loud.

"Just water, please," I said.

"I'm not much of a drinker, either. See how much we have in common?" His laugh was low, throaty.

"But you work at a bar?" I asked, genuinely curious.

"That doesn't mean I'm automatically an alcoholic. Water is my poison, too ... among other things." His eyes held a devilish glint of humor.

This man would be my poison if I wasn't careful, and I prided myself in being careful, and most of all, dedicated. Dedicated to my job and to my family. I couldn't mix business with pleasure with Cade.

"Truly an angel." He placed some ice in a tall glass and filled it with water. "Oh, how I'd love to corrupt you." His nearness was overwhelming.

He placed the glass on the counter and leaned his elbows against the bar. He was so close, the whiff of his masculine cologne made me stiffen and take in deeper breaths.

"So, how can I service you?"

I almost fell off my seat. All his sexual innuendos were driving me bonkers. He needed to stop.

I gripped the cold glass, hoping it would stop the heat wave inside me. "Stop flirting." My voice was a careless whisper, saying one thing, but meaning another.

He tilted his head and his intense gaze made my heart turn over in response. "Done. See? I can play nice. All you needed to say was stop." He straightened, seeming more businesslike. "So, what can I do for you?"

When I didn't answer, he simply stared at me, the gray in his steel eyes brightening. "You're beautiful," he said absently, almost as if he couldn't help himself.

I released a soft, silent sigh. "You're doing it again." I shied away, sweeping my hair to the front, using it as a curtain from his intense gaze, but that did nothing to quiet the zoo in my belly.

"I wasn't flirting that time. Just the truth." He shrugged as if it was nothing, but I couldn't deny that it meant something to me. His eyes were riveted on my face, appraising me.

No one has called me beautiful in such a long time ...

I cleared my throat and waved my hand, getting down to business and willing my pulse to slow down to a normal beat. "I just wanted to let you know that I'm taking over our downtown locations for Tene." Way to change the subject and go for subtle.

"So, you wanted to see me," he stated, that amused spark back in his eyes.

"No." My voice came out louder than I expected. "I mean, I'm visiting all our tenants to introduce myself. They were so used to dealing with my father and then Tene. Some I've never even met in person."

"Mmhmm."

I wanted to knock that all-knowing crooked smile off his face, then stupidly kiss him senseless.

"Believe what you want to believe," I said. "Now that it's done, I think I'll be going." I pushed back the stool, but he placed his hand on top of mine, stilling me. A jolt of electricity surged through me where we were connected. Would it ever stop, the tingle that traveled up my arm with the mere touch of his fingers?

One touch. His touch. I was amazed how my body reacted to him this way. It was forbidden and exciting at the same time. He was my tenant, which meant he was off limits.

"Sorry." His features softened, truly apologetic. "It's too much fun teasing you. You said stop, so no more teasing, okay?"

"Okay." My voice was soft, resigned.

His shoulders eased up, giving me an easy smile. "So, they're giving you more responsibility?"

"Yeah, with my father sick ..." I turned away, my chin trembling. "I mean ..." I hadn't meant for those words to slip out. Tene and I still couldn't talk about my father without choking up. Most of our long-term tenants knew of his condition, but Cade was a new tenant.

When I turned back to face him, his expression stilled

and grew serious, and there was a look I'd recognized that was so familiar, a look of ... understanding?

"I'm sorry." His voice got thick with emotion, and his grip tightened on my hand.

"It's kind of an unspoken topic. He had a heart attack last year, and my family likes to pretend it's not happening." I smiled again because that's what I did when things got uncomfortable—the forced Angelica Armstrong signature awkward smile. The center of my chest ached with a familiar pain.

He nodded, and a sentiment of sympathy filtered through his eyes. "I get it, Angel. I really do."

The business of the lunch hour was around us, but, once again, it seemed as if we were the only two in the room. Some unspoken words passed between us, an understanding of some sort. For some reason, I sensed he knew exactly what I was going through. His apology wasn't the automatic response that I was used to hearing from other people, and I wondered if he'd experienced some great loss as well.

"My mom's ... she's struggling, too," he blurted out softly but turned his head as though he hadn't meant for those words to escape his lips.

It was the first time in our brief encounter together that I had witnessed vulnerability in his confident, masculine demeanor. "I'm sorry," I said, the words heavy in my throat.

"Yeah, me too." There was an understanding in his look that comforted me, let me know that I wasn't alone.

Kristy called out his name behind him, needing some assistance down the bar.

"I'll be back." He pulled his hand away, breaking our connection. "Don't leave."

He turned before giving me a chance to respond, and I watched his retreating form.

I couldn't help but think there was more to Cade beyond his confident muscle man demeanor. And I couldn't help but want to uncover it.

———

After ten minutes of helping Kristy with the afternoon rush, Cade strolled my way. "Walk with me." He carried a bag of trash and nodded toward the back of the bar.

I followed him through a door that led back to the kitchen. The kitchen was in full swing as the cooks hustled and bustled around each other. A long stainless steel table was adorned with different plates of food garnished with what looked like sliced turnips rolled up and shaped into a rose.

Down the hall, into the back, he pushed a door open to the alley, and I trailed behind him and watched him lift the lid of the dumpster and toss the black bag inside.

"I'm sorry." He ran one hand through the top of his dark locks.

"For what?"

"You know, for revealing too much back there. The sad stuff."

I shrugged. "I did it first."

He turned away and nodded, and that awkwardness filled the air again. I hated it. I wanted that familiarity back, the short instant that we bonded back at the bar, so I filled the silence with words.

"Tene and I don't really talk about it because I start crying, and Tene gets all teary-eyed, and she hates that. She never cries—ever. To her, it's a sign of weakness. I'm just one big cry baby, and I don't want to start because I won't stop." I gave him a weak smile.

He nodded, his face careful. It seemed as though that one slip at the bar about his mother had been a mistake, and he was going to be careful not to make it again.

I leaned against the red brick of our building, staring at the concrete. I couldn't talk about my father with Roland, not anymore. And when I had tried before, I'd never believed it when he'd said that all would be okay. It always seemed forced, rehearsed, and only for my benefit. And he didn't truly understand the constant worry Tene and I had over Dad's health.

For once, it felt nice to let my feelings all drip out. "It's like my world bottomed out when he was in the hospital. All I could think of when he was in there, tied up to all those tubes, was that he couldn't go ... not yet."

My father was the glue that kept us together. Not only with the business, but he kept our family intact.

I swallowed a cry in my throat, getting lost in my own thoughts. "My mother cried the whole time beside him, and she's built like Tene; she doesn't cry at all. That's how I knew it was bad." I let out a long, low sigh and fidgeted with my fingers. "People say everything is going to be okay, but it's not. Nothing is going to be the same after this." I bit the inside of my cheek. One more word out of me, and I knew that I'd be a wreck. Maybe it was a mistake to talk to Cade about all this. I focused on the cars passing by, the soft breeze against my skin, and the clear blue sky above me so that the internal havoc inside of me would dim.

Cade leaned against the wall beside me, propped one leg up and retrieved a pack of cigarettes from the back of his pocket. He offered me one, but I shook my head. Then he placed the cigarette on his lips.

"I didn't figure you for a smoker."

"I don't smoke."

"What?" I frowned.

"I don't." He eyed me with a crooked smile.

Both of my hands fell on my hips. "So, you work at a bar, yet you don't drink. You carry cigarettes, but you don't smoke. Is there an underlying reason for this?"

"I do drink, but not in excess." His smile disappeared, and behind his vision, a thick cloud of darkness formed. "My sister had addiction problems."

I didn't miss the past tense, and the hairs on the back of my neck stood at full attention.

"She's dead," he added. He flinched as soon as the words left his mouth and his whole face faltered, his shoulders slumping.

Before I knew what I was doing, I rushed into him and hugged him, my head against his chest. "I'm sorry."

The move was Angelica automatic.

And I was so very sorry. I couldn't imagine losing a sibling and at such a young age. His loss made me think of Tene, and I couldn't even fathom losing her. I wouldn't be able to deal.

I caught him by surprise because he froze for a second, before his warm hands wrapped around my waist. When I realized I had seriously crossed some unprofessional lines on so many levels, I straightened and moved back, but not before his arms drew me closer.

It felt good to be this close to him, consoling him. I couldn't bear to look up because we were already in a compromising position, and staring into his face would only worsen our situation.

I brought my hands around to the firm span of his stomach, to the hard pecs of his chest. I meant to push away, but his words distracted me. "I get it, Angel. When you say nothing's going to be the same after this. I get it. My sister is gone, and she's never coming back. My family is forever changed because of it."

His hand caressed up and down my back. His voice sounded so distant that I wondered if he knew what he was doing or that he was even touching me. But I understood him fully. One event alters everything in its path. My family would forever be walking on pins and needles with my father's health. I wondered if the fear would ever go away.

"I don't let vices control me. Drugs, alcohol, and even cigarettes. It's a lesson I learned. I am in control of this life I lead. Addiction already took so much from us."

A silence settled over us. All I heard were the swish of the cars down the alley and the soft breaths escaping him.

"I've lost more than you know," he continued. "And family means everything to me. I sacrifice and will continue to sacrifice everything for my family."

His arms still caged me in. It was so wrong, yet felt so alarmingly calm to be next to him. I comforted him, knowing the truth. "It won't be the same for our families or for us ... but maybe ... just maybe it'll get better. At least, that's what I hope for."

He rested his chin on the top of my head, and, for once, since I'd stepped into him, my whole body relaxed.

I knew I was crossing all the boundaries, but I couldn't help it. There was no way I was pushing him away because, although I gave him comfort, selfishly he gave me comfort, too.

———

For the next few days, life continued as I knew it. After

work, I drove to my new place and walked into an unfamiliar room, placed my bag on a different table and kicked off my heels on the floor because I was without my usual shoe storage bench.

I plopped on the couch and reached for my cell. My phone indicated five missed calls from Roland. I stared, unblinking at his name and the picture of us together, and my heart sank to the floor. We'd been together since before I could even remember. He'd been my first everything, and I still couldn't grasp the idea that we were done. Done and over. Kaput.

But I'd made the right decision, hadn't I? Were we truly over? Did I miss him?

My finger hovered over the screen of my phone. I realized I loved and missed the old him—not the new him—and that I was in love with a ghost. Because the old him was permanently gone, and he'd been gone for some time now.

My birthday was coming up. To me, my birthday was my favorite day of the year. And this year, I'd be spending it alone. Roland had planned a celebration dinner, but I wondered if it would've actually happened if we were still together.

The thoughts brought me back to last year's birthday non-celebration.

⸺

A giddy smile filled my face as I applied my mascara, staring at myself in the immense bathroom mirror. This bathroom was Roland's sanctuary. That was why he'd had the builders import the granite from Italy and had installed a tufted gold tub that took up a quarter of the bathroom.

Today was my birthday.

It was the one day where, like a big kid, I saved all my wishes to make that one epic wish when I blew out all my birthday candles.

The exhilaration of knowing it was a new year—a new beginning—it was as though I was experiencing a new birth. Most made New Year's resolutions. I made birthday resolutions. For me, my birthday was a reset, a do over.

Pursing my lips together, I took in my reflection one more time. I had curled my hair to perfection tonight, knowing it was my special day. I'd received my birthday greetings this morning, ones I looked forward to every year, and tonight, Roland was going to take me out.

For the past five years, on my actual birthday, he'd surprised me. I never knew where we were going for our dinner date, and he always showered me with expensive gifts and planned a separate family dinner with both sets of parents, which was happening this weekend.

Strolling into our massive walk-in closet, I pulled out the new dress I'd bought for the occasion, a navy blue fitted lace dress that rested just above the knee.

I knew Roland would be taking me somewhere upscale, a place that donned no less than ten courses, plus dessert. He was a connoisseur of fine dining when work wasn't occupying his time.

After I slipped on the dress that clung to my hips, I tiptoed in front of my floor-length mirror and turned around once, loving the exposed lace around my neckline and at the bottom of the dress. My eyes sparkled through the mirror as a lightness spread through my limbs.

New beginnings. For him. For me. For us.

There was a bounce in my step as I sauntered to my jewelry box and pulled out a pair of one carat studs that Roland had given me on our last anniversary.

When I heard my cell ring, I ran back into the bedroom and picked up the phone.

"Happy Birthday, Angie." Roland's voice was hoarse, different. My stomach dropped to my toes.

"Is something wrong?" My first thought was that he'd been in an accident on his way home. "Roland!"

"Angelica ..." The way he said my name, his soft, apologetic tone, was so familiar. It's the tone he uses before sentences that end in 'I'm sorry.'

"What happened?" I held my breath and fidgeted with my earring.

"I need you to do something for me. Go into the closet in the foyer and your present will be there."

Immediately, I ran out our bedroom and to the front of our apartment. My heels clicked against the floor, ready for the night to begin. I loved surprises, and Roland knew this about me. When I pulled open the closet door, a rather large blue box greeted me, wrapped in silver wrapping paper and a bow that spanned the entire top of the gift.

"I have to say," I said, smiling. "You spoil me."

"I know you'll love it. I ordered it six months ago."

I took off the pieces of tape from the sides and unwrapped my present. When I lifted the box, my hand flew to my chest as I took in a 5x7 double silver picture frame of the two of us in high school, right next to the one of a more recent one of us during Christmas. On the bottom of the frame under each picture was the date that we got together and on the more recent one, it was engraved "Until Forever."

Roland had never been the sentimental one in our relationship, and as my fingertips grazed over the words, "Until Forever," a heat radiated in my chest, spreading to every part of me.

"It's so sweet, Roland. So romantic. I absolutely love it! I love you."

"It's custom-made, and there are only five just like it." His tone leaked with pride.

My hand flew to my heart, then I noticed the blue leather underneath the picture frame.

"Oh." Laughter escaped me as I repositioned the phone by my ear. "There's more." I placed the frame on the kitchen table and pulled out a beautiful, elegant Hermes purse, slipping it over my shoulder. "Roland. Seriously, it's perfect. It matches my dress. This must have cost a fortune. Thank you." I twirled around, and my skirt swished against my legs.

"I'm glad you like it, Angie. It suits you. Beautiful. Sophisticated."

Nothing could've deterred my mood. The day was getting better and better as it went on. Brunch with my sister, gifts, then dinner with my beloved.

"Happy birthday. I'm glad you love it."

"I do," I squeed, practically hopping on my heels.

"Angelica ..." His voice trailed off.

Something in his voice made my stomach roll. There it was again, the same tone as earlier.

My fists clenched the straps of the purse, slightly trembling.

"Angie ... you know that deal I've been working on? The one where I've been trying to get a meeting with the CEO of the company ...?" His voice lowered, as though he didn't want others around him to hear.

I chewed on my inner cheek, practically making it bleed. "Please don't, Roland." My voice broke as I dropped the purse to the floor. Both of my hands gripped the phone as though it was my lifeline. "Not today. It's my birthday."

He was silent, and the quiet seemed to drag on for a lifetime. "And I will be able to make a later dinner reservation. I'll call. I'll reschedule for later tonight."

"Like what time? Ten? We're going to have dinner at ten?" The words sounded ridiculous, even to my own ears. "Just tell your boss you can't go."

"I couldn't. I didn't know what to tell them."

At his words, I lost it, lost my cool, something that had never happened before. "You could've told them that it was your girlfriend's birthday." Tears burst from my eyes. There was no denying I was crying as my body shook with an anger so strong I felt dizzy. "That she looks forward to this day every single year. That you've missed and cancelled every event lately, but you'd never—ever—miss her birthday. Not in a million years. How about that, Roland? You could've told them that!"

"Angelica. You need to understand ..." His tone was authoritative, as though he were speaking to a child.

I was tired of hearing his excuses, tired of him blowing me off. "Are you going to meet that CEO tonight?" I held my breath, holding out for any last ounce of faith I had in a man I'd spent most of my young adult life loving.

"I have to, Angie." His voice broke with finality, but so did my heart. "I promise I'll make it up to you."

There was a first for everything, right? I just couldn't believe that this was my new beginning. I threw the phone across the room, and, for the first time ever, sobbed myself to sleep. On my birthday.

━━

Weary, warm, waterfall tears coursed down my cheeks and onto the pillow. I clutched the pillow closer to my chest and curled into myself. Deep down, I knew—I knew in my heart that this was truly the end. We weren't on a break, having a fight, taking a time out.

Work had been coming before me for a long time, and I couldn't take it. I couldn't suffer through that for a lifetime.

I wouldn't.

What I thought would be my happily-ever-after, my dream come true, had ended a long time ago.

It'll be okay. I'll be okay, I repeated to soothe myself. Though I thought my heart had known this was coming, it still hurt. It still hurt to think of Roland not in my life. But being in a relationship didn't define me, and once I was done grieving, I knew I'd come out of this stronger.

CHAPTER 8

LATER THAT NIGHT I ended up at Allswell. I needed
someone to talk to, vent to, and I craved the emotional inti-
macy that I'd experienced with Cade in the alley. My
family would never understand my frustrations with
Roland, whom they adored. And I wasn't ready to tell them
yet. I didn't know how.

The car sat in park as I watched a few patrons leave the
restaurant. When my stomach grumbled, indicating dinner-
time, I stepped out, pulled my suit jacket shut and entered
the restaurant. I had flown out of my new condo with such a
hungry desperation for food and wine that I'd forgotten to
change out of my skirt suit.

My hands wrapped around my middle as the blast from
the air vent sent a chill right through me. Cade was
nowhere to be seen, but I proceeded to the bar anyway.
There was no way I was going home, and I had no other
place to go. If I went back home, my father would know
something was wrong, and the last thing I wanted to do was
stress him out.

After plopping my butt on the stool, I lifted my hand for

service. Forget food and wine, I needed hard liquor. "Cranberry and vodka," I told the bartender.

The tall brunette's hands flew to the vodka bottle, the other on an empty glass.

"Is Cade here?"

She used the dispenser to pour cranberry in the glass and glided my concoction in my direction. "He's in the back. I'll get him." She called out his name, and when he strolled in, my lips parted, and heavenly havoc reigned in my heart.

The moment our eyes met, my whole body gravitated toward his as though he was fire and I needed the voodoo of my foul mood melted.

"Bad night?" he asked.

"You can say that." I slumped against the counter and reached for my drink.

"Men problems, money problems? Or is it your job? Is someone making it difficult at work?" The corners of his mouth tipped up, and the chill in me dimmed.

He leaned forward in a cocky manner. "I'm a bartender, which sort of classifies me as a psychiatrist, except I don't prescribe drugs, I make drinks. So, go ahead, tell me your problems." That damn sexy crooked smile was back on his face, and I couldn't help but be amused.

From below the bar, he took out a shot glass, poured some tequila and placed it in front of me. "Drink."

"I have a drink." I lifted my dark colored beverage.

"You need stronger meds."

I did. I'd come here to talk, to forget, to cool off. To all of the above and all at once.

Taking what the doctor ordered, I didn't even hesitate as I downed the shot. The hard liquor burned the back of my throat. I covered my mouth and began to cough.

When the patrons down the bar and Kristy all turned my direction, Cade let out a humorous, low laugh.

"I should've given you less."

He handed me a napkin, and I wiped some of the liquid that had trickled from the side of my mouth. Resting his arms on the bar, he gave me a pointed look. "Why are you here, Angel?"

"What, no flirting? Now you want to get rid of me?" I tried to make my voice light, but anyone could sense the tinge of sadness behind my tone.

His smile tightened, and concern crossed his features. "It's not fun flirting with you when you're like this. Talk."

My gaze dropped to my hands that were gripping the glass too tightly. "It's Roland." My hands trembled, matching the quiver in my voice.

He nodded once, understanding. "The boyfriend has a name."

"Ex," I corrected him.

"Really, now." He rubbed at his jaw with his forefinger and thumb. "This is interesting. Plot twist."

"I'm serious, Cade. It's over." There was finality in that one word. Death. Death of a relationship.

I needed someone to talk to who would simply listen. No snide comments. Joking aside, I needed a comforting ear.

From the look on my face, I sensed he knew it. "Okay, Angel. Talk."

Then the words I'd kept inside for days flew out. "I've just had enough. He's so involved with work. It's late nights, early mornings, and working all weekend. I was living with a man I barely saw, barely knew anymore. He'd changed. He is full of empty promises." The vodka and cranberry liquid swished in my glass. "I've always been second best to his job, and I'm sick and tired of waiting for him to come back to me." I was tired of pretending I was happy in front of everyone else and trying to convince myself that I was happy. Sometimes when you lie long enough, you tend to believe the lies. "I ended it before I started believing our fake fairy tale."

I was now lumped in as one of those people that went to the bar, drowned all their sorrows in liquor and disclosed all their problems to the local bartender. I peered up and pushed the shot glass in his direction. "Another dose, please."

He nodded and filled me up. When I snapped back the shot glass, the burn down my throat lessened.

"I can do better than his false promises, but then I think of all the time we've been together. I've been with him since high school. He's the first boy that ever kissed me, my first boyfriend, my first everything, and my family absolutely adores him."

I pushed my shot glass back in his direction, finally feeling warmer and more loosened up.

"Did you eat?" he asked.

"I'm not hungry anymore."

"That's not an answer."

I nodded toward my empty glass. He hesitated at first, but then poured me another shot.

"Our mothers are practically planning our wedding. I love his mother. She's sweet and kind, and our families get along so well. And I haven't even told them yet. I don't even know where to start." My stomach rolled, but I welcomed the feeling. It was this or feel sorry for myself. I'd take numb over self-pity.

I pushed my shot glass in his direction, my mixed drink neglected and forgotten.

He shook his head, amused. "I think you've had enough."

"No," I whined. "You're my shrink. Don't cut me off. I need more meds." There was an intense ringing in my ears as my eyes glossed over, but I wasn't ready to slow down. "More."

"Answer me this first," he said, his tone serious. "Are you in love with him?"

His question shocked me. No one had ever asked me that question before. The answer was obvious, wasn't it? "Of course, I love him." How could I not after all we'd shared together? My stomach churned, and I knew it was from one too many shots.

He shook his head. "Are you *in* love with him? Loving him because he's all you've ever known, or loving him because your family loves him versus being in love? There's a difference, Angel."

One hand flew to my throat. He was right. I'd been in a drawn-out relationship for so long that I'd forgotten the difference. "I used to write his name with hearts on everything I owned ... I can't believe we ended up like this." It wasn't an answer, but it was all I would give him. Anything else would be too personal. "It doesn't matter anymore. We're done." I pushed the shot glass again in his direction. "More."

Indecision crossed his features, but I added the puppy dog face and a "Please." He hesitated at first, but couldn't resist and poured me another shot.

Just what the doctor prescribed.

———

Time passed by. Kristy left, and the bar and restaurant were spotless. Who knew what time it was? Who the heck cared?

I sure didn't as I sipped my whatever-was-in-my-glass-drink, listening to Cade's stories and slumping against the bar.

Cade was drinking a bottled water in the stool beside me, displaying a wide grin. I slipped off my jacket, and my thin silk blouse clung to my body. One too many drinks had me a little warmer than normal.

All I knew was I was having a grand ole time, and I wasn't blaming it on the liquor. It was the gray-eyed, tattooed male in front of me. Learning about his past and his family intrigued me.

"Yeah, about my brothers," he went on. "My parents were foster parents, so there were kids in and out of our home. Jordan and Wyatt are my brothers, but not by blood. I bonded with them on a level I never did with the other kids. Plus, they permanently stayed."

There were so many facets of this man I barely knew that I needed to know more about. He was like an unfinished book, and I needed to get to the very end.

"Do you have any biological siblings?" I asked.

"Yeah." He turned, and pain passed through his features. "My sister." He choked out the words as though his throat was closing up and a huge, painful knot formed inside my chest.

The atmosphere turned tense when Cade tore his gaze from mine, and in typical Angelica fashion, it was my job to make things better, so I placed a hand on his forearm and squeezed.

"Do you want to talk about her?" I wanted to know more about his family without prying too much, so I let him take the lead on the direction he wanted to take our conversation.

He focused on where we were connected and cleared his throat before whispering, "No. Not right now. I just can't." A sad silence swallowed the space between us, and I stared at his face, bleak with sorrow.

He lifted his head and offered me a forced smile. "How about you? Do you have a big family?"

He was changing the subject on me, but I'd bite because I'd do anything to erase the desolate look in his eyes.

"I always wanted a bigger family. I don't have any brothers, but I do have Tene, and she's my best friend." I took a swig of my drink, thinking of my sister and all we'd been through. "She totally thinks I'm too good for Roland, but then again, I think she'd think no man is good enough for her little sister."

"What if I told you I thought you were too good for Roland?" The line of his mouth tightened, his steady gaze serious.

"I'd tell you that your opinion in the matter is a little biased. You want to get into my pants." I laughed and averted my gaze, embarrassed that the words slipped out. Funny how liquor was the truth serum. My brain to mouth filter seemed to be out of service.

"Pants or no pants, from what you've already told me, and what your sister—who I think is a no bullshit type of girl—has said, I think you made a smart decision by dumping the loser."

I sighed, then drummed my fingers against the bar while memories of our past and how our families were so interconnected bombarded my brain. "My parents think he's perfect for me."

"Do you always do what your parents want you to do?" He cocked an eyebrow.

His questions were making me dig deeper today. Although I was the obedient child, I was never with Roland because of my parents. And I certainly didn't stay with Roland simply because they thought he was perfect for me.

I blinked, and in response to his question, I downed my drink. My stomach flipped and flopped as a dizzying current ran through me. "Yes, I do. But parents want the best for their children, so what's wrong with that?"

I stood then gripped the chair for support. "More, please?" The room spun around me, and I closed my eyes to stop the nausea about to take over.

Warm hands gripped my shoulders, and I leaned into him for support, enjoying the heat of his body against mine. God, it felt good to be next to him, to feel the strength of him, especially since the liquor made me queasy and my emotional state was shot.

"You're cut off. Done." His voice was light, though I knew he meant business.

My arms wrapped around his middle for support, and I leaned into his steel frame. He smelled of sweat and beer and cologne and all manly goodness. I buried my nose in his shirt, and he laughed.

His face creased with a small smile. "I think you're officially wasted, Angel. Do you want me to call you a cab home?"

I rested my chin on his chest, staring up at him with teenage googly eyes. Gosh, was he thoughtful and handsome and everything all wrapped up in a pretty bad boy inked package, just like Christmas.

I licked my lips, and slow and seductively his eyes slid downward to my mouth.

The liquor was hitting me hard, and my head was spinning in circles. "I want to kiss you." I guess with the liquor came a lack of morals.

His smile was jaw-droppingly beautiful and drew me in

like a magnet. "We can't," he said, though his body language, the way he pulled me in, told me he very much wanted the same thing I did.

"Why?" I whined, sounding annoyed. The alcohol. *I'm blaming the alcohol.*

His smile disappeared from his handsome face. With one finger, he lifted my chin and angled forward until we were almost nose to nose.

His nose skimmed my chin, then glided up to my ear. "Those lips are so fucking kissable." I released an audible sigh as he kept speaking. "What I would do to kiss those lips." His nose made its way down my temple to my neck. He placed a light kiss on the crook of my neck that sent tingles throughout my body, a sensation that went from the top of my head to the tip of my toes. "But I won't." His lips trailed tiny kisses up my neck and back to my ear. "Because you're drunk, and when I kiss you," his warm breath tickled the outer rim of my ear, "I want you to remember."

"No fair." I rested my head on his chest as his hand went continuously up and down my back. The nonstop motion caused the tightness in my shoulders to loosen. "I'm sleepy. So tired." All the tension from work and my problems with Roland had worn me down.

"Sleep, my Angel," he said softly. Then he whispered three words that I was used to saying to everyone else. "I've got you."

My whole body relaxed against him, then I felt something tight wrap around my legs, and it was like I was floating on air.

CHAPTER 9

THE POUNDING in my head accelerated, and as soon as I opened my eyes, I shut them tightly again as light registered in my brain. It was as though every sensory element in my mind was heightened, making my stomach queasy and equilibrium unstable.

"The garbage is right by the bed," a familiar voice spoke.

Sexy. Sultry. Masculine. That voice could only belong to one person.

Cade.

I jolted to a sitting position, pulling the sheets closer to my chest. The abrupt movement had my head spinning.

Cade was in all his wonderful glory, shirtless with only his boxers on. He sat on the edge of the bed, placed a hand on my shoulder and ushered me gently against the headboard. "Rest."

Angelica Armstrong. Think, think, think. What have you done?

I remembered drinking.

And more drinking ...

And the last thing I recalled was laughing, though the

rest was fuzzy. I most definitely did not know the specifics of how I had gotten into his room, or worse ... into his bed.

My eyebrows pulled together as I tried to calm my hammering pulse. I drew my shaky palm to the top of my hair as my other hand began to fan myself. In about two seconds, I knew I was going to have a nervous breakdown.

I took deep breaths in my nose and out through my mouth in a repetitive motion to calm myself. But it wasn't working.

"Angel, uh ... you don't look too good." His tone heightened with worry. "Are you okay?"

I shook my head vigorously; the room was spinning faster and faster, my body uneasy, my stomach woozy. Then I tried to stop the dizzying effect the room had on my senses by staying as still as possible.

He knelt right next to me, asking me again, then placing one hand on the sheet that covered my thigh. "I'll grab you some water."

He shifted, and the small movement caused my stomach to flip erratically. And that's when the gurgling in my belly began, and the queasiness in the pit of my stomach spread to the top of my throat.

I threw one arm over my mouth and tried to push myself off the bed when the oversized shirt rose to the top of my thighs, and I realized I didn't have any underwear on, shocking me and stopping me in my spot. That hesitation had me done for, and it was too late. I cupped both hands to my mouth, but not before I threw up everywhere. On his bed. On his sheets. All over myself.

Tears sprang, from embarrassment, from guilt. I couldn't even wipe them off my face and prevent them from falling because there was vomit in my hands.

"Angel, you're going to be okay." He scurried to the bathroom and came back with a basin and washcloth in one hand, while he held a small trash can in the other.

I emptied my hands into the garbage.

"Don't. I can do it," I said through muffled sobs and wiping my mouth with the edge of my sleeve.

He leaned in, so close, I knew he could smell the foul stench of whatever had been in my stomach.

"Stop," I begged, not able to look him in the eyes.

He folded the soiled sheets over, knelt beside me and reached for my palm, not caring that I was still filthy, and wiped down each finger. He dipped the washcloth in the basin, rinsed it and repeated the motion of wiping me clean. "Relax. This is me taking care of you."

More tears surfaced at his gentleness, at the softness in his tone, at the tenderness of his touch. I wanted to tell him that wasn't his job, but I didn't, afraid to speak, afraid to move because my mind was mush and my stomach was uneasy, and the guilt was overwhelming.

I was sure I should've told him a million things last night, things a responsible adult should be saying, but I was certain I didn't, or I wouldn't have ended up here. If I couldn't resist him when I was stone cold sober, there was no way I could've resisted him when I was drunk.

When he was done cleaning my hands, he reached over to the side table and pulled a Kleenex from the box, dabbing at my cheeks. "There, all done."

The sentiment was so sincere, so sweet, that the tears welled up again. I was used to taking care of everyone else— Tene when she was butt-ass drunk; my mother when she couldn't function when my father was sick; and Roland, functioning as his live-in mother sometimes.

I stared up at Cade with newfound wonder and

straightened on his bed. It felt nice to be taken care of, for once.

One slight movement and he would've seen my hooha, though I knew he'd more than seen it the night before. Still, I didn't want to give him a second glimpse as I pulled the other sheet over my knees.

"Th-thank you." I had been crying so much that I was now hiccupping.

A fresh round of tears started to fall. All I could think of was my stupidity at getting so wasted that I didn't even remember what had happened last night. If I was going to have sex with the hot bartender, I should've at least remembered it.

He sat beside me quietly, staring, studying, not smiling. He placed one hand over the blanket, touching my leg. "Nothing happened, Angel."

I perked up and took in his face, the seriousness in his tone. "What do you mean?"

"I mean, we didn't have sex. You were drunk, and I'm not that guy." He smiled. "My mother did not raise three men to take advantage of women."

I dabbed my eyes with the Kleenex. I still didn't have the ability to find my voice.

"Though, damn, I wanted to. But I'm really not into paraphilia. I like my women wide awake, lively, and begging for more," he joked.

I lifted the blanket from my legs. Yep. Still no underwear, like they would've automatically appeared.

He cleared his throat. "When you—as you said it—had to 'tinkle' in my bathroom, you slipped off your underwear and refused to put them back on."

"Oh ..." My face turned tomato red, the heat rushing to the apples of my cheeks.

"Oh, yeah, Angel." He nodded. "And when I insisted you put them back on, you took off your silk blouse too." He smiled his crooked smile and blew out a low, hoarse whistle. "That was a sight to see."

"And then what happened?" I pressed, not wanting to hear more but needing to.

"And then, you passed out. Cold. Naked. On my floor."

He leaned in closer as this mischievous glint glimmered in his eye. "God, you're the sexiest little thing I've ever seen."

My forehead heated. Can your forehead turn red? Because I was pretty sure that it was. Visible sweating was taking place. "You managed to get my shirt back on, but not my underwear?" I asked, quirking an eyebrow.

He grimaced with humor. "Well, every time I tried to get your underwear back on, you kept kicking your feet." He let out a thick, throaty laugh.

I dropped my head in my hands. This could not get any worse. Or could it?

"Let's just say, I tried twice. I could've tried harder, but shit, baby ... that ass. That perfect ass of yours." He bit his fist, looking tortured. "I just wanted to take a bite."

I peered at him through my fingers. "You bit my ass?"

"No, but I wanted to. I did enjoy the view, though."

I dropped my hand and pulled the blanket closer to my chest. "Pervert," I muttered, not really upset with him. Just that my life was over. All of it. I could never face this man again, yet I knew I'd have to.

He raised one eyebrow, looking amused. "I'm only a pervert if you didn't like me checking out your ass."

His flirty look had my lips wanting to curl up in a smile. "I'm so embarrassed. I don't think I want to hear anymore. Would you please stop?"

"Okay. Stopped." He pressed his lips into a tight line as if gluing them shut.

We sat in silence as I wrung my hands in my lap. "Promise me you'll never make me a drink again."

His laughter floated up his throat. "But I haven't had that much fun in a while."

"Cade."

"Okay." His eyes were sincere, and he raised one hand as though saying an oath. "I promise."

I bit my lip and peered over at him sheepishly. "Thanks. You know ... for taking care of me and all." I twisted the bed sheet within my fingertips. "That's never happened to me before. Ever. Where I drank myself into oblivion."

He shrugged. "It's okay. Everyone needs to let loose once in awhile, and it's not like I've never got butt-ass wasted before."

He tipped his chin. "It's nothing, Angel. I'm used to taking care of people. It's what I do." He moved from the bed and stood. "Candice was an alcoholic, among other things, so I know all about cleaning up puke." He turned to walk toward the bathroom, taking the basin full of my vomit with him. "I took care of her until she killed herself in the car accident. My father was in the car, too."

I gasped, and my hand flew to my parted lips. I didn't see his face, but I could only imagine what he was feeling. The little tidbits I'd learned about his family explained so much about Cade, yet a big part of me believed I hadn't even scratched the surface.

CHAPTER 10

MY FIRST COUPLE of days handling the downtown locations was coming to an end. I had to say, I was pretty proud of myself and on an ultimate high. I was rocking my job, proactive in contacting our contractors and getting every complaint assessed and every repair fixed. The zoning and city ordinances were all up to date with all our inspections. I was starting this right and making sure that I didn't disappoint my family and I lived up to the Armstrong name.

Driving down Elgin Avenue after work, I slowed to a stop in front of Allswell. Thoughts of Cade and what happened a few nights ago surfaced—his careful attention as I vented all my frustrations, his gentle affection when he took care of me, his soft tenderness cleaning me up when I had thrown up all over his bed.

I touched my cheek, still embarrassed at the memory. I could still conjure the stink of everything that had come up from my stomach, the memory still fresh.

Yet not once did he make me feel uncomfortable like he was happy to take care of me.

Dithering there in my car, I decided I wanted to see him. If I was being honest with myself, I missed him.

I pushed through the door of Allswell, and as always, there was a line waiting to be seated. One hostess peered at her papers in sheer concentration while others cheerfully ushered customers to their tables.

After walking straight to the bar, I raised my hand and got the attention of another bartender. I leaned over the counter. "Is Cade in the back?"

"No. He won't be back for a couple of days."

My stomach dropped with disappointment. "Oh. Do you know where he went?"

"Home, to take care of his mom." This time it was Kristy who had spoken. She approached me and waved off the other bartender to tend to other patrons. "He goes home often because he has family obligations to take care of." She eyed me with disdain, skimming my suit and the Hermes bag slung over my shoulder. "I don't know what game you're playing here."

I leaned back and crossed my arms over my chest. Automatically, my walls were up. "I'm sorry. Cade and I are just friends. I'm not playing any games."

She raised a judgmental eyebrow, and her lips puckered with annoyance. "I know you spent the night the other night."

I shook my head vigorously, not sure why I felt the need to maintain my innocence with her. "Nothing happened. Nothing."

She shifted her weight and ducked in, propping her arms on the bar. "Sure, whatever." Her tone dripped with sarcasm. "All I know is that you have some sort of hold on him. He's been through a lot of shit. So, whatever you're doing, whatever you have planned, cut it out. He's got too much on his plate."

I sucked in my cheeks and bit back the words that I was going to say. We warred for seconds without words. Then her cutting voice sliced through the silence. "You rich girls think you can do whatever you want."

I reeled back, face tight. I didn't have to deal with her crap. I'd done nothing wrong. "You don't know me," I said flatly. "So, you can take your rich girl comment and ... and stick it up your ass."

My ears burned, my breathing sped up, and my nails dug indentations on the insides of my palms. I'd never wanted to punch someone so badly in my whole life.

I half ran out of that place before I did something I'd regret.

Being so busy at work, the next few days flew by fast. A new tenant was moving into one of our vacant properties, and since the property was on Elgin Avenue, it was in my territory.

Though I was busy, I couldn't help but think of Cade, hoping he was okay, hoping his mother was fine. I know that he'd said she was unwell, but I wasn't sure what that meant entirely.

I was standing in our vacant property, making sure the cleaning people were doing their job, and everything was up to code before our tenant moved in when my phone rang with an unknown number.

"Hello?"

"Hey, Angel."

Two words that made my body betray me and had a

shiver running down my back. The simple sound of his voice made my senses spin. "Hey."

"Kristy told me to call you and make sure everything's okay. She told me what happened the other day and wanted to make sure everything was fine with our lease." His tone was laced with worry.

I moved to the side of the room and rested against the wall, pleased with the shine on the newly-polished floors. "You signed a five-year lease with Armstrong. Just because one of your employees doesn't like me doesn't mean I can amend your lease, Cade. Even if I wanted to, which I don't, I'm pretty sure that's illegal."

He chuckled. "Where are you right now?"

"I'm just a few blocks away from Clark and Lasalle. You know, the hard life of being a landlord." Something plagued the back of my mind. Although he was my tenant, our relationship had crossed into the land of friendship with vomit and naked sleepovers without sex. "How is your mom?" I asked, knowing I should keep our conversation purely professional, but I had to know that everything was okay.

He didn't answer, but said, "Can you come by later? I'm not really a phone person."

I knew I shouldn't have. I should only go to Allswell on business and nothing more, but I found myself agreeing anyway. "Sure. I'll be over soon."

Thirty minutes later, I was walking into Allswell during the busy lunch hour. When he saw me enter, Cade's whole face lit up, and his signature crooked smile surfaced. Smitten, I staggered in my step, taking him in and needing a moment to collect myself.

Breathe.

There was no denying this powerful force of attraction I had toward him, an undeniable pull. Horizontal gravity.

"Hey," he called over when I approached.

After I sat on the stool by the bar, he handed me a tall glass of water with a slice of lemon. "Water by day. Shots at night, right?"

I grimaced, just thinking about the other night. "Yeah, I'll never be drinking like that ever again."

He winked at me. "Never say never."

I smiled, remembering why I had come. "How are you?"

"Good, now that you're here." He placed both hands on the bar, leaned in and scoured my face as though I was the light in the room.

Sigh.

I kept my face casual, though my heart fluttered widely in my chest. "You're flirting again."

"Maybe." He smiled, then tipped his head toward Kristy, at the end of the bar pouring drinks for a couple of guys in front of her. "Sorry about her. She's from home, and she kind of gets protective of me."

"So, you have history?" Curiosity ate at my insides. I wanted to know every single detail of his history, his life, what made him Cade.

His smile faded a little when his eyes flickered toward her. "We dated briefly, for a week. Biggest mistake ever. Totally incompatible as a couple, but we're great business partners. Now she heads up and trains at all our new locations. We normally get along until she gets all mama bear on me. Protective and all."

Suddenly, her reactions toward me became vividly clear.

Cade turned my way, lifted his arm, and made his muscle pop. "Like I need protecting, right? I think people need protecting from me." He dropped his head, his words low and seductive.

I coughed through the heat rising to the apple of my cheeks. "It's fine. I ... I just came in to talk to you about what happened the other night." I lightly fingered a loose strand of hair on my cheek, needing to do something with my hands because my fingers itched to touch him. "Thanks for listening. You're the best therapist any girl could ever hope for."

"Don't mention it." His eyes locked with mine, taking me in. His gaze was riveted on my face.

"No, I needed that," I continued. He didn't understand how much I had been craving his listening ear that night. I'd always been on the other end, listening to Roland, my sister, and my mother when my father was sick. I averted my stare, feeling sheepish. "So ... Thank you."

There he was. Doing it again. Scouring my face, searching me as if he was studying my soul.

I played with a strand of my hair, pulling some to the front. "So, how was your trip home?"

He quirked an eyebrow, and his smile widened. "Changing the subject on me? I'll bite. It was good. My brother Jordan came home."

"You go home often?" I sat on the edge of my seat, feeling eager. I didn't know half the things about my other tenants that I knew about Cade, and yet it wasn't enough. I needed to know more.

He shrugged one shoulder. "Yeah, at least twice a month. More, if my brothers can't make it. I told you my mother's not well, right?" A guarded look came across his face.

"You did." I took a sip of my water.

"Well, she's in a nursing home, and we make sure that someone visits her every weekend." He cut his eyes to the bar, the sadness in them showing.

"Does she get lonely there?" No one in my family had ever been put in a home. Not my grandfather or my grandmother. They had died in their house with home care and with my parents nearby.

"Lonely?" he scoffed. "My mother? Please." He waved a hand in the air. "She's the most social person I know. She put herself in a nursing home so she wouldn't be a burden." He let out a low laugh. "She's nuts, but I think we all feel better seeing her. I get homesick; so do the other guys."

"So, do you take turns to visit her?" I reached for my glass and took a sip of water, all the while continuing to study him.

"Yeah, it's basically on Jordan's schedule. He's filming constantly, so between Wyatt and me, we're picking up most of the weekends. But then Jordan will be off for months, and he'll take two months straight to see mom."

I blinked and held a hand up. "Wait. What's your brother's name again? You said he's in film?" Then it hit me as I put Cade's last name with his brother's first name, but it couldn't be. There was no way. "Jordan Ryder? Your brother is Jordan Ryder?"

He let out a deep, throaty laugh, one that I felt vibrate against my skin. "Yes. The one and only cocky ass. That's him."

"Oh, my god. You're kidding." My tone raised in pitch and I bounced on my seat, fangirling a ton and unable to hide it.

"I wish I was. Got his first gig over five years ago and then it was over. He rose to stardom. He's a good-looking guy," he said matter of fact, and I could hear the affection in his voice.

"Yes, he is! Can I meet him?" I fanned myself with one hand.

Cade's smile faltered, his mouth slackening. "I can get an autograph, but there's no way I'm letting my brother near a little sweet thing like you."

Is he jealous?

I lifted an eyebrow. "And why not?" I challenged.

"Because." He grabbed my glass and proceeded to fill it with a water gun connected to the bar. The conversation dropped; the topic of Jordan over.

I laughed, more flattered that Cade was jealous over me than I was disappointed that he was shutting me down. "Is that all I get?"

"Yep," he said. "That and another refill on your water."

In between Cade serving drinks and his down time, we spent the next few hours talking about anything and everything. About his family. About mine. About life. Everything short of world peace.

"Tell me one weird thing about you. Something no one would ever guess," I asked while he was wiping down the bar. A patron had spilled his drink a few minutes ago.

"I'm an excellent dancer."

I coughed out a laugh. "I remember." My cheeks warmed as soon as the words flew out of my mouth, my thoughts traveling back to the first night we'd met. His arms around my waist, his body flush against mine. "I mean ..."

"You mean, I bump and grind pretty well on the dance floor." His eyes danced with mischief while the warmth of my cheeks spread to the tips of my ears. "Angel, my mother was a dance teacher for years. Foxtrot. Cha cha. Quickstep. Salsa. We know it all."

My mouth fell ajar, and I jerked back, assessing if he was kidding. I hadn't expected that this tall, tatted male was a graceful ballroom dancer.

"Surprised?"

"Um, yeah. I think that's amazing."

"Do you want me to teach you sometime?"

"Teach me how to dance?" I squeaked in shock and reeled back. For a hot second, I thought he was joking, but the look on his face told me he was stone-cold dancer prancer serious.

His gray eyes intensified, and his voice lowered as he leaned in. "Or teach you other things, because I'm up for anything."

I snorted, trying to keep my wits. "I'm sure both of those are out of the question."

The glint of humor was heavy on his face. "Your turn. Name one thing no one would guess about you."

I tapped my fingers against my chin, thinking there was a list of weird things only a very select few knew about me. "I like to bake cakes, but not just regular cakes. I use fondant, and I like to build my cakes." I beamed, thinking of my talent that I obsessed over. "I've baked a cake for every one of my family members since before I could remember. It's a tradition."

He tilted his head, his eyes thoughtful. There was an almost an imperceptible look of pleading on his face. "You think you could bake a cake for me sometime?"

I slapped both hands against the counter, immediately excited for the challenge. "Of-freaking-course, newfound bartender friend and tenant. When is your birthday?"

He chewed on his bottom lip, his expression tender. "It just passed a couple of months ago, so you'll just have to wait till next year to bake me one."

A thought passed through my head, one that dampened my mood, an undeniable and dreadful fact that our time together was limited. My smile dimmed. "If you're still here in a year."

His eyebrows knitted together, and silence spanned the space between us. I wondered what he was thinking.

"Cade!"

We both jerked up, turning toward Kristy. She motioned to the group of people in front of her. "I could use a hand over here."

He nodded, never breaking eye contact. "Be right over," he called out.

Then he whispered under his breath, "You'd think she forgot who was boss."

I laughed and slipped my purse over my shoulder. "Bye, Cade."

"See you later, Angel."

I waved a goodbye and walked out of the restaurant, knowing full well his eyes were on me.

CHAPTER 11

THIS WAS THE FIRST TIME, in a long time, that I was alone. Alone on my birthday.

I stretched my arms over my head and glanced at the clock next to my bed. My phone was pinging loudly, indicating texts and voice mails. I could almost guarantee that I had a voice mail from my mother and father, Tene and Nana. And Roland.

I had avoided him completely, drowning myself in work, and he hadn't known where I had moved to, so he couldn't stop by.

Mustering enough courage, I reached for my phone and placed it on my ear.

The first voice mail was from my sister "ANGIEEEE. Happy birthday to the most beautiful and sweetest sister in the world. I love you to pieces. See you for our family birthday dinner!" She concluded with the worst rendition of "Happy Birthday" in her loudest voice. As obnoxious as it was, it made me smile.

The next was from my mother. "Angie, Happy birthday. I hope you have a great day. We're so proud of you. Have a fun time with Roland tonight, and we'll see you for our family dinner." I could hear my father shouting in the background. "I love you and Happy birthday," over my mother's voice.

I bit my inner cheek as a slew of emotions pounded through me. They thought that I'd be with Roland today, as I'd been every year since we'd been together. This meant that I would spend today alone.

I should tell them the truth, that we'd broken up, and I would, but today wasn't the day to do it. Not on my birthday. I didn't want to remember my twenty-fifth as a pity party.

The next voice mail was from Roland. At one time, the sound of his voice had sent butterflies in a frenzy in my belly. Not this time. This time, my insides filled with dread at what he had to say.

"Happy birthday, Angie. Don't spend your birthday alone." He sighed heavily on the phone. "Stop this nonsense already. Pick up your phone and call me. I still have reservations for Italia scheduled tonight. Don't you think that this has gone on long enough?"

My chin trembled, and I clutched my phone against my chest, swallowing down the desolation.

He still believed that I wasn't serious about our breakup, and the bitter pain of that realization hit me in my gut. He'd never take me seriously. Not now, and not in any scenario of a future together.

I didn't care how lonely I was or how pitiful it was that I was spending my birthday alone, there was no way I was calling him. Instead, I pushed myself off my bed and got ready for the work day.

That evening, when the bustle of the day had ended, I stuffed my keys and my phone in my oversized birthday present that Roland had gotten me last year and dined at my favorite restaurant, by myself. The time alone gave me a moment to contemplate my life, my history, and how I'd gotten to this point.

After that, I drove for hours, all over the city, not stopping until I had barely enough gas to make it home. After I had filled up my tank, I drove downtown. Around half past midnight, I found myself parked in front of Allswell. I stepped out of my car and readjusted my purse on my shoulder. My feet and heart had led me where my mind had been saying I shouldn't go.

I stood in the shadows in front of the closed restaurant, staring at the waiters and waitresses scurrying about, trying to clean up and close down. My sights zoned in on Cade by the register at the bar, calculating his earnings for the night.

I wished with a desperateness inside me that Roland could be Cade. I wanted Roland to look at me with the desire and seduction Cade did. I wanted Roland to take care of me like Cade did, comfort me when I was sick, cheer me up when I was sad. Make me laugh and feel cherished, not by what he could buy me, but by how he treated me.

But I realized you can't wish or want for someone to be someone they were not. And I couldn't settle for less. I couldn't accept who Roland was, and I most certainly couldn't accept how he treated me.

I didn't know how long I had stood out there, but one by one Cade's employees left for the night, and I pushed myself closer to the front of the door. I wanted another glimpse of him. I had told myself that I wouldn't come back here. I had made a solemn vow that I wouldn't invite danger, yet here I was.

My heart rate increased when he proceeded to walk to the front to lock up. I should've turned away, but I simply stood there.

When our eyes locked, he stepped out into the dark night and pulled me toward him. Though the brisk air had caused the cold to spread throughout my body, his one touch warmed me from the inside out.

"What're you doing out here?" he asked sweetly.

"I'm not sure." My voice was blank, devoid of any emotion, just like my mind.

He intertwined our hands, and it felt so natural I couldn't pull away, then he pulled me inside and led me to the bar.

I placed my purse on top of the bar, noting how the gold in the clasp caught the light. Other women would sell their souls for a purse like this. Practical women would sell this purse to feed their family.

The reality of my life and the circumstances that I'd been surrounded with rushed to the surface. Though I was the quieter Armstrong sister, I still held the Armstrong name. With that last name came power and wealth and prestige. I had thought Roland and I were the perfect match. He'd come from money and his last name held value. I had thought that, at one time, there was equality in that. Now I see how shallow I was being. How blind I was. I could settle for all that Roland offered. But it would kill my soul to do it, and I just couldn't.

Cade placed a mixed drink in a tall glass in front of me.

I shouldn't. But I was too bummed out to care.

"It's a virgin Margarita." He smirked. "I promised you I'd never make you a drink again, and I never break a promise."

My birthday drink, I thought to myself. Since I'd been born, there hadn't been a year that I hadn't blown out candles and made wishes. Another birthday signified a new beginning and that excitement from that newness of turning another year older. I gritted my teeth, realizing that Roland had taken that from me. I rubbed my chest, feeling the raw ache of my empty heart.

"What's the matter, Angel?"

I dropped my lashes to hide the hurt and stared intently on the slushy red liquid in my glass. "I thought today would be different. Last year he ditched me for work, but this year ... I thought ..." A familiar warmth spread behind my eyes, but I forced back the sadness, the tears that were about to burst through.

I refused to cry two years in a row on my special day.

Cade stiffened, his jaw taut. "It's your birthday?"

When I didn't speak, his features turned murderous. "What the fuck is his problem?"

I bit my bottom lip as it quivered. A feeling of utter despair washed over me.

I closed my eyes and focused on anything but the jerk I'd given way too many years to. "It's fine. He invited me out, but I don't want to move backward. I just didn't expect to be alone. Alone on my big day."

"Stop," Cade commanded, causing my eyes to fly open and meet his. "Don't cry."

I hadn't realized that I'd been crying. Again.

Damn it.

Cade jumped over the bar in one leap and reached for my waist, startling me. When his hands gripped my trembling chin, forcing me to look at him, my insides ignited with a flame I vaguely remembered a man could stir up.

This is dangerous.

He inched forward, forcing me to part my legs to make room for him, and caged me in against the bar. His fingertips grazed my bare thigh as my dark brown eyes met his gray ones. "What do you want to do for your birthday?" The way his sentence flowed out of his mouth in a staccato cadence made my pulse skitter.

My sullen mood suddenly shifted to an unbelievable deep want in the innermost part of my belly. A hunger that grew to dangerous proportions, just being around him.

"What do you want to do for my birthday?" I whispered.

I surprised him with my question because he stood silent in front of me before a seductive smile popped up on his face. He leaned into me, and I licked my lips, feeling light-headed.

With his nose, he outlined the curve of my jaw, leading up my neck to my ear. My breathing became shallow, my nipples pebbled at his touch. "I want to make this the most memorable birthday ever. I *want* to take you so hard that all you feel is the throb of me between your legs, all you hear is your voice screaming my name, and you forget everything about that sorry asshole." He pulled back, unaffected by his words while my pulse raced into overdrive. "So, don't ask *me* what I want to do. I'm going to ask you again, Angel. What do you want to do for your birthday?"

Everything south tingled with want, and the deepest, most honest part of me wanted what he wanted. I distanced myself, just a fraction, but enough for me to piece together some sort of conscious thought. "I want to blow out candles on my birthday cake. Twenty-five."

My response surprised him again, amused him even as the corner of his mouth tipped upward. He pulled back, straightened, then assessed my face. "Candles?"

I nodded because that's all I wanted for my birthday, to make that one wish.

He stepped back, giving me room to breathe and extended a hand. "You can't blow out candles without a cake. Let's bake a cake, Angel."

CHAPTER 12

I POURED myself my second glass of wine and took a sip before I placed the chocolate cake in the double oven of the restaurant's state-of-the-art kitchen.

"You know what's damn sexy, woman?"

"What?" I asked, almost dizzy at being able to spend this much time with him alone.

He eyed me with an adorable half crooked smile. "A woman who knows her way around a kitchen."

I patted my own back, proud of my creation and excited to have him take a taste. "I can't cook anything but cake and breakfast, so don't be too impressed."

He chuckled and dropped the rag he was holding in the oversized double stainless steel sink. What surprised me was the hands-free automatic faucets that turned on by sensor.

I took in his state-of-the-art kitchen. It must've cost thousands to build out this place. I could practically see my reflection against his appliances. Against the wall spanned a multi-unit range with a combination of gas burners, a griddle, a wok burner, and a fryer. Overhead there was a full-length hood to provide maximum ventilation and a wall rail for gadgets and utensils.

There were multiple ovens, and while Cade had tried to explain the functionality of each one, I couldn't remember. There was one to keep the food warm, one to bake items, and a smoker.

One thing I knew, I was in absolute heaven using all of his restaurant style gadgets.

"I would've loved to be a cook in my former life," I sighed.

He frowned as if it was the easiest wish I could've asked for. "Why don't you?"

With the spatula, I cleaned up the side of the silver bowl and licked the icing off it. "I don't know. I like real estate, too."

He grabbed the spatula and licked the other side of it. It was the sexiest thing. Almost like we were kissing but not touching.

"You like real estate or do you like pleasing your parents?" His tone was light, though I couldn't help but be a tiny bit offended, which forced my attention back his way.

"Both," I said honestly. "I like real estate and running Armstrong Realty, and, yes ... I like making them happy. They're my family." I'd grown up watching my father help my grandfather build up the Armstrong empire. I had always wanted to grow up to be him, to be my father, to build and create. And in a way, maybe that's why I liked making cakes, too. I enjoyed the art of creating.

"I understand about family." He approached my mixing bowl and watched me as I meticulously cleaned the bowl with the spatula.

I wanted to pry. I wanted to push him so badly and find out about her. "Do I remind you of her? Your sister,

Candice?" I had sensed this when he'd mentioned the sound of my voice.

"I don't think of you in a sisterly way if that's what you're asking." He let out a low laugh and averted his eyes so I couldn't read them. "But the good things, the things I want to remember. The parts where she wasn't drunk and high all the time." His broad shoulders heaved as he breathed. "The way her laughter filled a room, her goofiness, the way she was before ... The parts I miss; you remind me of those parts."

He dropped his head, and torment clouded his vision. "I hated seeing her toward the end. She was so doped up on coke that she was a totally different person—a person I hardly recognized." One shaky hand ran from the top of his head, down his face. "I don't want to think of those parts. I want to remember her before that stuff. The person I knew and loved."

He straightened when the timer dinged in the background, indicating that our cake was cooked, and, sadly, our conversation about his sister was over. As he strolled to the stove, I focused on her name on his forearm, written in black curlicue letters.

After he pulled the cake from the oven, a waft of chocolate filled the air, making my stomach grumble.

He placed the cake on the counter, and I proceeded to fill the pastry tube with icing. After allowing the cake to cool down, I began my favorite part of the process—decorating the cake.

"You know you bite your lip whenever you're thinking too hard."

"What?" I stopped midair, the pastry tube in my hands. I was showcasing my cake decorating skills, making pink rose flower petals along the edge of the frosted chocolate cake.

"Oh, I never noticed. Must be a family thing. Tene does it, too."

My hands moved toward the cake with purpose and a creative flair. One more rose and I'd be finished. "Tah-dah!" I backed away, smiling as I wiped my forehead with my forearm, careful that my frosting-covered fingers didn't touch my face.

"Impressive." He inched forward and eyed the cake with a seriousness that made me laugh.

"What? Is it not up to par, Mr. Ryder?"

"Hm." He rubbed his forefinger and thumb across his chin, as though he was thinking mighty hard.

"I want to see you do better," I countered, placing one light hand on my hip. "What do you know about decorating cakes?"

"I went to culinary school for two years," he said, shocking me. "I'm a certified chef."

"Oh." My smug smile left my face.

"Did you think I just owned a bar?" He cocked an eyebrow. "When I knew that this was what I wanted to do, I had to master the whole process."

Suddenly the thought that I was really being judged didn't sit well in my stomach. "Well, what's wrong with it?" I tilted my head, noting the perfectly made pink roses with the decorated border outlining the edge of the cake.

"It's missing something."

"What?" I tapped my fingertips against the counter, feeling impatient. When I picked up the pastry tube again, he shook his head and took out seven candles.

My shoulders relaxed, and a smile sat heavily on my face as I waited patiently for him to set up the cake. In one row, he set two candles. Right underneath that row, he set the rest of the five candles. Twenty-five. A quarter of a century year old.

As he lit each candle, my smile widened. I'd waited for this moment all year, for this new beginning, this new wish. Last year, I had wished for my father's health. This year, I decided I'd wish for something for myself.

When he set the lighter down, he stood right beside me and shook my shoulders. "Happy birthday, Angel." The corner of his mouth tipped up into his signature crooked smile.

"You're going to sing, right?"

He shook his head and let out a giant laugh, one that would've shook his belly if he had one, but the only part of his anatomy that shook was his chest. "I don't sing."

I playfully pointed a finger in his direction. "It's my birthday, and for my wish, I command you to sing."

The candles were going to burn out if he didn't do it soon.

I gave him my sweetest smile, the one I used on my father when I was playing cute and wanted something. "Please."

His smile disappeared, and just when I thought he was going to shut me down, he started to sing. "Happy ... Happy birthday ... to you." His voice was curt and broken. Boy, did he sound horrible, but the gesture was so terribly sweet.

I motioned my hands for him to continue, though he looked like he was in pain. "Happy ... birthday to you." His face turned beet red. My gosh, the big muscled, tattooed bar owner was blushing. I didn't think I'd ever smiled so big. My cheeks hurt.

"You're not done," I teased. "Seriously, the wax on the candles is melting." I motioned with my hands again.

"Happy birthday, dear Angel. Happy birthday to you."

The last words rushed out of him so fast, I almost didn't catch some of the words. "Turn around and make a wish."

He walked behind me and held my shoulders as I closed my eyes, just like I do every year. Tene and my whole family made fun of me about how I acted like a child for my birthday. I had a million wishes; too many to count. But today, I only had one. I inhaled deeply, thinking of this one wish, and blew out all seven candles, releasing my thoughts and energy into that one breath.

"Thanks," I said, turning around to face him. "I was afraid I wasn't going to do that this year."

His hands dropped to my upper arms. "I wasn't about to let that happen." His thumbs grazed my bare skin, and my whole body warmed, my pulse quickening and my mouth drying up from his touch. The air shifted with tension like a thin string wired with electricity. His stare flickered to my lips, which caused a hunger deep in my belly to overpower all of my senses. My knees felt weak as I angled toward him and tilted my head.

He leaned in, and I gave in just an inch. I should've wished for a kiss. A kiss that could never have been forgotten because, once I kissed this man, I doubted I'd ever forget it.

His eyes fell to half-mast, and when he inched closer, my pulse pounded loudly in my ears. He was about to close the gap between us ... so close. Closer ... closer.

Too close. Too soon. Too much.

I straightened as the thoughts awakened me from my trance, which forced him to still.

He was only going to kiss me, nothing else. But the last guy I'd kissed had been Roland. And our first kiss led to many kisses. Many kisses that led to me falling deep in love with him. And that love had led to heartbreak. I could see how things could escalate between Cade and me, and I couldn't get emotionally attached and have my heart broken again. A slew of emotions bubbled in my chest, causing me to clam up.

"I think ..." I lost any ability to think or speak or function as I gazed back up at him. "I think we should eat cake." It took me a second to recollect myself. I backed up, away from him and turned to said cake.

He stood there for a second, silent. I wondered what he was thinking as I took the knife on the counter and busied myself by cutting the cake into pieces. I separated two plates and set a piece on each one. I was afraid to see his reaction, to see the longing on his face that was mirrored in mine. Because even though I was crazy nervous, and my thoughts were a jumbled mess, I couldn't deny what I felt. I longed for this man.

He approached the counter. "Chocolate cake. My favorite." There was no huskiness in his voice, so I turned around and was awarded with his sexy crooked smile. My nerves relaxed at the sight of him.

"My favorite, too."

He dipped his fingertips into the chocolate and smeared my cheek with it.

My mouth dropped open, my lips curling into an 'O'. "I can't believe you just did that."

He chuckled and smeared chocolate on my other cheek.

I blinked. "Oh, you want to get dirty, huh?" I said, chin out, body ready to rumble.

His smile was blinding. Not the crooked, half semi smile I was used to, but a full-on grin. "Dirty is my middle name."

I wiped the chocolate from my face and licked my fingertips. His eyes flashed.

Good.

"You're going to get it." I stepped out of my heels. My fingers swiped at my other cheek, and I brought the chocolate to my lips.

With stealthy quickness, he rushed toward me, spread chocolate on my forehead, then hopped away.

My feet shuffled a step back. I didn't think it was possible to be shocked twice in such a short time frame, but I was. "You did not just do that." My smile widened, and my feet drummed on the floor, ready for my next move.

Full teeth were on display. God, it was the hottest thing on this man—a full-on smile, all teeth. I laughed, and just as fast as he approached me, I dipped my hands into a big chunk of the cake, feeling the squishy, sticky cake and frosting fill most of my hand, then I slammed him in the face.

My actions surprised me, or maybe the fact that he was too slow to dodge them. I stilled in my spot, wide-eyed and blinking. "Oh, god. I'm so sorry." The cake covered his eye, some falling on his cheek. I grabbed the white cloth napkin behind me and stepped toward him to help him clear off some chocolate, but in the next second, he reached behind me, and, with a handful of cake, coated my face.

"I'm sorry, too." He belly laughed, looking like a little boy, and I wondered what kind of silly antics he did as a child.

I narrowed my eyes, meaning war now. "Okay, I see how it is." I swiped at my face and pieces of chocolate fell from my cheek to the ground.

He bounced from side to side, like a boxer in a ring, knowing I'd get him next. And I would.

When my hands picked up the whole cake, he jerked back. "I don't think that's playing fair."

"Mmhmm." I advanced toward him, the cold of the tile floor against my bare feet. A sneaky smile creased my mouth, the kind that Tene used to throw me when we fought.

He maneuvered behind the center stainless steel table separating the room, separating us, separating himself from the cake shower I was about to give him.

"You think you can catch me?" he dared me. "I think you might be too slow."

My mouth dropped open, and I barked out a laugh. "That's what you think."

He flexed his muscles, causing the intricate tattoo that went up his forearm to tighten. I ran to catch him, but he flitted to the other side, the table still between us.

"You," I laughed. "I'm going to wipe that smug smile off your face." I whipped a handful of cake across the room, hitting him in the chest.

He peered down at his shirt with a glob of glowing frosting on it. "I happen to like this shirt. My mama gave me this shirt."

"It's an ugly shirt," I goaded him.

His eyes narrowed playfully. "Are you telling me my mom has bad taste in shirts?"

I lifted my chin in defiance. "Yes. Or maybe it's the person, not the shirt."

He took off his shirt, and I swore; I almost dropped the cake. Seeing him shirtless was glorious, and gosh darn it, I forgot we were even in a cake match.

"You all right over there?" he asked too innocently.

"Ahh," I stammered. No words. A mural of black ink etched half of his chest, trailing to both shoulders and up his neck.

"Ahem." His smile told me he knew I was ogling him.

Right. Carrying on.

I hurled more cake in his direction, this time hitting him straight in the face, and his look was epic. His eyebrows shot to his hairline.

"I'm sorry?" My voice didn't sound apologetic one bit. I shrugged, feigning nonchalance.

His smirk tightened, his face amused but oddly filled with purpose as he charged toward me.

"Ahh ... no!" I rushed to the other side of the table. Where he moved, I countered, as far away from him as possible.

Then he planted his feet apart in a wide stance, determination set in his shoulders and my pulse quickened. "One way or the other, I'm going to get revenge, Angel."

Well, crap, then.

His voice was playful, but I wouldn't want to get on this man's bad side.

I didn't know what came over me, but I fisted more cake and chucked it at him, hitting his neck.

He growled, but in the next second he darted toward me, grabbed the cake from my hands and slathered it all over my face as though he was giving me a cake facial.

I squealed under all the frosting.

"You said you loved cake," he laughed. He had me backed up against the wall, but that didn't stop my determination.

I coated his bare chest with chocolate. "My birthday is over." Slapped it against his back. "Thank you for everything."

We were inches apart as I pushed the whole cake that he was holding into his face.

He could barely see, and I couldn't stop laughing. My

fingertips lathered it through his hair like shampoo while tiny giggles escaped me.

He wiped his face clean, and then it was a full-on cake fight. Cake was everywhere. He stuffed it down my top and in my hair. "Happy birthday, Angel." He slathered cake on my neck as he pushed me up against the wall, anchored me, supporting all my weight.

"I'm dirty." My voice was hoarse, and my pulse beat erratically against my wrist.

"I like you dirty," he growled.

Suddenly, the air shifted, all amusement gone. His lips parted, and his eyes filled with lust.

My sticky hands slipped around his bare back, right by his backside. "Now you're dirty," I whispered. The sensation of warmth flooded my body.

He pushed against me, and I could feel his hardness against my stomach, which caused a dizzying current to run through me. My legs parted to cradle him, my skirt hitching up. His hands moved down to my bare thighs, and his fingertips made a sensual path up my legs until he was holding me up against the wall by my ass.

He rocked into me and his hard length pressed against the wetness of my panties. "You're a dirty girl, aren't you?" He rocked into me again, and a small moan escaped my mouth. He skimmed his nose down my cheek to the crook of my neck, where he licked the span of skin. "And because it's your birthday, I'm going to lick you clean." The warmth of his tongue set my skin ablaze.

All self-restraint disappeared as I tugged at the top of his hair and slammed my lips against his. Pure ravenous fire ignited between us, an inferno heating my body, all from the touch of his lips and the swirl of his tongue. He licked and flicked and bit my tongue in a long, lulling tempo that made me heavy with want and dripping in desire. I moved against him, loving the friction of our bodies. And it wasn't nearly enough.

One hand moved to the apple of my ass, and when he pushed me against him, my lips lost contact with his, and I trembled with pleasure.

"You like that?" He rocked into me farther, and an explosive current ripped through my body. My aching breasts rubbed against his bare chest, and my whole body sizzled against his.

He moved against me, creating this sensual friction that made my insides want to combust. "Angel ... I want you so bad." He rested his forehead against mine, his breathing labored and hot against my skin.

My pulse beat in every part of my body and my nerves were raw in the best possible way. "Well, take what you want," I whispered.

A hunger so strong, a thirst in the deepest part of me that I thought was gone, abruptly emerged as he lifted me and led us down the hall and to the freight elevator to take us to his apartment.

CHAPTER 13

OUR LIPS NEVER LOST CONTACT. Not when he walked out of the elevator. Not when he pushed his key into the lock. Not even when he walked us into the apartment and into the bathroom. The sound of the water running in the shower echoed through the room as his hands molded to my ass, but we didn't stop to even catch a breath.

I welcomed the way his hands, his lips, his words were making my body react. When my clumsy fingers could not undo his belt, my feet touched the ground, and he stepped back and worked to finish what I couldn't. After he undid his belt, he slipped out of his jeans ... no underwear.

For all that was holy!

His cock stood at full attention, saluting me, and I blinked, unbelieving at his width.

A throaty chuckle left his lips, and all I could do was stare. Simply stare and blink.

"See something you like?" he asked, his crooked smile widening.

My cheeks flushed as I just ogled it—stared at it pointing at me. I knew you shouldn't compare, and since I'd only really seen one dick in my whole life, I didn't have anything to compare it to, but yeah, Roland was no comparison to Cade.

"No words? Did I numb your mouth from kissing you?"

When he approached, I jumped back, and he laughed again.

He made his cock twitch, and I shuffled back another step.

"It doesn't bite," he promised.

"Uh." Once again, this man had me stupid speechless.

"Scared?"

"Of course not. I'm not a virgin." But when my hands reached for him, his dick jumped again, and I jerked back.

He shook his head, amused, and came toward me. "Angel, let me teach you a thing or two." He reached for my fingers and brought it to his hardness. "This is a cock. Touch it. Feel it. Kiss it if you want to." He guided my hand to lightly stroke his length.

"Shut up," I muttered.

He angled closer, and my head lifted toward the ceiling as his warm tongue licked the tender spot on my neck. Instinctively, my body arched toward him.

Not once did he stop me from stroking his satin-like skin, up and down, my fingertips light but firm.

His hands dropped from mine, letting me take the lead. Hot, horny, heavy breaths escaped him.

When I increased my speed, his lips lost contact with my neck. "Shit," he growled. His eyes were closed, skin flushed, and his eyebrows knitted together like he was on the verge of combustion.

"Do you want me to stop?" I whispered.

Now he was the one at a loss for words.

My insides soared with victory because, for once, he

was the one unable to function, let alone speak. Our roles in this crazy relationship were reversed, and I reveled in having the control, wielding this man with the power of my touch.

His eyes flipped open. "You're going to make me come. It's been a while."

His words surprised me. I had assumed—I didn't know why—that he had women falling at his feet.

"Move." He ushered me back, toward the shower, his cock against my stomach.

I smirked, still feeling powerful. "I own this building, sir. You don't get to tell me what to do."

His face told me he loved it when I fought back with some sass. He pointed his dick toward my stomach, urging me backward. "Move." With each thrust of his cock, he pushed me toward the shower. "Get going." His tone, his stance, his overpowering demeanor made my body hot and ready with want.

I enjoyed this tug-of-war between us, and I backed up a step. "You're not the boss of me."

"I can't boss you around, but I can control what he does." His cock jumped again, and my heart pounded an erratic rhythm in my chest.

After I shed my clothes, I grabbed his dick and pulled him into the shower. My boldness surprised me, but my body lusted for this man so deeply that any restraint I had was gone.

Warm water hit my skin, cascading to the floor. He towered over me as I watched the beads of water trickle down his chest against his tattoos, like a waterfall against a work of art.

Beautiful and breathtaking.

He reached for the soap above me and lathered up his

strong hands, bringing his hands up my thighs and over my taut stomach. "You need a little cleaning up, dirty girl." His voice was rough, ragged, raging heat that matched my insides.

"I am a dirty girl. Dirty, dirty girl." I'd never played a part before, never role-played during or before sex. But damn, the way he talked, his foreplay with words, was electrifying and erotic, and I didn't want him to stop.

He continued lathering me up with soap, starting with my breasts and making his way down. Lower. All the way down. Farther down. To the apex of my legs, where he slipped a finger inside me. One. Two. Then three.

My head fell back against the glass when he began to pump his fingers in me, slow and seductive and with purpose, all the while watching me.

When he dropped to his knees and spread my legs farther, I didn't have time to formulate my next thought before he grabbed my ass and flicked his tongue between my folds. Kissing, licking, sucking my clit with a deep-rooted ravenous hunger that made me buck forward.

I gripped his hair to steady myself. "Cade," I whispered. He needed to slow down, or else I'd combust. But he didn't stop. If anything, he feasted on me like I was his first meal of the day and the last meal of his life.

It didn't take long before I peaked and erupted, pushing his face farther into me. The magic of his tongue worked me over and over, making the orgasm last forever until I saw a burst of light behind my eyes and my whole body shook with sensation, and my legs gave out beneath me from utter and wonderful ecstasy.

Cade turned off the shower, and he carried me to his bed. He peered down at me through hooded, hungry eyes. All I could hear was the sound of the condom wrapper ripping and the beating of my raging heart. All I could see was him over me, the lust in his gaze, the hunger that made me feel like the most beautiful woman in the world, and all I could feel was his hard, wet body above me.

My body was still quivering from the aftershocks of the everlasting orgasm mere seconds before, but it didn't stop me from grabbing his cock and positioning it above my center, needing him, wanting him inside me. He entered me in one swift movement and stilled.

"Fuck," he cried out in one low, husky moan. "You feel too good."

I shifted to adjust myself to the width of him, to the feel of him inside of me.

At first, his movements were slow and sensual, and I felt each thrust of his body everywhere, sending a shiver of pleasure down my spine to my toes and then back. But I wanted more, needed more. I didn't want him holding back.

"Harder." I lifted my hips to get him to drive deeper.

He gripped my chin with force, watching me with a heavy, hungered passion. "You want harder." He rammed into me, his movements animalistic, raw, and full of passion. "This hard enough for you?"

"Yes," I screamed, digging my nails in his ass.

"You feel so good. So fucking good." His lips connected with mine again. Tongue against tongue. Thrust after thrust. Skin slapping against skin.

There was a thin line between pleasure and pain, but it felt so achingly amazing. Too good, and that's when the first spark deep in my belly initiated, building in the base of my spine, spreading to my toes, then overtaking my whole body and turning all my thoughts to mush.

I moaned loudly as the best orgasm I'd ever experienced shook my world and everything in it. I gripped Cade tighter against me, my legs wrapping around his waist as he took me higher and higher and higher, where every sliver of sensual sensation rocked through me while Cade's body pumped into mine.

Our loud moans of ecstasy echoed through the room as I tasted the sweetness of lips, smelled the scent of our passion, and every single part of me quivered with pleasure.

I should've felt guilty, or any type of remorse, but I didn't because, for once in my life, I'd never felt more alive.

When the bed shifted the next morning, I awoke to Cade's firm ass walking toward the bathroom. When he shut the door behind him, my mind wandered, turning over and over, while all my muscles felt like liquid mush. It was as though I had received a massage from the inside out. Well, I had—an orgasmic massage.

As I listened to the water run in the bathroom, I wondered, *what now?* Cade was inevitably leaving to set up his new restaurant. Where did that leave me? Where did that leave us?

Thoughts of the night before filtered to the front of my brain. At twenty-five, I'd never in the quarter of a century of my existence ever experienced what I experienced with Cade. Last night, his lips had worked magic over every inch of my flesh. The navy-blue cotton sheets rustled against my body and goose bumps prickled my skin as my mind flickered to thoughts of last night, after the shower, to round two and in the wee morning hours for round three.

You'd think I would be tired, but I wanted more, more of him, more of what I'd experienced. After being deprived of uninhibited, unselfish sex, I loved the way he made me feel—wanted and sexy—like he couldn't get enough.

My fingers drifted south as I thought of the pulsating tremors that Cade had caused. When I pierced myself, my eyes fell shut, and my breathing accelerated. My body tingled from my touch, still sensitive from hours before.

When the door creaked open, I pulled my fingers out and tugged the sheets over my breasts. A flush crept up my cheeks, as though I'd gotten caught in an inappropriate position.

With one hand, Cade towel dried his hair, while another towel was wrapped around his waist. His beautiful intricate tattoos were on full display, and I took in every inch of him, from the ones on his neck, down his arms and chest, and I marveled at that masterpiece in front of me.

He smiled his crooked smile. "You hungry?"

I straightened on the bed, my back flat against the head-board. "I could eat." I flattened my hands against my bed head, suddenly self-conscious.

He noticed. It seemed like he noticed everything about me. "Stop it, you're beautiful."

He gazed at me like he was photographing me with his eyes, a look as though he couldn't get enough of simply staring at me. "Let me cook breakfast for you," I said.

With a slight head shake, he approached the bed and kissed the top of my nose. "You're sweet, but no, I'll just grab some food from downstairs. It's still your birthday week, after all."

The cool masculine scent of his shampoo wafted through my nose, and I wanted to pull him close and take a deeper whiff, but I didn't know if that would be appropriate. As much as we had shared, there was still a newness about us, and I didn't know what his boundaries were.

He cupped the side of my face as his thumb grazed my cheek gently. "I'll get you fed." He bent down to kiss me, slow and thoughtful. "And then I have to get going."

I sighed, loud enough for him to hear, but I couldn't help it because I didn't want our time to end. "Okay." My voice was barely above a whisper. I didn't know where to go from here. For once in my planned life, I didn't know what to do after this. After I did the walk of shame out of his apartment, where did that leave us?

I didn't have a game plan, and as soon as he walked out of this room, reality would kick in. Could I work with Cade on a professional level given what we'd shared?

He seemed unbothered by it all as far as I could tell. He kissed my forehead, turned, and stalked to his dresser.

"When do you leave for Toline to set up your new bar?" My voice held a sad undertone, the same tone that matched the dead weight in my heart.

He must've heard it because he stilled. For a second, he paused, then his eyebrows knitted together as though he was thinking deeply. The air shifted between us, and the visible tension rose in the room. The unbearable silence took over the space between us until he said, "Two weeks, Angel."

"Oh." What had happened between us had been purely a booty call, so why did I feel so disappointed? I had never been intimate with anyone but Roland. I didn't know how to do one-night stands. I didn't know what would happen tomorrow, what the future held for me, but I knew that I didn't want him to go.

He slipped his shirt over his head and stalked toward me. When he sat on the bed, I shied away.

"Hey." He reached for my hand, forcing me to peer up at him. "I leave in a couple of weeks, but let's not think about tomorrow, okay? Or what'll happen the day after that."

I nodded, swallowing hard. What had I expected to happen? That after sex, he'd drop his life and settle in with me? The problem with living in the moment was that there were consequences. Consequences of the heart—my heart.

He added, "Let's not lie to ourselves and pretend it was more than what it was—really good sex and awesome company." He dipped his chin, clearly hiding some type of emotion he didn't want me to witness.

My jaw locked. Though it was the truth, it cheapened last night.

His fingertips grazed my chin. "You're not looking for a relationship with me, Angel. If you'd be honest with yourself, you're looking for a distraction and some fun. We both have complications in our life, complications with our family, that prevent us from taking this any further."

I jerked away from him and wrapped my arms around myself.

"Am I lying, Angel?"

"No."

"Then why are you mad?"

"I'm not mad," I moped.

He unhooked my arms and came closer, gathering me against him. His firm gaze landed on mine, never wavering, completely serious. "I like you, Angel. A lot. But you still haven't figured things out about that ex-boyfriend of yours. You just broke up."

"I slept with another man," I said, incredulous. "It's most definitely over."

"You broke up just days ago." He ran the back of his hand down my cheek. "I told you. You have more to lose here than me, and I have everything to gain. Things could change in a heartbeat. You could change your mind." His voice was whisper soft, but his eyes were strongly guarded.

He lifted my chin with the lightness of his pointer finger. "What's the matter?"

"I just don't know what happens now ... with everything," I blurted, honesty seeping out.

His face was thoughtful. "What happens is whatever you want to happen."

When I didn't answer, he continued, "I'm not sleeping with anyone else. I haven't in a while. My random hook up days are done because of my obligations to this job and to my family. I still want to have sex with you because, damn, last night was the best sex I've had since ..." He paused for a beat. "... ever. But I leave this all to you, Angel." He playfully tugged at the sheets of his bed, exposing me. "What're you doing this weekend?"

"Why?" I paused to examine him and readjusted the sheets over my bare breasts.

"It's ladies' night, and I very much want you to come so I can see you again." He climbed on top of me, surprising me, and I cradled him between my legs. "Is that a yes, you'll come?"

Automatic heat spread throughout me, my body arching toward his. "I think I came multiple times last night."

"Funny girl," he chuckled.

"Maybe." Because there was no denying that I wanted to see this man tonight and every night after that.

He tugged the sheet back, exposing my body and his lusty eyes raked over me before he licked his lips. His hand slid up my breast, and between his fingertips, he squeezed my nipple, sending a shock directly to my core.

"We stop when you say the word. Do you want me?" He pushed his growing erection, under the towel, against my stomach. "Because it seems," he chuckled, "that I will always want you. All the time."

My fingers moved to the edge of his towel, my silent answer to his spoken question. I pulled it from his waist, and he grabbed a condom from his side table.

My head fell back as he sank deep inside me, filling me and moving on top of me until I couldn't feel my legs.

Everything that filled me was Cade.

His clean, masculine scent. His hard, toned body against mine. The way his hands tightly gripped my thighs as he moved inside me.

My heart was racing.

My mind was mush.

I couldn't think.

But I knew that I didn't want this to stop.

I straightened out my skirt and applied gloss again before grabbing my purse and shutting the door behind me. The gust of wind blew my skirt up when I stepped outside, and a chill ran through my body. I remembered the last time I'd gone to Allswell to go dancing; Tene had been with me. So much had happened since then.

My feet hurried to my car, and I shivered as I placed the key in the ignition and started the vehicle.

Fall was approaching quickly. Soon enough, my family events would include pumpkin patches and carving pump-kins with my father. He insisted that we do this each year, even though we were adults. The way it went in our family, Christmas was my mother's event, Halloween was my father's, and birthdays were mine.

Roland's parents came over every year during

Halloween to pack bags of candy for our local orphanage. Where did all this leave us now? I wondered if our close families would still hang out. An ache spread through my chest when I thought about our mothers and their friendship. Would they still be as close?

Then I shook my head, breaking the guilt that rose within. I had dated Roland, not his family. I couldn't think about how my break up with him would affect both of our families because that would shatter me, quite possibly have me running back to him. I needed—for once—to put myself first.

Driving, I passed the post office, the corner bakery, and Roland's place of work. I knew he was still inside with his business associates, so late in the evening. We hadn't talked about it, but I knew soon enough, Roland would be in for bigger and better things, which only meant longer hours, and, inevitably, a move to a bigger city—New York City, most likely. But this time, I wouldn't be there following him around like a lost puppy or waiting for him to come home.

Live for today.

Cade's words brought me out of my thoughts, and I nodded once, thinking that was exactly what I was going to do. Live for today and live for me today and from now on.

After dropping my car off at the valet, I headed toward the back of the line that went on forever. The line was long. Super long. Like the Nile River long.

Ladies' night really drew in a crowd. This was by far a longer line than the first time I had come here, and this time, I didn't have Tene to talk her way in.

I lifted my phone to my ear and called Cade. I'd never confirmed that I was coming, and I doubted I was on some magical list that the bouncer had. When it went to voice mail, I stuffed the phone into my purse and headed to the front of the line, bypassing the people standing in it.

"Hey, girlfriend." A taller woman bumped me with her ass. "I don't think so."

"I know the owner." I grimaced as soon as the words left my mouth. God, if that wasn't the most cliché line ever. "And I own the building." I was overreaching now.

"Sure. Sure."

Everyone protested, but I forged ahead, dropping my gaze to the ground and watching my feet lead the way.

Would it have been better to say, "I'm sleeping with the owner?"

I should've just given up, but I was all dressed to impress in a black, skintight Chanel dress. I was determined to see Cade.

I maneuvered myself through the thick line, and when I reached the front, the tension in my shoulders relaxed. My head tilted to take in the over six feet of all hard muscle bouncer. He nodded toward me to speak. If these were the cooks or Cade's staff inside, they would've possibly known me. This guy didn't.

"Hi!" I piped up, smiling sweetly and waving my hand in front of him like he was across the room, but he was a mere foot away. "I'm here to see Cade Ryder." My demeanor was more cheery and bright, opposite my fun flirty sister many nights ago.

He blinked, his expression stoic. "Is your name on the list?"

"No," I said through a toothy smile.

"Back of the line, then."

"But ..." I blinked.

He cocked his head, then pointed to the back of the line.

"No. Please, I—" I was cut short by his pinched expression when a warm arm wrapped around my waist. I reeled back automatically. Glancing up, I stared into an unfamiliar pair of hazel eyes, then I stiffened.

The stranger's hair was slicked back into a man bun. He was broad and could've passed for one of the bouncers. Maybe he was but was just off duty. "Ted, she's with me."

He leaned into me to whisper in my ear. "Just go with it. You want to get in, don't you?"

I did.

He pulled me closer, and I allowed it. It was either that or let all the effort of getting dressed up go to waste.

The bouncer nodded toward the male by the red velvet rope, and he unclasped the rope to let us pass.

Music pounded in my ears as I stepped inside. The laser lights blinded my eyes, and immediately the sweat in the air stuck to my skin.

There were crowds of people crushed against each other as they swayed and bounced and bobbed to the music.

The man's hand was wrapped tightly around my waist as he ushered me in. When I turned around to thank him for getting me into the club, he angled closer, his warm breath on my face. "Let me buy you your first drink."

I rocked back on my heels, needing space away from him. "No, thank you. I'm meeting someone." I wanted to be upfront and not personal. "Thanks for getting me in, though. I would've been standing in line forever." When his hold didn't loosen, my smile tightened, and my eyes darted around me for an escape. "My boyfriend works here."

"Just one drink, pretty lady." His eyes were light with humor. "I did get you into the club."

When he angled his head toward the bar, I scanned the area for Cade, and, when I couldn't find him, I nodded once. "Okay." I decided to play nice. One drink in repayment for getting me in. He seemed harmless enough.

After I stepped away from him, not liking the feel of his body so close to mine, he held out his hand for me to lead the way.

The heat of everyone's body cramped up like sardines pressed against me as we pushed through to get to our drinking station destination. Though this stranger was no longer all up on me, everyone else was.

When we were by the bar, he wedged himself in the small space in front of me, turned and smiled. "What are you drinking?"

"I'll get a long island iced tea."

He raised his hand to get the bartender's attention and ordered our drinks. I didn't recognize the redhead, but then again, Cade had so many people that he employed. I continued to scan the space, but I couldn't find him.

"What's your name?" The man seemed to be in his mid-thirties, a little older than the mass of people around us.

"Angie."

"Nice to meet you, Angie. I'm Walter." He opened up a space so I could move closer to the bar. "You showed up alone? Usually you women travel in packs."

"I'm sort of meeting someone here." It was the second time I had mentioned it, but Walter seemed unfazed.

Kristy, at the very end of the bar, saw me and her eyes narrowed. I knew she didn't approve of me being with Cade. Gosh, who could blame her? For all she knew, I still had a boyfriend and was two timing both of them, and now I'd shown up with a whole different guy.

And although I wanted to deny it, I wanted to be friends with Kristy because Cade liked her. They were friends from back home. It was important for me to be friends with his friends. I wanted her seal of approval, though I doubted I'd ever get it.

Walter pulled out his wallet from his back pocket. His eyes furrowed, which caused me to focus my attention toward him. "Hey, I'm super embarrassed about this, but do you have an extra dollar I could tip her? I don't have change."

"For sure. No problem." I dropped my head into my purse and dug to the bottom, finally digging up a few dollar bills. "Here you go."

He threw the dollar bills on the counter, on top of his money, and grabbed our drinks. "Let's move away from the bar. It's too crowded over here." He handed me my drink and ushered me away toward the dance floor.

I tipped back the glass, feeling the cool burn of the liquid hit the back of my throat. As soon as I was done with this long island, I was searching for Cade.

And that was the last thing I remembered.

CHAPTER 14

A POUNDING HEADACHE and a deep overpowering voice brought me back into consciousness.

I squinted up at an unfamiliar pair of green eyes. The young woman was nose to nose with me. My back was slouched against the wall, and a draft drifted up my skirt, which was bunched by my thighs. I wanted to pull my skirt down to hide myself, but my limbs were weak. I was disoriented; I couldn't move. Couldn't speak. Couldn't do anything but lie there. The inside of my throat felt like old paper, dusty and dry.

My vision was blurred, but when I lifted my head, a larger male was pounding his fist into some guy's face. Squinting at the scene, I realized it was the guy I had just met at the bar—Walter?

"I'm going to fucking kill you for touching her." The voice was deep and deadly and dangerous.

Cade.

My sight sluggishly came back to focus, but my mind was slow to comprehend what was happening. We were in the back of the restaurant by the freight elevators. Three bouncers and Kristy were trying to tear Cade off Walter. Walter's face was bloody, his one eye swollen shut. I didn't know where the blood was coming from.

My eyes fell shut again, but Cade's voice still echoed throughout the room, his tone powerful and overwhelming and frightening.

"Who fucking gives you the right? Huh? *Fucker!*" His voice was seething rage. "Tell me!" He gripped Walter's shirt, anchoring him against the wall, choking him.

Slowly, awareness came back to me, and something clicked in my brain. I remember taking a sip of my drink. Feeling Queasy.

Dizziness.

Walter ushering me into the back hall.

Me saying no. Feeling unsteady. Sleepy.

Some of my thoughts came back with fearful clarity. I remembered him groping me through my clothes, and a silent cry escaped my lips.

How far did he get?

What happened?

My mind raced, and a tremor of terror shook my insides, but I was unable to move, my body still so weak.

I forced my eyes open and tried to move my legs to stand, but failed as though every limb on my body was in deep slumber.

"Easy." My vision focused on the blonde girl with the pixie cut. Slowly, her hands pushed my head toward a tiny bottle. "Just take a whiff of this. It'll bring you back."

One inhale had me wanting to gag, but abruptly the room was in sharp focus.

Kristy was now holding Cade back while Walter slumped, his head lolling like a doll and his body almost sagged completely to the floor. The only thing holding him up was the wall behind him.

Kristy pushed at Cade's chest, but his furious eyes were focused on Walter's beaten body. His nostrils flared, and the veins of his forearms were bulging. He lunged at an already defeated Walter and pummeled his face again, which forced him to finally drop to the ground.

Cade lifted his fist, ready for another hit, but this time Kristy jumped in front of him before he could get another shot in. "You want to get your license revoked for this?"

She shoved at his chest, but he didn't budge. "Do you want to go to jail?" Another shove. "Killing him will not bring Candice back! It won't, Cade!"

Cade couldn't see anything, hear anything, his hard hate focused only on Walter's bloodied and helpless body on the ground.

When Cade stepped forward again, not done with his punching bag, Kristy shoved at his chest with all her might and shouted over his head. "Get that piece of shit out of here before he kills him."

The bouncers nodded and carried Walter out of the room.

Thoroughly pissed, Cade threw his arms up, stalking backward from her, pointing a finger in her direction, his muscles tense, his jaw tight. "Don't ever fucking tell me what to do," he roared. "No one tells me what to do." His chest heaved in and out as though he had just run a marathon, and he was still running.

"I do. When you're acting like an animal, I sure as shit do, Cade." She jutted her chin, and my insides churned as I watched their confrontation. She had balls; I had to give her that. Just listening to Cade's tone had me cowering.

"I don't want blood on my conscience. Nothing happened, Cade. You got here just before it did."

The blood drained from my face as the reality of what could've happened hit me like a bat. I released a long, shaky sigh and shivered at the coldness running in my veins. He had been close, so close to violating me in the worst way possible.

Kristy's voice boomed, but nothing seemed to break Cade from his daze. "She's fine, Cade. Okay? She's going to be okay."

"And awake," said the girl with the pixie cut in front of me.

All eyes in the room moved to my direction. I would've sat up from my slouched position, but the only functioning part of me was my mind.

Cade stalked over to me, but Kristy blocked his way. "No. She's your fucking trigger. I'll take care of her. You can't think straight when it comes to that woman." She turned to face me, her voice lightening. "Do you want me to call the cops? Do you want to press charges?"

My head shook no automatically, my thoughts jumbled like computer code. I didn't know what I wanted.

"Kristy. Move." His harsh tone meant business, and one look on his face had her side-stepping to let him through. In the next second, he was right beside me.

He bent down, and for the first time, his facial features softened. He cupped the side of my face, his knuckles still red from Walter's blood. "I've got you." In one big swoop, he scooped me up, tucked my head into his chest and walked us down the hall.

"Cade!"

Kristy yelled his name, but he ignored her, moving us to the back of the bar and up the freight elevator to his place.

I took in his scent of sweat mixed with beer, which made my nostrils twitch. But I snuggled closer because this was Cade and I was in his arms, which meant I was safe.

The sounds of the freight elevator creaking to the second floor filled the silence, and when I buried my nose into his neck, the tension in his shoulders and his chest finally relaxed.

"One second, Angel." He placed me on the floor, but his hold on my waist didn't relent. And I was thankful because I was sure if he let me go, I'd fall flat on my butt.

With his free hand, he keyed into the door and then I was swooped up again, his arms under my knees.

Gently he laid me on the bed, and my head hit the pillow. I was too tired to move, let alone do anything else.

It was only when he tore off my heels and my nylons—which were ripped to shreds—did I realize how close Walter had been. With the fog lifting, my emotions pushed to the surface and tears gushed down my face as the adrenaline of what happened hit me full force.

He knelt by the bed, right beside me, where I could feel the warmth of his body and the strength of him. "Nothing happened. I swear it." My tears continued, and the torment in his eyes heightened. "We caught him in time. I promise you nothing happened, Angel. I swear to God if it did ..." He took both of my hands in his, staring into my eyes with such conviction. "If he did, he'd be dead." The finality in his words sent a tingle of dread through me.

I nodded as the tears continued to course down my face and tremors shook me like I was surrounded by ice.

So many questions raced through my head, but I was afraid to ask them, afraid to relive the night because I didn't remember.

He slid into the bed next to me, held me in his arms and

ran his fingers through my hair. "You're okay. I have you. I'm here. I've got you."

He kissed the top of my head and pulled me into him. The warmth of his kiss, the continual movement of his fingers through my hair, and his comforting words dimmed my bubbling nerves.

"You're okay." His tone was shaky but soft. "You're okay," he whispered.

I didn't know if his words were for his benefit or mine, but all my energy drained. Whatever Walter had given me had been strong. I tried to force my eyes open, so I could focus on Cade but failed. "I'm tired," I said groggily.

"Sleep, my Angel. I'll take care of you." He lightly rubbed my back, his touch protective, gentle, comforting. "You're okay," he softly said again.

I drifted away, but not before I felt his whole body relax against mine. He held me closer, locking me against his chest.

And when a shudder left his body, only then did I realize that having me close was consoling him, too.

CHAPTER 15

THE HEAT WAS UNBEARABLE. When I opened my eyes, half of Cade's body was practically on top of mine, his arm around my chest, his head on my shoulder and his leg wrapped around my waist.

Like an artistic masterpiece, his tattoos were like a painting against a blank canvas, only this canvas was lean, rippled, and toned. When I ran my hand through his hair, feeling the softness, he exhaled softly.

My chin trembled as I cuddled closer, remembering the horror of last night. Thank heavens he'd been there. This morning would've been a different scenario if he hadn't. A shudder ran through me at the thought.

"Thank you," I whispered. I shifted and pressed my lips against his.

He stirred and automatically both arms wrapped around my waist.

And I kissed him again because he was my savior in more ways than I could count. It was as though he'd been purposely put on this earth to save me—from the only life I knew, bringing me out of my comfort zone, protecting me from Walter.

His eyes slowly opened. "You okay?"

"Yes." I was. Because of him.

He kissed me back with such force and heat and sweetness that the touch set my body aflame. It was as though he wanted to know and feel that I was truly okay.

He repositioned us where I was laying on his chest, and I rested my chin on one of his pecs. "I want to know what happened last night."

I sensed he didn't want to tell me for my own protection, but it was better to know than to be in the dark. "I need to know, Cade."

He nodded and his whole body tensed beneath me. "Kyle, one of my bouncers, saw you go into the hall with that asshole. He could tell you were incoherent, not all there." The muscles in his jaw worked. "He recognized you and called me down."

He scrubbed one hand down his face and then his arms tightened around me. "I'm sorry ..." His voice rattled with heavy, sullen regret. "I'm so sorry I didn't answer your call, Angel. I'm so damn sorry."

I drew circles on his bare chest, snuggling closer, needing him to warm the cold chill running through me. "It's not your fault." My fingers trembled against his beating heart, tracing the lines of ink that spanned above it. "I'm just glad you got there when you did. What if ...?" I couldn't even voice my fears aloud.

He pressed a tender finger to my lips. "No what ifs. If he ..." He cringed. "I'd be in jail, Angel, I promise you that."

I squeezed my eyes tightly at the reality of what could've happened. I was so grateful I hadn't been hurt, but also grateful that Cade hadn't murdered him. Simply grateful.

Kristy's voice from last night rang in my head: *You're not going to bring her back.*

"Was Candice attacked?" I asked carefully.

He nodded.

"Did you almost kill her attacker?"

"We almost did," he answered, and I wondered who he meant by *we*.

His voice was thick with emotion. "She started using after that ... that happened."

He didn't need to go into more detail. I cuddled deeper against his chest, wanting to take away his anguish, his sadness, his pain. I'd ask him more later, but I knew now was not the time.

So, I just let his warmth soothe me and hoped that having me near was soothing him, too.

———

The next night, we had dinner and Netflix in his bed. He hadn't touched me like I wanted him to. After the almost attack, it seemed as though he was keeping his distance.

I snuggled close, laying on his chest and feeling his even breaths on my cheek. "I like this," I said, letting a little of my feelings slip out.

"What do you mean?"

"Doing nothing but lying here with you." I had told myself to be careful. Told myself to keep my heart guarded. He would be off and gone to his next destination in no time, leaving me here in Rosendell, in the background, thinking of him constantly. But I couldn't help the honesty that slipped out.

He kissed the top of my head, and his arms wrapped tighter around me. I breathed in his masculine scent, one that I had already committed to memory. I would never take our time together for granted.

"I know what you mean."

I listened to the sounds of our soft breaths cutting through the muted sounds of the television, feeling his firm body against mine. My hands against his hand, my chest against his chest.

I could lay in this happy heaven forever. I was falling deep for Cade. And it frightened the crap out of me, yet I couldn't help it. I couldn't stop feeling more for him if I wanted to.

"What are you thinking?" he asked. His fingers traced tiny circles on my thigh, tiny little circles that caused huge butterflies to take flight in my stomach.

"I'm thinking how much fun I've had over the last few days. How I don't want it to end." I nuzzled my nose against the crook of his neck, my words getting muffled against his skin. "How much I like you."

His chuckle vibrated from his chest. "What was that?"

"Nothing," I said, embarrassed and cowering into him, my nose jammed into the spot between his shoulder and his neck. I'd let too much slip already.

He pulled back and captured my chin between his fingertips. "What did you say, Angel?"

I averted my gaze, knowing he'd be able to read me and know how deeply I felt for him, that this was more than a fleeting crush.

"Angel." His eyes were like a dark polished shard of metal. Staring up at him, I knew there was no pretense. No reason to fear saying the truth, but before I had a chance to blurt it out, he said it first.

"Angelica Armstrong, I'm very much in like with you."

His words seemed like something a little kid would say, but it was endearing coming from a grown man of his stature and build.

I beamed, and my stomach did flip-flops like a gymnast at a competition. "And Cade Ryder, I'm very much in like with you, too."

His thumb brushed lightly on my bottom lip and a familiar warmth, one that only he could stir up, radiated in my chest. "I want to spend every waking moment with you. It's like I'm on borrowed time."

I nodded, agreeing wholeheartedly. "Like it can't be this good. So effortless."

He kissed my lips. "Exactly. So effortless." Then again. "So happy." Then again. "So sexy."

His hand tightened, squeezing my outer thigh while his tongue outlined my mouth. And my whole body warmed with arousal.

He took in my face, his thumbs caressing my cheek. "I might have to prolong my trip because of you."

I pulled back, reading his face to see if he was serious. "Really?" My heart skipped two, three, four beats.

"Yes, really." Then his lips captured mine in his. And then I was lost. Lost in his kisses. Lost in his touch. "You're absolutely beautiful." Lost in his words.

And then I sighed. Out loud. And I was pretty sure he heard it. When Cade called me beautiful, it was like he was saying it for the first time. He said it with conviction, like in the dictionary my picture would be under the word. He didn't say it in passing or out of habit or to be nice. He honestly thought that I—Angelica Armstrong—was beautiful, and my heart soared.

"You make me feel beautiful," I whispered.

He pulled back, want and need heavy in his eyes. His thumb lightly grazed my cheek in soft, graceful caresses. His eyebrows furrowed, and I searched his face for what he was thinking. His eyes were transparent, clear gray and endless. He was being careful with me.

Slow and seductive, he nipped at my flesh. "This okay?"

I bit my lip and nodded. "More than okay," I said, urging him on.

His fingers reached for the hem of my long T-shirt. "I don't think it's fair that I'm shirtless and you still have your clothes on."

I lifted my arms, and as soon as the shirt was off, he chucked it to the side.

His tongue explored my breasts, paying each one equal attention, all the while watching me lose control. If this were anyone else, I would've been embarrassed by my heavy breathing, but not with this man.

This man made me feel beautiful, even naked in the full light. All my imperfections were plain for him to see, but he marveled at them, not making me feel shy. Instead, he made me feel like the sexiest woman alive.

He gently guided me to my back and lifted his head, staring at me with such reverence. It was as if he was painting a picture of me in his head, and my whole body tingled as I felt every stroke of his imaginary paint brush.

After slipping off my underwear, he bent down to capture my lips in his and entered me in one slow, agonizing sweep. He stilled, and a shudder ran through his body before he pulled back and reentered me, creating a sensual tempo between us.

His voice was husky, hoarse. "Your body ... your body was meant to fit with mine."

The slick of sweat from his chest stuck to mine, and I

trembled from the feel of him. "You feel so good, Angel." He voice was guttural, his tempo increasing. "It's never felt this good."

I gripped the top of his hair, so dark, so soft, so wonderful between my fingertips. Our bodies moved as one in a beautiful sexual dance. His body, his being, his whole self was meant for me, too. I believed it. I believed it with every thrust of his body against mine, with every word that left his mouth and with every kiss he planted on my lips.

This wasn't hardcore, uninhibited sex as we'd had many times before, one where I'd experienced instant, body-crushing satisfaction. This was planned, slow, and soul-crushing lovemaking. I felt his every push and pull inside of me, not only with my body but with my soul. I felt him everywhere, places that were broken and healing and being put back together. And I was afraid to admit it, afraid to say it to him, and more so admit it to myself. But I couldn't deny my strong feelings for this man any longer, I more than liked him. I was falling in love with him.

And I never wanted to let him go—ever.

CHAPTER 16

AFTER SLAMMING the door of my car shut, I organized the receipts and stuffed them in my portfolio. I had paid the contractors that fixed the broken pipe and checked on the work myself to make sure it was done. On the new job end, I was rocking it.

On the man front, I was rocking it, too.

On the family front, I was drowning like a kid without a floaty.

The next few days I spent with Cade, I ignored the world around me. My mother had called me, and we spoke like everything was normal, and that was how I knew that they didn't know that Roland and I had broken up. So, I continued to live in the alternate universe, because in this world, I was happy, and I was living for myself. It was as if I was on my own little planet, just Cade and me. And it was a hella happy bubble of joy.

Tene knew something was up, though. She had texted last night, asking me to call her and saying that it was important. I'd promised myself that today would be the day I told her the truth about my relationship status because, out of everyone, she'd understand.

After checking on the rest of my downtown tenants, I strolled into Allswell during my lunch break. Kristy stared at me like I needed to ask permission to even be here.

She cared for him. I knew this. But what she didn't realize was that I cared for him, too. She didn't know what was happening with Cade and me. She just didn't know, nor was it really any of her business.

The scent of tomatoes and fresh basil and spices filled my senses when I stepped into the kitchen. The staff was at the peak of their afternoon rush. Multiple dishes adorned with garnishes spread along the metal center table. The cooks in their white aprons scurried about in every corner of the kitchen. I scanned the area, but Cade was nowhere to be seen.

Tamara, Cade's head chef, was directing the others when she noticed my arrival. "He's in his office," she said with a smile.

I turned the corner and entered Cade's office. His back was toward the door as he shuffled through the papers on his desk. I paused to admire the view, taking in all of him. The way his fitted T-shirt hugged his body, outlining the defined muscles on his back. The way the ink on his arm traveled up, stopping at his sleeve but then continuing up his neck. I was lucky enough to know that the beautiful art spanned his whole arm, and into most of his upper chest.

When I shut the door behind me, he flipped around.

His eyes zoned in on mine. Locked, lustful, and loaded. The connection between us was like the click of a gun. Instant. Deadly.

His gray eyes smoldered as he took me in from the top of my dark brown hair to my button-down silk blouse to my fitted black work slacks. His stance screamed authority and possessiveness and need. He stalked toward me, stealthy like a cat, and with every single step in my direction, my body became more feverish.

I opened my mouth to speak, but he didn't even allow me to get a word out before he slammed his mouth against mine. His tongue intertwined with mine; it suckled and teased. With one hand on my hip and the other at the base of my neck, he brought me closer. We were chest to chest, pelvis to pelvis, and my temperature went from feverish to holy hell hot.

Will it always be like this? Is it only like this because it's new or because it's us?

I had so many questions because I had come to realize, even though I had been in a serious relationship for years, I'd never felt like this. Never this passion. Never this insatiable lust. Never this deep need that I would wither if he walked away from me.

I wanted to believe it was just us, how we were together.

Every touch prickled my skin with goose bumps and awareness, and my every pore radiated with sensitivity.

When he pushed his arousal against my stomach and his mouth devoured mine, my nipples pebbled and everything inside me screamed for him to take me.

"I missed your mouth." He peppered kisses along my neck as my fingers threaded through his hair.

"You just had my mouth," I moaned back. "If I remember correctly, it was on your dick." I rubbed at his hard ridge between us for emphasis.

He groaned. "Why do we have to work?"

I sighed, fully agreeing. "I wish we didn't." We'd be locked up in his bedroom if it were up to us, forgetting responsibility, forgetting everything.

The back of my knees hit the desk behind me, stopping me from moving farther. When he lowered me onto my back, I stilled. "Cade," I lifted my head and glanced toward the door, "it's the middle of the lunch rush."

He unbuttoned my slacks—his hands, his demeanor functioning with hot-blooded purpose. "Yeah. And I'm hungry." The guttural sound he made at the back of his throat had my panties soaking wet.

He ushered my slacks down my legs and onto the floor. When his fingers went to the waistband of my panties, my hands gripped his. "We can't. They'll hear us." My voice was hoarse, hot, and horny.

"Then try to keep it down, will ya?"

The devilish gleam in his eye had my back arching for him to take me. The ache between my legs was almost unbearable. The live wire that was my body was ready for him to release the tension.

"Be quiet." He pushed my panties to the side and slipped a finger in me. I gasped at the pleasure of his touch.

"That's impossible with your skills," I panted.

He threw me a crooked smile, and then I knew I was done for as he slipped my panties off and flung them to the floor.

When he cupped my sex and slipped another finger inside me, my head flew back, and my eyes shut tight. My body arched, and my hard nipples pointed toward the ceiling as he pumped his fingers in and out of me.

"Shit. Angel." He unbuttoned my shirt with one hand while the other hand continually and seductively teased at my clit. He cupped my breast with his free hand and then trailed kisses against my stomach. "You're so wet."

I bit my lip as his mouth went lower, nipping tiny bites down my inner thigh, then lower.

My hands ran through his hair, and my breathing labored. His tongue dragged down my inner thigh until he reached my center, and I bit my tongue instead of screaming. "Cade," I drew out as quietly as I could, "you have to stop."

My man was an oral genius. He had a master's degree in oral sex, and I was the recipient of this gift. He knew where to find the G-Glorious spot, and it was glorious.

"Cade," I moaned, my hips bucking forward, the steamy sizzle between us heightening.

I shivered against his hold, as his mouth continued to feed on me. "Angel, I love the taste of you."

My moans increased with each flick of his tongue, and it didn't take long for the pinch at the pit of my belly and the tingling in my toes to begin.

I breathed hard, pulling at the end of his hair. His movements were electrifying and erotic as he fed on me with new fervor. "Please." My back arched against his desk and then I decided I didn't care. I didn't care about anything else but his hands and his mouth on me and the inevitable orgasm that was coming. "I'm close ... Ahh." I tried to stifle the moans leaving my mouth, but it felt oh so good. Too good. I forgot about every single thing around me. The whole restaurant could've been burning down, but I wouldn't have cared.

I gripped his hair, pushing him lower, closer, and he suckled my clit, working it over and over. When I shifted, he steadied me with his hands, increasing the flick and push and pull and magic of his tongue, while my body wriggled and bucked above him.

I felt a familiar tug in the deepest part of my belly, and I knew I was close. So close that I bit my lip to minimize my cries of ecstasy.

"Don't stop, Cade." Forget it. Forget them outside. Forget everyone else but us in this moment. "Don't stop, baby. Don't st—"

"Omigod. Please stop." A familiar voice brought me from the edge, my orgasm robbed as horror instantly overcame me. The door slammed shut, and I jerked up to see Tene staring directly at me, fully exposed.

CHAPTER 17

"WELL, LOOK WHAT WE HAVE HERE." Tene's eyes widened, but her voice stayed evenly calm. "This is definitely not something a sister should see." She strutted in, readjusting her Chanel purse on her shoulder and shut the door behind her.

I jolted up to a sitting position so quickly my head spun. I blinked, eyes wide, mind disoriented. My vision clouded and my body in orgasm-robbed-shock quivered at my sister simply standing there.

"Oh, my god. I'm blind. I'm fucking blind." She gawked at me, a slow smile building on her face as Cade picked up my panties and slacks, handing them to me.

Nothing seemed to faze him, but I was mortified.

I wanted to run or hide or something. Anything but lay naked in front of my sister.

Cade brushed his fingers comfortingly down my arm, simultaneously stepping in front of me to block Tene's view. When he handed me my panties, I slipped them back on.

Tene piped up, "Please, Cade. She's my sister. We used to bathe naked. But I can say I've never seen Angie at that angle before. I could've lived without it, quite honestly." She clicked her tongue against the roof of her mouth like I was the one in trouble. "No wonder you aren't answering my calls. I tracked your phone, then I saw your car outside, but would've never guessed this." Her eyes took me in, as though she were looking at me for the first time.

"Don't," Cade commanded, his face hard. "This is all me. Not her."

"Tsk, tsk, tsk." Tene propped a hand on her hip. "Like the saying goes, 'it takes two to tango.'" She eyed Cade with a mischievous grin. "Or it takes a guy with a thick tongue to give good oral."

"Tene," I gasped, finally finding the ability to speak. My hands shook as I slipped into my pants. "Cade, can you leave so I can talk to my sister?"

His jaw tightened, his protective stance not changing as though he had to shelter me from my own sister, but she was the least of my problems at this point.

I placed my hand on his chest, begging him with my eyes. "Please."

He hesitated at first, but then he reached for my hand, kissed it, and turned to the door. "You know where I'll be."

"Oh, Cade," Tene sassed. "Just a word of advice, maybe you should brush your teeth before you go out there." She pointed to me and back to his mouth area. "Ya know, good hygiene and all."

He grunted, and his eyebrows pulled together before he walked out and closed the door behind him.

"Oh, Angelica Armstrong!" Tene chided. "I didn't know you were such a freak. And to think you've picked the unattainable Cade Ryder. The finest man in Rosendell." She appraised me, looking impressed and pleased, shocking me yet again. Then she shook her head. "It's always the good girls. I would high-five you, but I don't know where your hands have been." She grimaced.

I backed up and leaned against the desk for support. The room, my world, my life was crazy messed up. I rubbed the back of my neck, unable to look her in the eye. "Please, Tene. Not now. Please stop." I swallowed hard, on the verge of tears, mortified at the position she'd caught us in and not knowing where to start, how to explain the fact that I'd slept with our tenant.

"Stop?" Her eyebrows rose to her hairline. "I just got started. You'll never live this down, little sis. You know I like to tease you, but nothing will top this." She stood right next to me and crossed her ankles, leaning against the desk. "So, baby girl. Do tell. How long has this affair been going on? Does Roland know? Are you still with him?"

"No!" I snapped. "Roland and I were over a long time ago."

She lifted an unbelieving eyebrow. "Does he know that? He doesn't know where you are, but I think in his mind you are still very much together. How about dear mama? Does she know?"

"We're not together," I sighed mournfully. "I've been blatantly clear to him. And no."

My parents ...

A sourness hit the pit of my stomach. Gone were the days of my alternate happy universe. Reality had hit the fan. Our families were so tightly interwoven together that I knew our breakup would hurt my parents.

"Not like I'd let this leak, but I just want to snap a picture of mother's face." She held her fingers in a square as if demonstrating snapping a picture. "Just to spite her. Her reaction would be epic." She grinned with malevolence.

"Tene. Enough." I couldn't handle her jokes. Not now.

My voice lost its gusto as the guilt and pressure finally surfaced.

She lowered to my level, and her face pinched. For once, her cheery features fell, and her lips pressed together in a slight grimace. "Tell me you didn't, Ang."

I turned away, but she ducked in to get in my line of sight. "Shit, baby girl. You did." She quieted, her face less animated. "I thought this was just a fling. I thought you knew what you were doing here." She searched my face for answers—answers that I would soon have to own up to—then her eyes leaked with sympathy. "I should've known. I know you. You don't do flings." She blew out a long breath, as though she were the one in this predicament. "You did, didn't you? You fell in love with him."

As soon as the words left her mouth, tears erupted, like a dam bursting open, finally after all this time, flowing down my face. Because it was the truth. Above getting caught, tears flowed endlessly because I was in love with Cade, and my family and history would not make it easy for us.

When I cupped my face with both hands, Tene's arms and warmth surrounded me. She rested her chin on my head. "What are you going to do?" she whispered. "What are *we* going to do?"

———

When Tene left, Cade entered his office. He walked right up to me and raked in my features, his lips pulled together in a slight grimace. "Are you okay?"

"Yes," I replied. Because although my life was totally discombobulated, like a 1000-piece jigsaw puzzle mixed in a box, I was weirdly centered, and it had everything to do with him being right in front of me.

My life had been turned upside down and inside out because of him because I'd chosen him, but for some reason and everything that mattered, together we were rock steady. Even though our future was uncertain, I at least felt that.

He put his hand in mine and intertwined our fingers.

My eyes locked on where we were connected, the warmth spreading down my arm. Then my nervous jitters from my conversation with Tene evaporated.

"What happened?" He brushed a tender finger through my hair—light, soft, comforting.

"She wanted to know what I was going to do."

"And?" Conflict reigned in his eyes. Was he afraid I'd end it? This affair? Us?

"I don't even know where to go from here," I said, feeling lost.

He squeezed my hand and opened his mouth to speak, but then shut it again. After a beat, he spoke, but for some reason, I didn't believe it was what he was originally going to say. "You take it wherever you want it to go, Angel. This is your decision. Your life."

My life.

I sighed.

Roland was selfish in our relationship, but with Cade, I was on an equal playing field. He let me decide, take the lead. But I knew I was falling for him. Last night and my conversation with Tene confirmed that. And I wanted more.

I glanced up at Cade and his crooked smile and took him all in. His steel grey eyes were guarded.

"What are we doing here, Cade?" The thoughts in my head, what I'd been wondering about this whole time we'd been together came out, super fast, without hesitation, without restraint, with all honesty.

He wrapped his arm around my waist and pulled me in. "We're having fun, Angel."

I winced. What was happening between us was more than that.

He cupped the side of my face, and I leaned into the warmth of his hold, reveled in his touch. I was in too deep with him. Tene was right.

Inhaling deeply, I put everything out on the line because I had to know. "Is that all this is? Fun? Because ..." I shied away, my voice trailing off, but when I met his gaze again, I said, "Because, for me, this feels ... different."

His fingertips skimmed along my jawline. "If you think you're just an easy lay for me, you're not. I haven't been with another girl for a while. What I said the other night, it's all true. I like you, Angel."

I wanted to ask him, for how long. Until he got tired of me? I couldn't look him in the eye, afraid he'd know I was in too deep.

He gripped my chin to force my focus up to his. "I've got baggage, okay? Things you don't know about, and things I'm not about to tell you."

Pulling his hands down, I said again, "Why not? Why can't you tell me? What are you going through that's keeping this from going any further?"

He was silent for a moment. "I've got obligations."

My body warmed with irritation. "What the hell does that mean?" I asked, my tone sharp. "What kind of obligations?"

Cade was giving me control, so I seized it, dragging things into my playing field. I stepped back, away from him. The man who lit a fire in me. The only one in my whole world who had never treated me like I was some little child who needed guidance.

"I can't." I shook my head, crossing my arms over my chest. "Because at the end of this ... you move away and I'm the one left behind. And I won't be able to handle that. I won't."

When his arms went limp, and he nodded once, an intense pang hit the center of my chest. "You walk away now, that's your choice." He stared intently with a seriousness I hadn't seen before. "But that's you, not me. I'm here, and I'm staying for you."

I shook my head, unbelieving. "You said you're prolonging your trip. That's not the same thing."

"But it is, Angel," he urged. "I would be long gone now if it weren't for you. I have no other reason to stay." He let out a long breath, his look pensive. "Have you ever thought that I'm protecting myself?" I scoffed, but he continued. "You've been with Roland for years. *Years.* You haven't told him about me, right?"

"I broke up with him," I argued.

"It's not enough. Ninety-five percent of your stuff is still at your old place. Have you even told your family that you're no longer together?"

I blinked, unable to speak because he had me there. I hadn't told Roland I'd moved on. I hadn't told my family.

"It's complicated," I said, knowing that was a loaded answer.

"And my life's just as complicated." He softened. "I understand. I do. But you have history with him, and your families are close. So, yeah." He leveled his gaze with mine. "How do I know you're serious about me? I know what Tene's thinking. I saw it all over her face when she stormed out of the restaurant today. But how do I know you're not playing *me?*"

He was right. About every single thing. I could see his

reservations, and if that was one of the reasons that was keeping us from being fully together, I could fix this. I could and would rectify the situation.

I wrapped my arms around his neck and went up on my toes to get even closer. "I'm telling Roland. To finalize things with the apartment and finally move out. And I'm telling my family, too."

A beaming smile touched his face, and he cupped my face and gently brushed his thumb against my cheek.

And when our lips met, I knew with every fiber of my being that I was doing the right thing.

CHAPTER 18

MY FIRST MISTAKE was calling Roland to tell him I needed to talk. My second mistake was going over to my former apartment to talk to him. But I needed to pick up more clothes and toiletries and tell him that I was setting a day to move the rest of my belongings out.

My biggest mistake was getting in his car to go to dinner. He insisted that we discuss our relationship over a meal, and I contested, but then listening to his unusually sullen tone had the guilt eating me up.

Maybe finally and forever and formally ending our relationship over dinner would lessen the blow, so I hopped in the car with him, knowing full well this would be the last time I'd ever get in his vehicle.

My cell buzzed in my purse, and I dug to the bottom and silenced it. It was Tene; I'd call her later. Roland drove, while his hand stayed politely on his side. His fingers had traveled to my knee, and when I pushed it away, he didn't try a second time.

"Angie, I wish you'd understand. Just because work is important to me doesn't mean that you're not."

His constant excuses about putting me second in his life were no longer good enough.

"Roland, this has to stop." The best way out of this was honesty. "Our relationship wasn't healthy anymore because our priorities are unaligned. Our time ... it's run out."

"You're just angry about your dad's birthday, and I get it." He tapped his fingers against the steering wheel, his attitude nonchalant. "I had something grand planned for your birthday, but you weren't picking up my calls. I'll make it up to you."

He wouldn't. I knew. I'd played his game before, ridden this rodeo.

I didn't say another word as he weaved in and out of downtown Rosendell. I'd speak my piece when we were seated at dinner. But when he parked in front of Allswell, my world bottomed out.

"Surprise." He turned to me and gave me a shaky smile. "I know you cover this area, but this restaurant was all over the paper the other day, rated number one in the up-and-coming new restaurants in Rosendell."

I blinked, unable to form words or think through my next plan of action. Nausea slammed through me, making my stomach roll. My hands trembled at my side as I gripped the car door for support.

Did he know? Did he know where I'd been spending all my evenings lately? Why would he take me to this particular restaurant?

I needed out of this situation and stat.

I rubbed at the back of my neck, every one of my muscles twitching. "Roland, I'd rather go somewhere else."

"No, I've got another surprise for you." He ran to my side and opened the door, like the gentleman he'd been groomed to be. I stared at his outstretched hand, hoping, wishing, and waiting to wake up from this nightmare.

This could not be happening. I stood without assistance, and when my four-inch heels hit the pavement, Roland ushered me to the doors with his hand at the small of my back.

It was as if my heels were weighted to the ground, my pace matching my heavy, sluggish heartbeat. Every step toward the door hurt. Hurt my stomach, hurt my heart, hurt my head because I could not figure out how to get out of this. Both of my worlds were about to collide in a big, atomic explosion.

As soon as we stepped inside, I spotted our parents at the long rectangular table at the edge of the room. The familiar crowd shouted "Surprise!" at once, and I nearly buckled to the ground from the shock of seeing everyone together, my family and the patrons in the packed restaurant. My vision blurred, and a full-on panic attack was about to take over.

I scanned the bar for Cade. I couldn't spot him, but my eyes zoned in on Kristy. If I had any doubt whether she hated me before, there was no doubt now as her eyes told me she'd rather see me dead than alive. I couldn't blame her, even though what she was seeing was not reality. Maybe she thought I was doing this on purpose, that I was a vindictive bitch who wanted to make Cade jealous.

What woman showed up to her lover's restaurant with her whole family and her boyfriend? Ex-boyfriend, I must add, but Kristy didn't know that.

Kathleen, Roland's mother, engulfed me in a hug so tight I thought my dress would rip. "Angie, happy birthday, beautiful." She kissed both of my cheeks and tipped her head to the stack of gifts at the edge of the table. "I hope you love what I got you. It's perfect." She clasped her hands together and reached for her son next, taking off a piece of lint from his suit. "Roland."

And then I was passed around like a rag doll. Kissing and hugging and acknowledging their presence—my mother, my father, Nana.

Tene stood alone in the corner, her eyes skittering around the room. Nervous was an understatement. If my heart was beating a mile a minute, she was about to go into cardiac arrest.

She rushed toward me and wrapped her arms around my shoulders. "Don't worry. I don't think he's here."

An exaggerated sigh left my body. *Thank goodness.*

But then in the next second, her body stiffened, her head flipped up to something behind me, and I just knew he was watching this scene unfold.

When I tried to move away, she pulled me tighter against her chest. "You're fine." I didn't know if her words were meant to comfort me or her. "Everything's fine," she repeated. "Fine. Fine. Fine." There was a tremor in her voice, contrasting her normal confident demeanor.

I pushed from her grasp and turned around to see Cade, standing by the bar, his eyes hard, his jaw tight.

God, it hurt. It hurt to look at him when I couldn't talk to him. I wanted to rush over there and tell him that this was not my plan at all. That this was all for show, a façade, and that when I'd hopped in the car with Roland, I'd expected to tell him I'd moved on. I'd expected a different outcome, one where I was free from him and our old relationship.

Cade's eyes had once held so much reverence and adoration for me, and now they were filled with fury. I wished I were anywhere but here. Anywhere but in this moment.

Roland pulled out my chair, breaking me out of my trance, and I didn't dare look up at Cade as dread filled me and the ache in the back of my throat spread to my chest.

How do you know that I'm just not protecting myself?

His words, his honesty, rang loudly in my ears.

Who was I? I didn't recognize this person I'd become, hurting people around me, the ones I cared about the most.

"Let's get a bottle of wine to celebrate this girl turning twenty-five." Roland slipped an arm around my shoulder, but I shied away with an awkward smile. Though I couldn't see Cade watching, I knew he was. It was as if I could feel him boring a hole into the side of my face, lighting it up like he had laser vision.

"Yes, let's. I need some wine." Tene shifted in her seat. I wondered who was more uncomfortable in this moment. I appreciated her empathy, but what I really needed was an escape.

"Finally, there's our waitress." Tene's voice was soft, shaky, and so unlike her.

The waitress recognized me as soon as she approached, her eyes flickering first in my direction, and then to Roland's arm around my chair. Heat rushed to the apple of my cheeks, and I ducked my head into the menu.

Kathleen and my father's laughter boomed in the background, but I didn't hear a word. All I could hear was the intense ringing in my ears and the rapid beating of my chest.

"Angelica?" Roland's voice raised to get my attention.

"Huh?"

"What do you want to order?"

All eyes were on me, and I smiled awkwardly. My teeth hurt from clenching my molars, and I rubbed the back of my neck and spit out the first thing on my mind. "Burger, please."

Roland's face pinched. "You want a burger for your birthday?" He opened the menu and pushed it in my direction. "What about the lobster or the steak?"

I glanced behind me. Though Cade wasn't in the same spot, his eyes were laser locked on mine. A dizzying current took over, and I clutched my stomach to keep myself steady. "Burger is fine," I repeated, glancing up at the waitress glowering down at me with her judging eyes.

All I wanted to do was cry. Cry about the craziness around me. But here I was, maintaining composure when my whole world was falling apart.

"Honey, you don't look too well." My grandma proceeded to stand, and I held my hand out. "No, Nana, I'm fine. Really."

"I'm the one not feeling too well." Tene seemed as if she were going to puke. Her eyes teetered between Cade, Roland, and me. She was going to go cross-eyed.

"You know what," I said abruptly. "I think I need something other than water." Water was on the table, but our drinks had not come yet. "I'll get it at the bar." The need to get to Cade and explain was overwhelming.

"The waitress is coming right back," Roland said as I shot up from my chair.

"No, I really need a walk."

"Fine, I'll get it." Roland placed his hand on mine, possessively, stilling me.

"It's okay," I blurted. "I think I need to walk off this queasy feeling in my stomach." I pivoted toward the bar and rushed away before anyone else could stop me.

"Fuck." It was Tene. Everyone turned in her direction, and she replied, "I think I broke a nail."

My steps quickened, but not before I heard my mother scold Tene for her use of language.

I walked straight toward him, past the first and second bartender, all while he tracked me from across the room.

"I'm sorry." The words rushed out in one soft, broken sigh. I didn't care that he was serving a patron. The apology had to be said. I was tired of the guilt, of being the bad guy, of being unfair to the people around me. "I'm sorry. I had no idea Roland was taking me here."

Both hands fisted the top of his hair. "You agreed to go to dinner with him?" His anger turned incredulous.

"What?" I reeled back. "I did, but it's not what you think. I didn't know he'd throw me a surprise birthday party. If I'd known, I wouldn't have come. But you have to stop looking at me like that."

I flipped around, noticing that the only eyes on me were Tene's.

"Like what?" His gruff voice had me flipping back around.

"Like you hate me."

"I don't hate you."

"Then why are you looking at me like that?"

His eyes hovered above my head, and I knew they were fixed on my table. "Nice to see you're all out enjoying family dinner." His curt tone and quick change of subject gave me whiplash.

"Cade, please stop."

By this time, the patron in our area had left, and I was glad because I was reaching desperation.

"Stop what?" His glare cut through me, slicing my insides like paper through a shredder. "Are you back together?"

"What?" His question was ridiculous. I could tell he was pissed but trying his best not to show it. He wasn't very good at hiding his emotions.

I leaned in, my voice soft but firm. "You're the one with the commitment issues. You're the one who just wants to 'have fun.'" I used air quotes around the words.

"This is fun," he deadpanned. He fixed his stare behind me again for a brief second before saying, "It's fine."

"It's not fine!" I whisper-yelled. "I'm not with him, okay? Our relationship has been dead for a long time now." It had been. With or without Cade, I was forever done with Roland.

My true feelings fell out of my mouth, the fear, the reasons as to why I was holding back, not giving myself fully to whatever was happening between us. "At the end of this, you're leaving. You're going to your new destination, and I'll just be a blip in your past."

He stretched his hands over the bar, and when I didn't take them, he shook his head, and his voice softened. "You don't understand anything, Angel."

With my arms wrapped around my chest, I said, "Well, then tell me. Tell me so I can understand. Don't be indifferent toward this, toward us, like if we end, it won't matter to you." I tried to control the quiver in my voice but failed. "Because ... because it matters to me."

He lifted his head, focusing behind me, and I turned to see Roland approaching the bar.

"You were taking a while." Roland placed his hand on the small of my back, causing tiny spiders to crawl up my arms, a feeling that his touch shouldn't have given me.

Cade crossed his arms over his chest, and his lips flattened, his eyes icy cold. He didn't move from his spot, and they stared at each other through the ring of silence.

Roland's eyes wavered between the both of us. "Everything okay here?"

The tension in the air shifted to arctic icy cold, making

me want to hide. If I could only speed up time. "Yes." I nodded. "Cade was carding me, and I didn't have my ID."

I stepped away from Roland, but he grabbed my hand when I did. Cade's focus flickered to where we were connected, and his eyes hardened.

Roland laughed. "It's her birthday."

"She said her birthday was days ago," Cade snapped.

Roland's eye twitched, his stance changing. "Whatever, man. I totally vouch for her. Long island." Roland reached in his back pocket and threw money on the bar like it was trash.

"Rules are rules." Cade didn't budge, didn't move, didn't try to pretend. And I blinked rapidly at their interaction.

"Really?" Roland scowled. "She's not eighteen. If you're going to be a total dick about this ... Angie, go get your purse and get your ID."

Cade hunched forward, his fists perched on the bar like a gorilla about to hop over. His voice, though, was calm but deadly. "Is that normal for you? Barking orders at her?"

Roland stepped up to the bar, squared his shoulders and lifted his chin. "What's your problem, asshole?"

"Asshole?" The muscle in Cade's jaw twitched, and anxiety rose within me, my whole body tensing.

I reached for Roland's hand and tugged him away from the crazy scene about to unfold. "I don't want a drink anymore. Let's go back."

Neither man moved. They stood statue still, their eyes warring without words.

There was going to be a full-on wrestling match if I didn't break this up, and there was no doubt in my mind who would win.

Kristy approached from nowhere and pushed Cade back. "Don't. Leave. I have this." She shoved at his chest again, though he didn't budge. "Cade!" she barked. "Take a breather."

His eyes flickered between us.

"Cade, you're not going to fix anything here right now, and you know that." Her eyes burned with a feverish desperation. A desperation to stop a fight from escalating.

Cade's gaze turned my way before he stormed toward the kitchen, the door flying open then shut as he stomped through.

Roland's eyes met Kristy's. "Are you the manager here?"

Kristy nodded. "I'm sorry. He's a bit temperamental, and I have no idea why. He was in a good mood earlier." Her voice dripped with sarcasm. She stared directly at me, not even acknowledging Roland in front of her.

"Well, he needs an attitude adjustment. Can you get my girlfriend here a long island?"

"Sure thing."

I turned to Roland when she was making my drink. "Friend, Roland. I'm not your anything anymore." Maybe with repetition, he'd finally believe it.

But Kristy didn't seem to hear or care or believe me as she slammed the cocktail into my hands, shooting daggers in my directions. But what she didn't know was that she didn't need to hate me because I hated myself enough for the both of us.

CHAPTER 19

DINNER WAS HORRIBLE. Seconds, minutes, and over an hour ticked by, and all I wanted to do was go home. My mother chatted with Kathleen while my father chuckled at James's jokes. The scene in front of me only reiterated how much our lives and families were intertwined, how much our families got along and loved each other.

I rubbed at the back of my neck as the chummy scene felt like my walls were closing in, choking me, forcing air from my lungs. But I had a plan. I had planned to formally and finally end my relationship with Roland, discuss the logistics of our apartment and our belongings. Then I had planned to break it to my parents, but Roland had deterred those plans tonight, a grand detour that had led me into this deep ditch.

Tene was talking to Roland, and when his phone vibrated on the table, we both stared at it. His gaze flickered to me first before landing back on his phone. It was as though I could hear the wheels turning in his head. To pick it up or not pick it up ... that was the question. But I already knew what he would do. What he would always do.

When he didn't budge, and it went to voice mail, he seemed to relax and turned to Tene once more. And then it rang again, and he sat straighter in his seat. He cracked his neck from side to side while his hands twitched at the end of the table.

"You can pick it up, Roland." I needed to put him out of his misery. It was just as tortuous watching him watch his phone.

"I need to run to the washroom anyway." He stood without giving me a second glance back.

This. Coming here. Was a mistake. All of this was giving him hope, and more guilt rose within me. I couldn't win.

When Roland left, Tene jumped in his chair. "You know you can no longer handle this property, right?"

"I'll be fine. Everything will be fine," I said. My whole body and mind were numb. How could I come into this bar and talk to Cade about business when I had clearly crossed that professional line?

I'd failed in every possible way—in my love life, with my family, at work.

She placed a hand on my knee. "It's okay. I'll talk to Dad."

My life was turning upside down. I wanted to show my father I could handle Armstrong Realty, the downtown properties, the more lucrative tenants. Not cave in and sleep with the hottest tenant. "Can we just not tell him? Please?" My father had so much faith in me. If there was anyone in the world I didn't want to disappoint, it was my father. "It'll be business as usual when he leaves. I told you I can handle it."

Her eyes were cautious.

"Please, Tene."

Tene pinched her bottom lip, her look pensive. She reached for my hand under the table, gave it a little squeeze, then nodded.

When Roland tapped the chair, Tene scooted over to make room. He snaked an arm around me, but I distanced myself.

"Did you take care of what you needed to take care of?" I asked.

"Yes. And that's not important. What's important is that we're getting to the very exciting part of the evening. Your favorite part." He smirked.

When I glanced up, Cade was trudging toward our table at an incredibly sluggish rate. He held a chocolate cake in his hands, lit with candles.

Roland stiffened beside me and angled closer, his arm protectively slung over the back of my chair.

When Cade locked eyes with mine, my stomach rolled, causing nausea to hit my acute senses. His mood had changed like a flick of a match.

He smiled, which seemed to indicate that his anger had dissipated, but it was his eyes; his eyes gave him away. The eyes that held so much mischief were tinted with sadness.

He placed the cake in the center of the long glass table, his arm was just a few inches away from mine.

The night of my real birthday flashed through my thoughts. Making cake. Making love. New beginnings.

A gush of emptiness filled my veins as the cake's candles lit everyone's face around me.

Though Cade didn't touch me, the heat from his closeness was only amplified when he leaned into me and whispered, "Happy birthday. Cake may mean the beginning of a new year, but when some things begin, other things end."

I drowned into the eyes that held such woeful sorrow.

Something passed between us, and I tore my gaze from him, watching everyone's reaction around me. The start of everything that was exhilarating and new had ended tonight. We both knew it.

When Roland coughed, breaking the silent tension, Cade pressed a hand on his shoulder, and said, "Sorry about earlier. I've had a rough night." He shook his head before glancing at me one last time and walking away. And then the singing began.

Both of our families clapped along as everyone's eyes zoned in on me. The only person not smiling was my mother. Her eyes flickered between me and Cade walking toward the bar. I wondered if she saw things, if she knew things. And the wondering had my blood turning to ice.

When the chorus died down, and the ringing in my ears ceased, Roland leaned into me. "Make a wish, birthday girl."

I took a silent moment, and, as I blew out the candles, I wished for the one thing, the only thing I wanted. I wished for him.

After cake, Roland paid the check, and when everyone stood, I followed all of them outside.

A sense of relief washed over me as I turned to Roland's family to bid them farewell. Kathleen's arms snaked around my waist, pulling me into her. "Happy birthday, my beautiful girl." Guilt rose within me as I embraced her. She pulled back and palmed my cheek. "Roland told me you were having some issues lately. Be patient with him. He loves you. I've had to deal with the same from his father for years. They're married to their work, dear. It's built into their DNA."

Her words were meant to comfort me, but they did the opposite to my heart. When I glanced at James Spencer, I noted he was head deep into the screen of his phone. His sandy brown hair matched Roland's, and I realized they were much more similar than Roland wanted to acknowledge. Didn't he know the one person he had such animosity toward was his spitting image?

"Issues? What issues?" my mother asked. She slipped her arm around my waist next. "Fights are normal in every relationship. It's just little tiny blips in your endless years together." She touched her cheek against mine. "Nothing a little birthday party couldn't fix, right? You have got one sweet boyfriend. Happy birthday, honey." She patted my hand, then strolled toward the car, leaving me a heaping, frightful mess.

They'd never accept my decision to leave Roland. They thought he was *it* for me.

My father approached, walking over with his cane. His color was a little off, and my eyebrows pulled together, assessing him.

"You okay?" I asked.

"Why wouldn't I be?" he smiled. "The question is, are you okay?"

I blinked, and it took a few seconds to answer. "Better than ever."

"You wouldn't be lying to your dad, would you?"

I bit my lip and wanted to cry because he looked at me with eyes that saw all. But he had enough to worry about, and I wasn't about to add another problem to his list.

"No, I'm fine, Daddy, really." There was a sourness in the pit of my stomach, and I dropped my lashes quickly to hide the hurt.

"I think you're lying, but since it's your birthday, I'm going to let it pass."

When he pulled me in, I hugged him tighter and snuggled into his Santa-Claus chest, wishing that I could keep him safe forever, free from any stress. Maybe if he wasn't sick, I'd be able to confide in him because we'd always been close. Maybe I could've asked the most important man in my life—the one I adored, the one who kept our family together—maybe I could've asked him what I should do with my situation with Cade.

He stepped back but not before I took him in, everything that was my father—his warmth, his love for me and his family.

My earliest memory of my father was me riding on his back. I was four years old and had cried because I'd wished for a pony for my birthday and didn't receive one, and it was my father who'd stepped up and saved the day, cheering me up by being a papa pony.

He reached for my hand and squeezed. "I hope you made a good wish. You won't get another one until next year."

And I squeezed his hand right back just as tightly. "You know me. I always count my blessings and have never wasted a wish."

Roland ushered me back to his car, opening the door and shutting me in. My mind was tormented with thoughts and feelings and ideas of what I wanted, what I was going to do next, how I was going to set my life straight.

When Roland placed a hand on my thigh, I snapped out of my thoughts. Terrible thoughts because my mind was on another man when Roland sat directly beside me.

"After I pick up some of my things, I'm going back to the

condo tonight." The way I said it, he knew that I didn't mean our condo.

"What? Why?" Roland asked, braking to a stop and pulling to the side of the road.

"Because that's where I'm staying."

When I didn't budge or move or break my gaze from his, he blew out a breath.

Roland was pissed. Pistol pissed, if he had one.

He had never been the vocal fighting type, but when he went silent, he was trying to calm himself down.

His eyes were resolute. "Your tantrum has gone on way too long."

My whole body stiffened, and I jerked back. "Tantrum?" I blinked. He thought I was kidding, that I couldn't possibly leave him, that it wasn't in me. I wasn't strong enough. Did he think that I'd moved out and told him it was over again and again to prove a point?

Of course, he did.

Because according to him and everyone else, Angelica Armstrong was unable to make her own decisions.

"I promise you this is not a tantrum." I snapped. "Your birthday dinner is days late."

He slammed his palm against the steering wheel, causing me to flinch. After weeks and weeks of tension, I finally got a reaction out of him. Finally.

His laughter held a sharp edge. "You're going to throw years of our relationship down the drain? For what? Me, trying to do better for us? For *us*, Angie! For fucking *us*! I do everything for this relationship, for our future, and you're going to break up with me because of that?"

I fisted my hands in my lap, my nails biting the insides of my palms. "You're blaming me for our failed relationship?" Calm composure was replaced with aggravated fury.

"This was not one event or one day. This has been many events across multiple months, years of broken promises and me waiting and hoping and wishing that things were going to change, but they haven't, and I've come to the realization that they never will." I stared at him long and hard. "Don't lie to yourself and say you're doing this for us when you're blind to the fact that you're doing this for you."

He shook his head, not wanting to hear me. "You're ridiculous."

"Your job, your desire for power and to move up in the workplace, have trumped any love for me. I'll always be second best, and I'll never have a say in this relationship. You're always going to dictate what's important, how we live, and that's not how I want to live going forward."

"You're mad, and you're just spewing words you don't mean." His face was dismissive, and my insides burned with fury.

Though I'd spoken my mind, here he was, still telling me what I was thinking, and I'd had enough. He wasn't listening to me anymore. We weren't listening to each other. I pushed open the door and stepped out.

"Angie, get back in." His voice roared with authority.

"No."

He stormed toward me and gripped my upper arm, jerking me to a stop.

"Let me go."

"Stop this," he commanded.

"I've stopped. You are the one that wants to keep going. I'm not in love with you anymore, Roland! It's over. Let. Me. Go!" I yanked myself from his grasp and half ran down the block.

"Angie! Get in the damn car." I ignored his calls, his commands to come back, just like he'd ignored my pleas for attention—his attention—for months. "Angie, I'm not coming after you this time."

I flipped around, eyes hard. "When have you ever come running after me? When, Roland?" Then I walked faster into the dead of night. I didn't have to turn around to know that Roland wasn't behind me.

CHAPTER 20

THE INSIDES of my palms were slick with sweat as I wrung my hands together, twisting my fingers in front of me. "This is it." I spoke to no one but the silent night, staring at the pitch dark Allswell.

I had walked in circles, down blocks. I could smell the rain in the air, the tingle of my toes indicating a storm was coming. I should've sought out shelter, taken a cab and headed home, but I ended up in the very place I wanted to be. The shelter that I wanted belonged in the arms of a man I didn't have anymore.

The thunder began to roar above me, and drizzles of rain dampened the top of my head. Rain indicated a new start, a new beginning, but for me, this indicated the end.

"It's over. We're over," I said to myself. My stomach sank to the ground at the thought of never having him touch me again, never hold me, never kiss me.

"This is good," I said out loud again, almost trying to convince myself that, out of all the places that Roland could've picked for our family dinner, he had to pick

Allswell, forcing my worlds to collide, causing my life to come to a full stop.

More rain continued to crash down. I welcomed it, welcomed the cold. The cold was better than the overwhelming numbness spreading through my body and my dead heart, devoid of emotion. Full, bright, and circular, the moon cast a shadow of the post and garbage can onto the concrete. I lifted my head, getting soaked by the droplets of water pouring all over me. My dress clung to my body like Saran Wrap, and my hair was glued to the sides of my face.

I commanded my feet to move forward, to get a glimpse of him. That's all I wanted—a glimpse—because that's all I'd ever truly get anymore. From this day forward, I would only love him from afar.

Why did it feel like we were breaking up when we had never been officially together? Because there didn't need to be any explanation. We didn't need to talk things out. We both knew it was temporary until he moved to his next destination.

But I felt like I owed him something. Deep down, something was off. If I didn't care for him, as a person, I wouldn't have cared otherwise to be here, to give him an explanation, an apology.

I could see him closing up by the bar, and I walked closer to the window as the shower of rain continued, running down my back, my legs and through my hair.

His head popped up as though he sensed my presence.

He walked toward me, and I heard the click of him unlocking the door. "Angel." My name on his lips sounded like a blessing, not a curse. Through all I had put him through, he said my name as though he didn't believe I was here.

My tears fell down my cheeks, mixing with the rain that dropped from the heavens above.

Instead of forcing me inside, he walked outside. The droplets of rain wet his hair, trailing a stream down his shirt. He took another step toward me and cupped my chin and with that one touch, my lungs filled with air.

"Dance with me," he whispered.

"In the rain?" I half laughed because it sounded ridiculous.

"Yes, in the rain."

And then I did.

He held me close. One hand went to the small of my back, the other clasped mine, and my head fell to his chest like it was meant to be there, against his beating heart.

God, I loved him, the smell of him, the strength of him.

I pulled back just a tad. "Cade ..." I began, wanting to apologize a million times over, repeat what I had said earlier, tell him I'd had no idea that Roland was coming here, that I had only agreed to going to dinner with him to end things peacefully.

"Shh, we're dancing."

I stayed silent and rested my head against his chest again, hearing the sound of the rain pounding behind the thunder, of lightning crackling in the air.

We were soaking wet, and to others watching, we probably looked incredibly awkward just holding each other as a storm built around us. But it felt ... right.

It was a weird juxtaposition. Where the world around us was pure chaos, Cade and I, together, were calm and complete.

I closed my eyes while the world around me disappeared, my soaked dress, the slush of water in my expensive designer shoes. Everything disappeared but the two of us in each other's arms.

Who knew how much time had passed, but then the rain lightened up and eventually stopped. All I could hear was the slushing of my clothes together and a few cars whizzing by.

Then silence.

Silence of the night. The moon shined bright above us, cascading a bluish light around us.

His feet moved from side to side, and I followed his lead. I had always wanted to lead, in life, at my job, but with Cade, I'd follow this man anywhere.

Eventually what replaced the silence was our intermingled breaths, and soon, we were dancing to the beats of our hearts against each other. First his, then mine, then his, then mine, until eventually, it was hard to distinguish when his heart began beating and where mine ended.

And for a brief moment, the tiniest of moments where I pretended that I could get anything and everything I ever wanted in my life, I pretended he was mine.

A shiver ran through his body.

After releasing a long sigh, he stepped back, reached for my hand, and pulled us back into the restaurant and to the bar. The sizzle between us, that thin line of connection, the live wire between our bodies when we were outside suddenly snipped as soon as he let go of my hand.

He didn't turn to face me before he reached behind the counter and grabbed a stack of dishrags, handing one to me.

He lifted his shirt over his head and dropped it on the floor in a large slop.

I wanted to see his eyes, read what he was thinking.

"I can go grab you some clothes upstairs and bring them back down here." He lifted one dish rag to the top of his hair, toweling it off. The muscles in his back moved, like a work of art, the ink rising and falling as he continued to dry off.

"Cade," I drew out. "I'm sorry," I said in one final swoosh. "I promise you that I had no idea he would take me here."

He dropped the rag on the counter and gripped the bar, his head bent, his gaze lowered to the floor.

"Say something, please," I begged. I wanted to know his thoughts, and since I couldn't read his face, I needed to hear them.

Then two words had my blood turn from cold to boiling water hot. "It's fine."

"It's not fine!" I yelled behind him because this, whatever was happening, was anything but freaking fine.

Only then did he turn around to look at me, and the Cade I had fallen for was not there, just a mask of the man I knew. "What do you want me to say, Angel?" He smiled his easy smile that, for once, made my insides want to burst. For once in my mediocre life, I wanted to slap him silly because he was lying. His mouth said one thing, but his eyes indicated another.

He was angry with me, which he had every right to be. I wanted him to own up to his feelings. Cuss me out. Yell at me. I wanted this—us—to be eating him from the inside out, just as much as it was tearing me apart.

How could he maintain composure, normality in this craziness? Did he not ache or feel anything?

Warmth spread from my cheeks to the tips of my ears as anger engulfed me. I willed my pulse to return to a normal rate.

"Angelica, everything is how it's supposed to be," he said, devoid of any emotion.

Stay calm.

When he turned to pick up the boxes and walk to the back of the bar to the cooler, I followed behind him, irritated and sopping wet.

He dropped the boxes to the floor, and when he bent down, I took in his toned muscular thighs and his perfect ass. My insides rose a notch in temperature as my anger mixed with passion for this man, wanting him and hating him for not wanting me enough.

"That's it," I snapped.

"What's the matter?" he asked.

All hell broke loose as my anger pushed to the surface at his stupid question. I charged him and pushed at his chest. "What's the matter?" I asked, exasperated. "What's the matter, you ask? What do you want me to say, you ask?" I continually pushed against his chest, yet he didn't budge an inch. Damn him and his wall of a body. "I want you to say that *this* is driving you crazy!" I yelled, every one of my limbs shaking. "That you can't stand seeing me with Roland. That the thought of him with me makes your skin crawl. That you *hate* it. That you have any other reaction than indifference to me, to us, to whatever is happening between us."

His mood changed in a nanosecond, his look pensive. He pulled both of my arms against him. When I stared into his eyes, his pupils turned dark as night. "I hate him. Is that what you want to hear?" he growled. An internal battle happened within the span of gray staring down at me. "That I hate a man I don't even know? That I hate myself for hating a man I don't even know? That I can't see beyond reason because of your history? That all I can see is red when he touches you?" He gripped my arms tighter, pulling me against him. "That I can't breathe, can't think, can't function when you're not with me because my mind is going crazy, thinking you're with him? He's inside you?" His eyes softened with pain, his tone shaky. "Do you know ... do you know how many times I've tried to reason with myself, tell myself to let you go, tell myself you're not good for me, that what this is doing to me is unhealthy?"

His gaze was as soft as a caress. "But I can't leave you. I've tried. I've avoided vices because of my sister. I'm a fucking bartender, yet I don't drink. I hold a pack of cigarettes in my back pocket, yet I don't smoke. I don't let things control me. It's the reason why I've never done drugs. I don't want *anything* to alter my way of thinking. But this ... with you." His voice cracked. "I can't see beyond us. I can't see beyond reason. I'm addicted to you. This is beyond what I can control now."

He gripped my chin with a gentle fierceness and ducked in where I could smell the mint on his lips. "My Angel." He brushed his nose against mine. "I'm not indifferent. If it seems like I don't care ..." he whispered, "it's because I care too much. I fake indifference because ... because I'm in love with you."

His words stilled me. I blinked, unable to believe what he just uttered because he spoke the words that I'd been feeling all along.

My fingers lightly traced his jawline. "And I'm in love with you, too. So much."

He turned his head and kissed my fingers, each and every one, then he guided me into his arms, all of me, chest to chest, hips to hips. "I'm leaving, Angel," he said in a soft whisper.

His words shocked me from the warmth he provided, and I pulled back and peered up at him. "You can't."

"I've been meaning to go for a while now. To go back

home, check on my mom, spend more than a weekend with her."

"You're leaving me?" I stepped back, feeling desperate. "You just told me you loved me."

"And I do." He let go of me and ran both hands through his hair, gripping the tips. "Maybe you can think things through. Maybe it's just the best for both of us. I need this space, and so do you. We both need time." His voice cracked.

"No," I said, gritting my teeth as a slew of emotions hit me directly in my chest. "I have nothing to think through. I've already made up my mind." Hysteria bubbled within me, at the thought of being without him. "Then take me with you." I gripped both of his hands and brought them up to my beating heart. "Take me away from this small town. Away from this drama. Away from it all. Just take me with you. Wherever you go, I want to be."

His eyebrows furrowed, his eyes debating.

"Please. If you love me like you say you do, then you'll take me with you." Desperation leaked in my tone.

"Please, Cade."

After a beat, he pulled me close again and kissed the top of my forehead. "You know we're trouble when we're together."

I relaxed in his hold, knowing he had made up his mind. "Then trouble is where I want to be."

CHAPTER 21

AFTER I PICKED up my car from Roland's and dropped it off at my new apartment, Cade and I drove out of the city. I didn't tell Tene or anyone that I was leaving. The worries of work, my mother, Roland, and responsibilities of my tenants could wait until I got back.

I needed to escape. Escaping with Cade, who was choosing me and the life I wanted to live, and I knew as I stepped into the car that it was the best decision I'd ever made.

We left the city lights behind us. It didn't matter where we went. All that mattered was that I wanted to go anywhere and be everywhere with him.

I reached for my phone in my purse to silence it in case anyone called. "Crap." I kept digging to the bottom, then realized it wasn't in my purse. "I left my phone at the apartment."

He eyed me carefully. "Did you want me to go back for it?"

"No. I don't need it." *Escaping meant escaping from it all.*

"No, you don't." He leaned over and chucked his phone into his glove compartment. "And I don't need mine, either. Everything that matters is in this car and where we are going." He gripped my hand then gently placed a chaste kiss on the top of my fist. "There's no emergency at Allswell or anywhere else that Kristy can't handle or that can't wait until I get back."

When I stared back at the beautiful gray-eyed male in front of me, I knew with every fiber of my being that I was doing the right thing and escaping with him, even if it was for a little bit.

The comfortable silence ticked between us, and I yawned as he caressed the inside of my wrist with his thumb.

"Sleep, Angel. We're going home."

The way he said "we" and "home" together had my stomach doing non-stop flips.

"I'm taking you to where I grew up," he said, his crooked smile appearing. "You'll get to meet my mom. We're celebrating her birthday this weekend."

"Way to bump up the pressure," I mumbled sleepily.

He squeezed my hand. "You have absolutely nothing to worry about." Cade stared into the open space in front of us, his smile faltering, his gaze unfocused. It was as though he'd gone somewhere else.

"Cade? Where did you go?" I asked. "What were you thinking?"

"I just have some things on my mind."

I angled closer to him, reveling in the warmth of our clasped hands. "Like what?"

"You. Work. My mom. My dad. My sister."

"Do you think about them often?" I asked.

"Yes. Even more recently." His voice softened, and a

subdued sigh escaped him. "I just keep remembering how we lost them so soon. My sister, she would've loved you. And ... she would've loved you for me."

I inched closer, leaning over the center console and kissing his lips. "I want to know more about her. More about your family."

"We were close, my sister and I." His tone broke with a heavy, sullen huskiness. "Her name fit her perfectly. Candice was sweet, full of life but naïve at the same time. You already know that my parents were foster parents. And I already told you about my two other brothers they took in —Jordan and Wyatt."

The warmth of his smile echoed in his voice as he talked about his brothers that weren't blood. "Wyatt has always been quiet. Came from the wrong side of the tracks. When he walked into my house on the first day, I thought he was mute." He shook his head, but a small laugh left his lips. "The only person that could handle him and forced him to talk was Candice. They bonded on a level Jordan and I were never able to touch. They'd talk about deep things, and he told her things he had never revealed to me about his family."

"And they fell in love?"

"Hell no." He cringed and chuckled. "Wyatt and Candice were more like best friends. It was Candice and Jordan who fell in love."

"Jordan Ryder, right?"

He narrowed his eyes, then threw me a playful glance. "Don't get any ideas, Angel; you're mine. End of story."

I sighed openly. His. I could totally get used to being his.

As he recalled memories of his past, his eyes grew animated. "Jordan was Candice's twin. He was funny, spunky, and full of life. As soon as he walked into my house, I knew he was just a good guy that got dealt the wrong cards. We got along well until he saw my sister. I didn't think anything of it until she saw him back. She never was interested in boys, so I didn't think I had to worry, but I should've known better. Jordan was a looker. Best looking guy on earth. Practically every girl wanted him, but he only saw Candice." He eyed me carefully, and I grinned, liking jealous Cade—possessive Cade, *my* Cade.

My hand brushed against his collarbone. "I'd like to cast a vote on the best-looking guy on earth."

"Jordan, I already know," he said, feigning disdain. "Or maybe it's Wyatt. You haven't seen him yet."

"There's only one guy I have my sights on." But then I reeled back. "Oh, yeah." I'd remembered that his brothers were in business with him. "You guys make up CJW LLC investments, don't you?" *Cade. Jordan. Wyatt.* His brothers were his silent partners.

No wonder Cade had more than enough capital to set up restaurant after restaurant in the poshest areas of North America. One of the investors was the biggest rising star to grace the planet. His last movie had paid him millions.

My curiosity spiked. "So, what happened between them? Candice and Jordan. Could you blame her for falling in love with him?"

He shook his head, amused. "He wasn't the actor you guys all know now. He was this tall, handsome, confident kid. I warned him to stay away, and I warned her about guys like him."

"And then what happened?"

"He took her virginity."

Cade's guttural roar had goose bumps forming on my skin. This time he wasn't smiling. "He took her virginity—

my sixteen-year-old, virginal sister, who had never had a boyfriend." Cade's jaw tightened. "And I beat the living shit out of him."

I gasped. "Cade!"

"At one point, though, Candice threw her body on top of him, sheltered him from my punches, so I stopped. His face was a bloody mess, and he didn't get up from the floor. I was pretty sure I broke his nose, but when I started yelling at Candice, that's when he pushed to his feet and put her behind him." The visible tension in his arm tightened. "He said he loved her. That I could yell and beat the shit out of him, but I wasn't allowed to yell at her." He let out a subdued laugh. "And when I looked at him, then at her ... my sister ... I knew she loved him, too. She wasn't the little girl I was used to taking care of."

He released my hand and rubbed at the center of his chest, as though it hurt to think of her.

"I'm sorry, Cade. I'm sorry that you lost her." What he painted wasn't a drug addict, but a young girl who'd fallen in love. Though my curiosity to know more almost killed me, I didn't pry. I didn't enjoy seeing the same hurt on Cade's face every time he talked about her. I knew she'd been attacked, but I didn't know how that fit into the picture.

"We all loved her." His voice was thick with emotion, and his eyes darkened with pain. "We all experienced loss. But she was taken away from us way before she killed herself."

His eyebrows pulled together, his gaze growing distant again. "She started using when she was assaulted and that ... that was the beginning of the end."

"Cade ..." I didn't know what to say, how to comfort him.

"She had a stalker at school. Real messed up kid

obsessed with her." The muscles in his forearms bulged as he gripped the steering wheel with both hands. "See, Candice was nice to everyone. Every single person. And he took her kindness to mean she was interested in him." He blew out a long-winded sigh, one that was filled with sorrowful emotion.

"Cade, you don't have to talk about this," I said.

He cleared his throat. "No, I do. I want to. I want you to know everything." He winced, reliving his past. "She shut down. Totally. We didn't even know it happened. For weeks she seemed not all there. Numb. I didn't even realize that anything was wrong until Jordan came crying to me, a grown man breaking down and telling me she had broken up with him for no reason at all. It wasn't until Candice told Wyatt that we all knew what had happened."

A tear escaped me, but I tried to control it. He needed consoling—not me—but hearing it through his strained, shaky voice made me realize that their loss had affected them all. Though Candice had died years ago, the pain was still fresh, real.

His eyes didn't waver from the road, though his mind went back in time, back when tragedy hit. "Candice was strong. She wasn't the weak one between us. She didn't tell anyone because she didn't want anyone to bear that cross. Little did she know, we were all one unit. She hated Wyatt for telling us, but he had to." When the tightness in his eyes heightened, the hairs on the back of my neck stood on end. "Jordan lost it. Totally lost it. Happy go lucky since the day he moved in, and yet I'd never seen him angrier. He knew who it was. He was going to kill him and not care if he went to jail. I wanted the very same thing."

He let out a slow, shaky breath that shook his whole body. "But I didn't have to do anything. Jordan reached him first. When I found them, the bastard was barely breathing, an inch from seeing the devil who created him. I was going to finish him off. I was going to fucking kill him for taking the life out of Candice." He closed his eyes, and when he opened them, they held a blazing faraway look in them. "But Wyatt stopped us. He was our voice of reason."

Reliving the moment was too much to take. He pulled the car to the side of the road and hung his head, his arms resting on the steering wheel. "We tried to save her. She said if we told our parents, she'd kill herself." His arms started to quake, his chest concaving.

"We tried everything. We'd take her out. Wyatt would cook her favorite meals. Jordan did everything short of bleeding out for her. I didn't even know she was using until Jordan found drugs. Hardcore drugs."

He scrubbed one heavy hand down his face. "She wanted to block it out. She wanted to forget it even happened. I understood. I did. To a point. Every day we were losing her. More and more she wasn't the same girl we used to love. Jordan begged me. He said he'd handle it, but I couldn't watch her dwindle to a fucking junkie." His voice cracked with torturous heartbreak, and I reached for his hand, tears coursing down my face like a waterfall. "I told my mom, and ..."

His tone lacked strength, lacked life. "And the day that my parents confronted her, she was so high." His face crumbled in utter devastation. "My dad begged her ... but she didn't want to give up her keys." His voice softened to above a whisper. "So, they got in the car with her." His face pinched with unbearable pain, a stabbing pain that I could physically feel. "And that's the last time I saw my family whole."

The ache in the back of my throat spread to my chest,

and my tears gushed down my cheeks. I jumped on his lap, straddling him, legs on both sides of his waist, kissing his cheek and gripping him tightly to take the hurt away, wishing and wanting to consume his anguish.

He shivered against me, as though he was cold from his revelation, reliving his agony all over again by retelling what had happened. I now understood the magnitude of suffering he'd gone through. I understood why he'd been so angry when that man had attacked me at the club. I understood it all.

"I'm sorry," I whispered, framing his face with my hands. Because I was. Sorry for his loss, for his pain, for his family.

His eyes filled with depths of despair. "I had to tell them." His lip quivered. "We were barely kids and I ... we couldn't save her. I knew we couldn't."

His words only confirmed what I had thought—he blamed himself. He held himself responsible for his sister and his father's death. "It's not your fault." My voice was soft, yet firm because he had to know. "It's not, okay? You did what you had to do. You were barely kids."

I angled closer, forcing him to look at me. "It's *not*. How could you predict that freak accident was going to happen? How were you supposed to predict what she was going to do? You said it yourself. You guys were kids, crying for help. Pulling on your last strings of hope."

I wasn't getting through to him, so I pulled him close. "Baby ... It wasn't your fault." I framed his face and kissed his lips again to reassure him.

His voice was so quiet, so miniscule that I had to strain my ears to hear him. "I need you, Angel." He tapped his head against mine and held my hands that were framing his face. "So much."

This time, he met my lips and kissed me. Feather light.

"I can feel you, but in any second ... it's like you're too good to be true and you'll disappear."

There was a spark of a definable emotion in his eyes—hope, longing, love. "Don't leave me." He sounded like a broken child, vulnerable and in need.

As another layer of Cade's toughness was stripped away, I felt closer in knowing the real him. The scariest part was it only confirmed that, although I didn't know what the future held, I knew that I loved him. I was irrevocably his.

And as I stared into his eyes, the dark gray eyes that held so much pain and yet so much life, I knew I wasn't going anywhere.

"You're never going to get rid of me," I promised him. "I'm staying right here."

CHAPTER 22

I AWOKE to the bright sunlight and the breeze of the warm air on my face. Rows and rows of cornfields were laid out before me.

"Morning, beautiful." A deep, sexy voice awoke every nerve in my body, making me straighten in my seat.

"Morning." I glanced around and admired the endless rows of golden corn husks in the horizon and long grass speckled with wildflowers. "Are we there yet?"

"Almost. I stopped to take a little nap, which delayed us a bit." He lifted a playful eyebrow.

After he turned down the corner, the scenery transformed. Boarded up shops and graffiti on buildings lined both sides of the street. The farther we drove, the shadier my surroundings became. Overgrown weeds spanned neighborhood front lawns, bars on windows, boarded up homes.

"Not the best of neighborhoods, but Mom didn't want to sell the place we grew up in, even though we could afford to buy her anything she wanted."

"It's nothing I haven't seen before," I said, half-joking,

half-serious. Rosendell was clean and wealthy, and aside from the local soup kitchen volunteer event, I wasn't exposed to a lot, but still, if I needed to, I was sure I could handle my own.

"We're not in Rosendell anymore, Angel. This is the hood like you've never seen it. My brothers and I, we've earned a lot of respect in these parts. No one touches us or the house or messes with anything that's mine, and since you're mine ..." He threw a playful glance my way. "Are you mine?"

I leaned over and kissed his cheek without hesitation. "Exclusively and forever yours."

"Well then, no one will be bothering you, either." He pulled into a driveway, and as I stepped out of the car, I took in the quaint house, with its white windowsills accenting the gray siding and the white wooden fence that caged it in. The lawn was manicured with lilies and roses and hostas lining the pathway to the door. It seemed very well-maintained like it didn't belong on the block of outdated houses with barred windows.

"Ready?" Cade asked. "You get to sleep in my childhood bed where I filled all my teenage dreams with Adriana Lima."

I grimaced. "Okay, gross."

"But Adriana has nothing on Angelica Armstrong." His eyes danced with humor and he laughed.

"Mmhmm."

He popped the trunk, then gripped my fingers fiercely.

"So, I get to meet the infamous Jordan Ryder." When his jaw tensed, I added, "But Jordan Ryder has nothing on Cade Ryder."

He looked cautiously pleased. "And that's what I like to hear."

People were out on the street. Some wearing bandanas, others wearing the same distinguishable colors as though they belonged together. Cade made eye contact, tipped up his chin to the men and the women congregated outside and kept walking toward the house.

As soon as I entered the house, I let out a silent yet over-whelming huge breath out of my system.

Cade dropped his bag on the floor. "You're okay." He pulled me in and kissed the top of my head. "I'd never let anything happen to you."

I reveled in his hold, enjoying the way his lean body pressed against mine.

Hardwood floors gleamed from the sun shining through the windows. The walls were painted a neutral cream, and pictures hung on the walls, decorating the room in matching dark mahogany frames.

Cade reached for my hand and pulled me deeper inside. "Where's everyone at?"

"In here," a deep voice rumbled from the kitchen. Laughter carried us from our destination in the family room and into the kitchen.

I took in the two good-looking men sitting at the table that could not contain them. It reminded me of full grown adults trying to fit in a grade school desk, their legs spilling over the chairs.

Jordan Ryder, actor extraordinaire, stood first to greet me. His eyes were a sharp piercing blue. His baseball cap tipped backward, and he was sporting a Dodgers T-shirt and jeans. He reminded me of a frat boy, but with tats that spanned both of his arms. I was used to seeing him in a suit on TV during those award ceremonies or shirtless on the big screen. I was a little starstruck despite myself.

"Angel!" Jordan cooed, which made Cade push me behind him.

"She is off limits," he growled. "You can say hi from across the room. She's already starstruck stupid when it comes to you." I didn't know if Cade was joking or if he was being possessively serious.

Jordan stuck his hand out, and I peered at him behind Cade. "Hey, Angel. We've heard so much about you." He raised an eyebrow at Cade. "I'm Jordan." His five-star gleaming smile surfaced, the one that won awards, sold movie tickets, and I was sure bedded many women.

It didn't make my heart pitter-patter, but internally I was fan-girling a tiny bit.

"Nice to meet—" As soon as I put my hands in his, he tugged me forward and engulfed me in a big hug. "None of those formalities. We're practically family now. Cade hasn't brought someone home in forever." He tipped his chin, looking thoughtful. "Or ever, actually."

I patted his back. "Well, it's nice to meet you." He smelled terribly good like clean aftershave, but glancing at Cade's tight expression, I doubted that would be a smart move to voice my thoughts.

"All right. Enough manhandling my girl." Cade plucked me from Jordan's arms and kissed me fully on the lips. The girly girl in me gleamed at Cade staking his claim.

Cade gestured to the equally stunning man at the table. "And this is Wyatt."

Wyatt stepped forward, and I took in his over-six-feet lean frame. His dark, reddish brown hair flopped over his chocolate brown eyes. Wyatt rocked a little scruff on his chin, as though he was growing out a beard in a sexy lumberjack style. He took both of my hands in his. "It's great to finally meet you." His voice was evenly calm and sweet, a direct contrast to the other men in my vicinity.

Wyatt extended his hand and gestured to a seat by the table. "I cooked steak and mashed potatoes if you're hungry."

Cade slapped his back, his eyes appraising him. "Wyatt over here is our cook at home, while I'm the cook at the restaurant." When Cade pulled out the seat at the table, I sat down.

Their stature, their tats, their overall persona was over-whelming, overpowering, over-the-top. They looked like thugs in a nice, clean package, a walking contradiction. They weren't blood related, but there was no denying their family bond.

"We heading to Mom's now or going to get our ink?" Jordan asked, dropping his butt on the chair opposite me. "You getting one today, too?" He smiled again, and all I could think of was Tene and how she would die to know who Cade's foster brother was. I made a mental note to tell her all about our meeting later and rub it in.

"No, I'm afraid I'm tat free," I admitted sheepishly.

Cade slapped his brother on his head. "Don't be an idiot. When do you have to leave?"

"Tomorrow night," Jordan sighed. "My agent wants me back in Cali the day after tomorrow."

"How about you, bro?" Cade turned to Wyatt.

"I can stay for a while. I don't have to go back to filming for two weeks."

My stomach grumbled, and I picked up a fork and stabbed the steak and guided it on my plate. "You into making movies, too?"

Wyatt shifted uncomfortably in his seat. His stare went blank before he averted his gaze. "Um. Not really. More like directing documentaries or reality television."

"Don't be modest, bro," Jordan teased, knocking on the table. "This guy owns the BCB Network."

"Shut up, Jordan," Wyatt muttered, his face turning a light shade of red. "I just work there, I don't own it."

"Well, you're the only heir to Hendricks, so I'm sure if he keels over, you'll be taking over."

"Bill Hendricks?" My eyes practically popped out of their sockets. Bill Hendricks was the biggest media mogul in all of Hollywood. He owned multiple radio stations, TV stations, and, more importantly, he ran all the biggest cable networks.

"You're his son?" I asked again.

Years ago, Bill's face had graced the cover of every gossip magazine sold on every grocery aisle. Some titled *Bastard Son*. Some titled *Heir to Hendricks Dynasty*. I guessed this woman was paid a hefty sum to get interviewed about their multi-year affair, years back, that revealed that she had conceived a son. There was no way that she could get child support. Wyatt was way over the legal age, but some magazines had said she'd gotten paid over three hundred thousand for being on camera.

Wyatt's downturned eyes told me this conversation was over before it even started.

"Yup, Wyatt over here is a billionaire baby." Jordan playfully ruffled Wyatt's hair.

"Would you shut up already? Seriously. Shut the fuck up," Wyatt's voice boomed.

When he stood, almost making his chair fly backward, Jordan stood and jerked back. "Dude, that's something to be proud of."

Wyatt glared at his brother. "Like I said, shut up already."

Cade stepped in between them, placing a hand on

Jordan's chest. "Quit messing around. We need to figure out what we're doing for Mom."

The boys glared at each other, but in the next beat their faces relaxed, the fight fizzled and over.

"Balloons, cake, and tats? Like every year?" Jordan asked. "It's what Mama wants for her big day, and I've set it all up. We're all ready to go."

"Is today your mom's actual birthday?" I asked, turning to Cade.

"Our mom," Wyatt corrected. There was such joy in Wyatt's tone when he uttered those words.

"Yes, it is, and I can't wait for her to meet you." There was a twinkle of pride in Cade's eyes that made me swoon and blush and want to grab his ears and ram my lips into his.

"You'll love her. Mom is crazy fun." Jordan winked.

I marveled at the change in their moods and the banter between the boys as they talked about where they got the balloons and the kind of cake they ordered. They discussed getting cupcakes and the decorations and they wondered what tattoo they were getting today. Their easy banter and loud booming laughter was amusing.

"How about we get Angie's name this year?" Jordan asked, laughing.

My eyebrow lifted, and I reeled back, crossing my arms over my chest. "My name?"

"That's one name that's only going on my body and no one else's," Cade said, eyes hard and meaning no argument.

"We all got Candice's name." Wyatt stuck out his arm and embedded under the tattoos of Chinese characters was Candice's name, neat and discreet.

The table went silent for a second, and my stomach twisted at the loss of their sister. My thoughts flickered to our conversation in the car, the devastation in Cade's eyes, the destruction in his voice as he briefly relived his past.

"Where's yours?" I asked, turning to Jordan, curious.

For the first time since I had walked in the room, he stiffened, and his facial features dropped. "It's somewhere no one can see." His voice was curt and closed and warranted no more questions.

Candice was a sensitive subject, and I wondered if time would make it easier. I only hoped it would.

"Don't be a dick," Wyatt commented. "It's right next to his heart."

A heaviness spread throughout my chest. I wished I had just shut up.

"Whatever." Jordan stood, seeming vulnerable, and took a cigarette from his back pocket. "You want a smoke?" He offered Wyatt a cig, then me.

"No, I quit," I joked, trying to erase his sullen look, but it didn't work.

"I'm going outside, and when I come back, we can go." I watched his retreating back walk out the patio door, all the while thinking Jordan Ryder still wasn't over his dead ex-girlfriend.

CHAPTER 23

THE DRIVE to the nursing home took thirty minutes. We parked outside a resort-like facility with its circular driveway and Bellboys that ushered a couple of ladies in wheelchairs through the doors.

"This place looks nice."

"Yeah, we upgraded Mom as soon as we found out she checked herself into a nursing home," Wyatt said, from the shotgun of the car. "You should have seen that first place she checked herself into. Talk about a dump."

"This new place has its own built-in gym, pool, and spa." Jordan chimed in.

When we pulled to the front of the palatial nursing home, the valet held my door open, before my heels hit the cream marble floors.

Jordan threw his keys to the bellboy, and he caught them on the fly. "Danny, my man." He slapped the teenager on the back. "Take care of her, will ya?"

"Sure thing. Hey, can I get another picture?" Danny asked, already taking out his phone.

"Yeah, no prob." Jordan threw his arm over Danny and

smiled his signature smile that I'd seen many times before on the big screen.

Cade intertwined our fingers, tipping his chin toward Jordan. "That guy. Always the center of attention."

I laughed. "How long has your mom been at a nursing home?"

"Two years or so. At first, it was just me taking care of her. I wanted it to be all me because Jordan and Wyatt, they have lives."

"How old is your mom?" I asked, curious to why she needed 24-hour care.

"Sixty. She's young, but ..." He averted his gaze, where I couldn't read his eyes. "I guess you should know before we walk in there." He pulled me to the side, right before the doors. "When my parents jumped in the car with Candice that night, my father lost his life. But my mother ..." He swallowed. "Her legs are amputated."

"Oh, Cade."

"It happened so long ago, but the repercussions of that night ... how it changed our family, how it affects us every day ..."

I kissed his lips because I didn't want him to say it out loud, regurgitate his thoughts in his head. I knew that the pain would never go away, but I didn't want him to relive it in this moment.

"She called the nursing home to pick her up when we flat out told her 'no' and we weren't putting her in a home. I know she doesn't want to be a burden, and she's not. I mean, it was a lot on me at first, but when we split the responsibilities amongst the three of us, and we had a caretaker here, it was fine."

"You're such a strong man, so loving, so kind. You know she just doesn't want to put it all on you."

He spoke in an odd, yet gentle tone. "Yeah, I know. It's just hard to have her there. I mean we visit often. It's just ... for someone that lived her life taking care of others, it feels like we just stuck her in a home."

"Don't think of it that way," I reassured him. I loved this man. My man. From the outside he was big and buff and hella intimidating, but from the inside, his love for his family was limitless.

"Serious conversation can continue later." Jordan tugged at my arm and pulled me through the doors.

"Let go of my girl, Jordan."

Gleaming, newly-polished floors welcomed us at the lobby, and we passed a sign-in desk that was adorned with two beautiful vases of green and pink orchids, reminding me of a hotel. The scent of bleach that permeated the air, the multiple sanitizer stations and wheelchairs scattered in front, reminded me that this was a swanky nursing home.

A woman with a cute blonde bob with a clipboard greeted us in the front.

"Hi, Cade. Preparations that Jordan called in are all ready. Hey, Wyatt." She raised a hand to Wyatt walking in and spoke super fast, not getting a breath in.

"Oh, I'm so sorry. I'm Bella," she said, finally noticing the stranger amongst the men and extending a hand and friendly smile my way. "I'm kind of the party planner here."

"The best party planner there is," Jordan said. His eyes ate Bella up like she was his favorite candy at the candy store. But she seemed immune to his big, starry Hollywood stare.

Cade cleared his throat and eyed Jordan with a slight shake of his head.

I wasn't sure if Cade was the eldest brother, but one thing that was certain was that Cade led this family. He took responsibility, and he instructed the other brothers, and they listened. That was blatantly clear since the moment I walked into their house.

Jordan swept his hand in front of him. "By all means, Bella, why don't you lead us toward the party."

The boys were the life of the nursing home, and my smile could not be dimmed as they hugged practically every old woman they passed and high-fived every old man that were in our path. All of the boys knew everyone by first name, and Cade introduced me to each and every person.

Balloons were placed outside the party room, and music played from the inside of the room that was outlined with mirrors. If I were a betting girl, I'd guess this was where they took dance or aerobic classes.

Every inch of the space was decorated in pink and purple. From the balloons strung to each chair to the streamers hanging from the ceiling to the pink and purple décor on the long table against the far wall. A cake that spanned half the table and appetizers and dip were placed in glass dishes were neatly lain around a cake that could feed a hundred people.

The whole area rattled with rowdy cheers. Cade's mom was seated in a wheelchair in the center of the room.

Her hair was the darkest shade of brown to match Cade's. She was beautiful and seemed like the youngest woman in the nursing home, with not a gray hair in sight.

Wyatt and Jordan practically jumped their mother, lifting her chair with her in it and getting in her face.

It was endearing and outright adorable seeing them interact like five-year olds with all their boyish charm at the vicinity of their mom.

A mile-wide smile popped on Cade's face right before

he grabbed my hand, and, in the next second, I was in front of Mrs. Ryder.

He must have sensed my unease or maybe it was the feel of my sweaty palm against his because he gave me one reassuring squeeze.

I tried not to focus at her lack of legs or the fact that her knees were stubs. And it didn't take long because her smile was contagious when she motioned me forward. I walked toward her, and when I leaned down, she embraced me in a full-on cherry-topping hug. "Angelica, it's so great to finally meet you. I'm Stacy."

Her words and the way her voice eased out made me realize that Cade had told her a lot about me.

"It's so nice to finally meet you, too," I said, pulling back, reaching for her hand and squeezing it. She was stunning with her cute chin-length bob. She couldn't have weighed more than a hundred and ten pounds. She seemed fragile, but I knew that couldn't have been further than the truth because there was strength behind her gray steel eyes that matched Cade's.

"There was a while there that I thought Cade was into men." There was a chuckle from his brothers behind him. "Not like there's anything wrong with that, but just the fact that he hadn't brought anyone home."

Cade threw one arm over my shoulder. "Just waiting for the perfect girl, to introduce her to the infamous head of the Ryder family."

I shifted with unease as everyone's eyes were on me—Cade's brothers, the whole room.

"Don't let the Ryder family or this little ole woman in the wheelchair intimidate you."

"Ryder or die." Jordan yelled behind me. "Hm, yeah that sounded bad."

When Wyatt nudged his brother on the shoulder, the room erupted in laughter.

More people began to trickle in. The chatter heightened, and a line formed behind me, waiting to greet the birthday girl.

"So, Angelica, are you in town long? I'd love if we could have breakfast tomorrow, just the family. It's a family after-birthday tradition. Today is going to be a little crazy. Old people like to party."

I didn't know how long I was staying, through the weekend for sure, until I had to face reality. "Yes. I'd love that. Wyatt can cook a killer meal." I'd experienced it first hand back at the house.

She peered lovingly over my shoulder at her son. "Cade's ability to cook is taught, but Wyatt, my sweet boy, has a natural ability and a great taste for food."

"What?" Jordan asked, his tone feigning offense. "I'm not your sweet boy?"

She rolled her eyes and chuckles around us answered Jordan's question.

"Mom, you can grill Angel later. Plus, we have breakfast tomorrow. " Cade motioned to the people behind me. "There is a line waiting to give you your gifts."

Cade pulled us to the side, making room for everyone else to wish Stacy a happy birthday.

"I think I need to get you a sweat bucket for your palm."

I tore my hand from his grasp. "You're horrible."

"You're beautiful." A smile ruffled his mouth. "I don't even know why you're nervous because there was no doubt in my mind that she'd love you just like I do."

Is it possible to turn into a puddle of mush every single time he mentioned the "L" word? The butterflies in my stomach took flight. Again. Yep, very possible.

Bella approached us, walking in her cheery, happy pace. There was a natural bounce to her step. "Let's blow out the candles. Some of these people are going to leave early to take their naps." She chuckled, her eyes filling with an inner glow.

"Sure thing." He leaned in to whisper in my ear. "I want you to blow one candle tonight, but it's not on top of the cake."

I threw him a dubious look, and his gray eyes smoldered with promises of tonight in response. My cheeks flushed a dark shade of pink at his words. "You better behave, or you're not going to have your cake and eat it, too."

His gaze was as soft as a caress, and he pinched my side playfully while ushering me to the front of the room by his mother and his brothers, right by his side.

The two-tiered cake was beautiful in all purples and pinks and yellows with elaborate flowers etched on the edges. When it came to their mother, these boys knew no limits.

A giddiness stirred within me when they lit her two candles, the six and the zero. After all, birthdays would forever be my thing, and my birthday was what brought Cade and me together. Silver lining and all.

"Make a wish!" Jordan said, shaking Stacy's shoulders lightly.

Stacy beamed at her son, her eyes crinkling with pride. "I wish for what I wish every year. For my boys' happiness." She pointed to Jordan with a gleam in her eye. "And for Jordan Ryder to finally settle down with a nice girl."

His smile faltered, his mood dampening, and I knew what had triggered the change—Candice.

"Mom, you're wasting your wishes," he said, his voice whisper soft, his joyful demeanor flipping off like a switch.

She reached behind her and grabbed his fingers, placing both of her hands on top of his. "Someday, it'll happen. It happened once. It'll happen again. You'll see. You'll fall in love again, Jordan. I know."

He nodded, and in that very instant, he seemed so lost, so vulnerable, just like a child. His eyes became distant, a cloudy murky blue, and I knew in the deepest part of me, he could only be thinking about Candice.

Stacy closed her eyes tightly, and I held my breath.

Her new beginning.

And then she blew out her old life and wished.

Everyone in the room cheered and clapped and hollered.

Cade kissed my head again, which made me think about Jordan's wish. "How about Bella?"

"What?"

"For Jordan," I clarified.

My eyes darted between Jordan and Bella, the happy-go-lucky nursing home planner, but Cade slowly shook his head. "Nope. She's off limits. She's too nice of a girl."

My head tilted, weighing out the reasons why they should be together. "You don't want your brother to be with a nice girl?"

"Of course, I do. But Jordan needs someone just like him. He's not ready to settle down, and he'd chew Bella up and leave nothing left. And I like Bella. She's a good girl and that's why I told Jordan to stay away."

"And he'll listen?" I asked staring at the actor extraordinaire.

"It's not like he hasn't before. And he knows better." I peered up into my boyfriend's eyes and made note of the hard lines on his face. I doubted that there was anyone that went against Cade's wishes.

After I assisted Bella in passing around the cake to Stacy and her friends, I sat in the corner with my dessert taking in the scene before me. Jordan occupied the vacant seat beside me. "So, Angelica ... when is the date?"

I blinked. "What date?"

"The wedding date."

I laughed, half coughed on the cake I was picking at. His words weren't too far-fetched. I thought of forever, more with Cade in the short time we'd been together than with Roland and the many years we'd spent together.

"There's no date. We haven't been together that long."

He peered over to his brother who was chitchatting with Wyatt, making their mother cry with laughter. "Cade is a serious settling type. Once he's committed, he's committed for life. I've never met anyone so loyal. So, baby girl," he said as he patted my knee, "it's only a matter of time, so you'd better pick that dress now."

"You're nuts," I said, half-laughing, half-crazy myself because it had crossed my mind.

"Yes. I don't doubt that. But in all honesty, I'm just happy he's finally found someone." He leaned back in his chair, staring at his brother. "Cade has been taking care of this family for so long. Taking on the burden of caring for mom. He didn't want any help at first until we didn't give him an option. Thing is ... she's Wyatt and my mom, too. Not by blood, but by everything a mother is." A soft smile touched his face. "He's always worried about everyone else's happiness. I'm just glad he has someone that makes him happy for once."

In the short time I'd known Cade, there was no doubt he was one with character and strength and felt the pressure of making everything right in the world before tending to himself. He took care of me with such fierceness, and

because of that, I loved him beyond what was compre-
hendible. "I'm glad, too." I placed my palm over Jordan's on
his knee and gave it a little shake. "How about I invite you to
the wedding?"

He scoffed. "I better be in the wedding. I think I'll be the
best man since I called your wedding first."

"Jordan," Wyatt called over. "You getting fresh with
Cade's girl?"

Cade's whole body flipped toward our direction, and his
eyes narrowed. But Jordan egged his brother on and pulled
my chair closer to his and threw an arm over my shoulder.
"Play along, little sis. Let's see how pissed we can get him."

When Jordan leaned in closer to whisper something in
my ear, Cade stalked toward us, lips pressed together, face
serious. He didn't even have a chance to pull Jordan off me
because Jordan jumped to a standing position with both
hands up. "Just playing, big brother. I know what's off-
limits."

Cade huffed. "Not funny." He intertwined our hands
and kissed the top of my fist, claiming me for himself.

"Aw, how precious," Jordan cooed.

I could tell Cade was irked by Jordan's teasing, aloof
manner.

"Don't you have to fix the sink at the house before you
leave?" Cade asked.

Jordan scratched at his eyebrow. "Yeah, shit. I need to
get that done before I go back to Cali."

"Not before Mom has her dance." Cade tilted his head
toward Wyatt who was holding a remote control.

"Oh, yeah, bro. My favorite part of Mom's birthday.
That and the ink."

With one click on Wyatt's remote, the song "Mama" by
Boys II Men began to play in the background. "Excuse me,

beautiful. Mama needs her dance." Cade planted a chaste kiss on my lips before joining Jordan and Wyatt in the center of the room where their mother sat in her wheelchair. Cade was the first to lift her from her chair. He carried her as though she weighed no more than a feather and they swayed to the music, to the beats and words of the sweet song.

Unfallen tears trembled beneath my eyelids as I watched their closeness. My mind flickered to their past when tragedy hit. Cade had said she was a dancer and that she taught dance classes for a living. A pain squeezed my heart thinking that fate had not only taken Stacy's daughter and her husband but her legs, too—her livelihood. But as I continued to marvel in the interaction between mother and son and their happiness, I realized she was completely whole.

She pulled back, and they shared some words that made her laugh. The upper body strength that Cade had was amazing that he could hold his mother for half the song and still balance while she pulled away to hold a conversation.

The two other boys stood in a horizontal line, their faces anxious, waiting for their turn, and it took all my strength to stand there and not bawl my eyes out at their love for their mother, their strength through their tragedy and the force of my man, not just his muscle strength but the depth of his heart—their hearts.

After Cade guided Stacy into Jordan's arms, he walked toward me, his eyes misty. He extended a hand, and when I placed my fingers against his, he twirled me around and pulled me toward him, chest to chest.

"Just so you know, I have two left feet," I said.

"Just so you know, I'm a great dancer." The warmth of his smile echoed in his voice.

"Of that, I have no doubt." I noticed the people around us moving toward the dance floor, older couples dancing. Others standing around swaying side to side. My eyes moved to Jordan and Stacy. She was laughing uncontrollably, and you'd think he'd be someone struggling as he carried her weight and held up a conversation, but he glided around the dance floor effortlessly and with ease.

"Cade, that is the sweetest thing. "

"She thought it was ridiculous, at first. Until one day, Jordan just picked her up to dance, and she began to cry. My mother was nicknamed Twinkle Toes because of her ability to dance. She made it look so easy." He smiled as Wyatt took over as lead, dancing with less grace and style. "And now it's a birthday tradition."

Wyatt counted steps while dancing. One-together. Two-Together. Slide-one. Slide-two. He didn't struggle carrying her, but he did struggle with not knowing where to lead them next.

I watched him and Stacy dance with awe and thought of all the heartache they'd all endured.

The music changed to an upbeat tempo, and Cade motioned us to the side to sit. Soon, Bella and Wyatt joined us. Minutes turned into an hour as we all watched and witnessed the senior citizens getting down and dancing their arthritis out.

Soon after the dancing was done, the crowd cleared out, and the only ones left cleaning the room were Bella, Cade, Wyatt, and me. Jordan had left earlier after his slow dance to take care of things at the house.

Stacy sat in her wheelchair rereading cards that people had given her.

Her smile was infectious, and I'd given anything to get a sneak peek at what some of her friends had sent her. The first card she opened was a picture of a guy's ass. Who knew what was on the inside of the card, but his ass was on the outside for everyone to see.

She threw back her head and let out a great peal of laughter that carried throughout the room. I'd bet that there were more raunchy cards in the mix. Cade and Wyatt merely smiled.

"Do you ever wonder why people are put in nursing homes?" Wyatt asked. There was depth to his thoughts, and I read a storm brewing behind his dark brown irises.

Cade rolled his eyes while Bella piped up to answer him.

"Well, for different reasons. Some just can't provide the twenty-four-hour care for their parents anymore. They have kids and work and life."

"So, they just get tossed in here because they don't want to be bothered or burdened," he stated matter-of-factly. There was a hard, cold bitterness in his tone. "Just like kids in a foster home." Although Jordan and Wyatt came from the system, there was no doubt that Wyatt was still battling with some abandonment issues.

"Wyatt, some people come here because they want to, too. It's not a jail. They want to associate and live in a community that's welcoming." Bella placed a consoling hand on his forearm. "It's not a prison sentence being in here, Wyatt. This nursing home is not like others. We're a family here."

His chin dipped to his neck, and his gaze dropped to the floor. "I'm sorry," he said.

"Or you come here like Mom because you don't want to be a burden to anyone else," Cade spoke up.

Wyatt clenched his jaw, his face clouding with unease. "I fucking hate that she thinks that."

"I can hear you," Stacy chimed in with her cheery cherry-on-top voice. She wheeled herself over to where we were seated. "Just so I'm clear for Angelica because I've repeated myself a million times to my boys, I came here because I wanted to. For a multitude of reasons, but at the end of the day, I'm happy. I don't feel like a cripple here. I have friends, and as long as your mom is happy, that's all that matters, right, Wyatt?"

She placed her hand in his, and his whole posture relaxed. In the quietest voice, he said, "Yeah, Mom. All I want is you happy."

"Hello, my family." Our heads poked at the entrance where Jordan strolled in.

"I thought you were fixing that sink," Cade uttered.

"Well, I brought you all a surprise."

We all peered up, and I blinked, stunned speechless.

A dead weight filled my chest, and a dread filled my veins.

Automatically, I stood.

It was my sister.

CHAPTER 24

TENE RAN in wearing white shorts and a black, fitted tank top. Her hair was pulled up in a high messy bun. Sheer black fear shown through her eyes.

My every nerve was on end, and the hairs on the nape of my neck were standing at attention. Something was wrong. We were hours away from Rosendell.

She rushed toward me and threw her arms around my shoulders. "Angie," she gushed out, "I tried calling you, but your phone kept going to voice mail."

She fell into me, forcing me to support most of her weight. "I left my phone in Rosendell. What's the matter?"

I pulled back and searched her face. The fact that Tene was showing weakness in front of people she didn't even know meant that this was bad, like third-degree-burns bad. "What're you doing here, Tene?"

She shook her head and surveyed the room, her back straightening, her chin tipping upward as though she just noticed that we weren't alone. "I need to talk to you in private." Desperation, stark and vivid, filtered in her eyes.

"Well, before you talk to her in private, let me introduce

you to the group." Jordan grabbed Tene's hand. You couldn't ignore the way Jordan's eyes roamed my sister's beach-bomb body, or the way his stare traveled up the length of her legs, lingering on her chest, then stayed planted on her face.

Cade must've sensed it, too, because his eyes zoned in on their intertwined fingers.

"Mom, this is Christene, Angelica's sister. She doesn't watch television much or movies or award shows." He lifted both eyebrows and slowly nodded like he couldn't believe it himself. "Basically, she's not on the up-and-up with pop culture."

It took all my energy to compose myself. And was she serious? My sister was pretending she didn't know who Jordan Ryder was, as in *the* Jordan Ryder? She had his damn calendar on the back of her bathroom door.

Tene, with her sweet seductive smile, peered up at him. "Too busy leading our real estate company, I guess." She shrugged, and that earned a chuckle from Cade.

She eyed him in warning as if to say, "you better play my game or else I'll cut your balls and feed them to you."

As I glanced around the room, I realized Jordan was the only one who was fooled.

"Well, it's nice to meet you, Christene. Are you hungry? We have left over cake." Stacy motioned to the table of goodies at the far end of the room.

Tene gnawed on her lip and shook her head, her eyes darting at the slew of people around us. "No, thank you." Her eyes flickered over to me, as though she remembered why she'd driven hours to see me. "Angie, can we have a moment? We have to head home."

My stomach dropped, and I stepped toward her. "Is it Dad?"

Her eyes glazed over, and, in that instant, I knew that it

was. That her trip here had everything to do with our father.

My voice reached a hysterical tone, fear choking me. "What is it? What happened? Is he okay?"

"Let's give them a few minutes," Stacy said, reading my thoughts.

It wasn't like they were going to clear the area, so I ignored their worried faces and gripped Tene's hand, dragging her to the bathroom on the side of the room and locked us both in.

As soon as I shut the door, she let the tears flow. "Dad ... Dad ..." she said it in a rushed, broken puff, on the verge of hysteria.

I grabbed her shoulders and shook her once. "Tene! What happened?"

She took a deep breath. "He wasn't feeling well and passed out, so he went into the hospital, and now he needs bypass surgery."

The air pushed out of my lungs like a wind tunnel, the gust strong enough that I had to grip the sink to keep me steady.

One hand cupped my mouth as tears filled my eyes. "Is he okay?"

"I think so. He's staying in the hospital until the surgery. But Angie ..." She sobbed. "All he asks is for you, and Mom said to bring you back. He just wants to see you and talk to you, and, when I couldn't reach you or Cade, I went to the bar, looking for him, and that bartender girl at Allswell told me where you went."

Both of my hands gripped the counter to keep me upright. Maybe I had caused this. Maybe he knew what was going on. He had sensed something was wrong at my birthday party.

"Does he know where I am? About Cade?"

She wiped her cheeks with the back of her hand. It was one of the very few times I'd ever seen Tene so vulnerable, and it broke me.

"No, I don't think so," she answered, her cheeks stained with tears.

I extended my hand, palm up. "Give me your phone. I need to hear for myself that he's okay." She'd said he was okay, but I wanted to talk to my daddy.

She dug her phone from the bottom of her purse and handed it to me. Since he was in the hospital, there was no way he was answering his cell, so I called the hospital directly and asked to be connected to his room.

When the operator picked up, I asked for my father. "This is his daughter, Angelica Armstrong."

My mother picked up on the second ring, her voice soft and tired and defeated.

"Mom, it's me. Can I talk to Dad?"

"Where are you, honey?"

"I'm with Tene. Mom, can I just talk to him?" The need to talk to my father overtook everything else.

"Okay," she said softly. "I'll give the phone to him, but please, honey, just come straight here."

I slumped against the side of the sink, while Tene bit at her pinky nail, watching me through tear-filled eyes.

When I heard my father's voice, the tears started rolling down my face, like boulders down a mountain. "Daddy?" I choked out. "Are you okay?" God, it hurt; it hurt that he wasn't well. It hurt that I wasn't there to hug him. It hurt to think I had somehow contributed to his stress.

"Angie ..." His voice was gruff and tired and all-my-daddy. "Are you crying?"

"No," I said through all my sniffles, lying through my teeth.

"Don't cry, Angie. I swear I just like to keep things inter-esting for your mother." He was silent for a beat before he spoke again. "You were the only one not here when it happened."

"I'm so, so sorry, Daddy." More tears blinded my eyes and choked my voice. Tene fidgeted beside me, biting her lip to control her sobs. Her eyes were swollen and puffy and red. She most likely had cried all the way here.

"I ... I just had to tell the people that mean so much to me that I love them. How very proud I am of you, and ..."

"Dad, stop talking like you're going to die." My voice was whisper soft, choked with heavy emotion.

He let out a low laugh. "I'm not dying any time soon. Who will look after your mother? Tene?" His tone was amused, which I took as a good sign. At least his sense of humor hadn't left him.

I shook my head through the blur of water in my eyes. My sister would be the first one to ship her to a nursing home.

"Dad, what did the doctor say?"

"I'm having surgery again tomorrow morning. Bypass surgery."

I swallowed hard. "I'll be there. I promise."

"Where are you, honey?"

"Somewhere close." I wasn't specific because I should be the last of his worries. "Rest up tonight because tomorrow you have another big day."

"You know me." I sensed the smile in his voice. "Go big or go home."

I could picture him rubbing his Santa Claus belly, which eased the pain in the middle of my chest.

"I love you, Daddy."

"Love you, too."

When I hung up, Tene, my sister who is usually void of any emotion, pulled me into a hug. Not her regular shoulder bump or fist pound, but a full-on hug that I felt everywhere.

I think she hugged me for her benefit, to be her anchor because I knew she was on the verge of losing it.

"You think he'll be okay?" she asked quietly.

Usually, it was she who comforted me, the older sister taking care of the little one, but today she leaned on me with most of her weight. And like she had always comforted me in the past and had been that rock, I knew I had to be hers right now. "When have you ever known Dad to lie down and not fight?"

She nodded against my shoulder, and we held each other in silence. When she finally pulled away, there was a glimmer of curiosity and something else in her eyes. "So ... um, Cade's brother is Jordan Ryder? And he's adopted. Jordan filled me in on the way here."

She swatted me playfully. "I mean, really? Ryder is a common last name, but what were the chances?"

"I so know," I said. "And you don't watch movies?" I quirked a dubious eyebrow.

She pulled back and popped out her hip in a signature Tene move. "Well, I can't be filling his ego up any bigger than it already is. I'm sure he has the whole world to do that."

We both smiled. It felt good to smile.

Tene sighed. "We better start going. I want to get home as soon as possible. If we leave now, we'll get home at around three or four."

I nodded. Right now, the only thing that mattered was getting home to my father.

CHAPTER 25

JORDAN, Wyatt, and Tene were on our heels as I entered Cade's house to pick up my belongings.

"What time is your father's surgery tomorrow?" Jordan asked. His sweet smile melted hearts across the universe, and my sister seemed a little dazed and a lot confused at the look he was giving her.

Cade had noticed, too, and the muscle of his jaw ticked.

I answered for us both because, for the first time in the history of Tene's life, she fell silent.

"Early morning. Seven o'clock. Something like that." All I knew was that I had to be there before my father woke up. I'd promised. "That's why we should start heading back."

"It'll take you hours to drive there," Jordan said. "Why don't you take the jet?"

"You have your own personal jet?" Tene piped up beside him.

"Well," Jordan grinned, his dimple popping from his cheek. "Not mine; it's Wyatt's."

Wyatt's eyes protruded, his voice deepening. "It's not. It's our jet."

Jordan waved a hand in Wyatt's direction. "His Daddy bought it for him."

"Daddy?" Tene mouthed, turning toward me for answers. I could see her mind churning, trying to work things out in her head, but there was no way she was going to figure this one out—that Wyatt was the bastard child of Bill Hendricks.

Wyatt's face reddened. "Fuck you," he muttered to Jordan. He stormed up the stairs, the house shaking when he slammed a bedroom door.

"Why do you taunt him all the time, Jordan?" Cade's eyes were hard, his voice authoritative like a parent. "You need to stop that shit."

Jordan ran one frustrated hand through his hair. "Okay, I didn't know he'd go all PMS on me." Jordan threw up both hands. "Fine, fine. I'll go apologize and rub his balls." Jordan loped toward the stairs and stopped, turning back to us with a grin. "You can use the jet, but you'll have to go with us to get our tattoos."

He didn't even give us a chance to respond before he ran up the stairs and I heard him banging on Wyatt's door. "Open up, bruh. I'm sorry, a'ight? You know I love you. So, open up and forgive me so we can get some ink." *Bang, bang, bang.* "Come on, Wyatt. We're family. You can't hold a grudge forever. Dude, let it go. You know you're the reason that we have a better life now. That we can put Mom in a good home, that we started the businesses. It's all you, Wyatt." A lighter knock echoed down the stairs, but the walls of the house were so thin that there was no way you couldn't hear it. It sounded as though Jordan was tapping his head against the door. "Wyatt, I'm sorry, all right?" Another tap. "I'll stop."

Tene's face brightened, her mouth forming an "O." She

pointed at Cade. "C-J-W Investments. You're the invest-ment company that owns all the restaurants and bars around the nation." She clasped her hands together, over-joyed that she had figured something big out. "Wow." The woman with oh-so-many words had only one to say—"wow."

She tilted her head, eyes curious, and I could read all the questions filtering through that brunette head of hers. "Aren't you guys going to explain this to me?" She dropped her hands to her hips. "Angie, did you know that CJW Investments was part Cade's?"

I nodded guiltily but also feeling impatient. "Yeah, but it's a long story, and we really need to go. Go home. I promised Dad." We'd be stuck here until tomorrow if I answered all of her questions.

Jordan strolled down with one arm wrapped around Wyatt's shoulder. Wyatt appeared sullen still and in a sour mood, but whatever Jordan had said had gotten him to open the door and come down.

"You guys aren't going home until we go get our tattoos," Jordan reminded us.

"Tattoos?" Tene's eyes brightened. Her body was untouched by ink just like mine.

"We get tattoos to commemorate our sister and Dad who passed," Wyatt said. "We get one every year." Given that they were pretty tatted up, I wondered where else they were going to place their ink.

Cade tilted his head from side to side, releasing the tension in his neck. "They can't go. They have to go home."

"The jet will get them there in forty-five minutes," Jordan argued. "I can just have their car shipped back. No big deal." He eyed my sister with a little smirk. I was surprised Tene could form words given the way he ogled her.

I bit my bottom lip, twisting my hand together. "I promised Dad I'd be there before his surgery. We just can't waste any more time." My pitch was low, steady, and serious. I'd made a promise, and I needed to keep it. "Plus, if we leave soon, we can get some sleep."

My sister peered up at me, listening to my voice of reason and nodded. "You know what? You're right. We need to go."

Cade lowered his head, but not before I caught the downturned look in his eyes that mirrored mine. "Take the jet anyway," he said, softly. "You'll get there faster."

I was packed, and we were in Cade's car in under ten minutes. Cade held my hand fiercely through the whole drive, as though he never wanted me to leave his side. I wanted to enjoy it, sink into it, but I couldn't sit still. All these thoughts of our mortality were really getting to me. Minutes and seconds ticked by like we were on borrowed time. Both of our families had money—we were lucky—but one thing we'd never be able to buy was time.

When the car pulled into the private airport just outside the city, tears nearly burned the back of my eyes. I didn't want to leave. When would I see him again? We were together, so I had nothing to fear, right?

Jordan put the car in park, right by the private plane that said CJW in letters sprawled right above the wing. Wyatt sat right next to him in the front, waiting for direction.

"Let's give these two lovebirds a moment alone." My sister cleared her throat beside me.

Jordan peered behind him and nodded. "Yeah. Come on, Wyatt, let's give Christene a tour of the plane."

When the door shut behind them, I buried my head into Cade's chest, my whole body falling into his.

"I'm not ready to leave yet." I unbuckled my seat belt and hopped in his lap. "Thanks for taking me here to meet your mother, your brothers. I ... I had so much fun in the short time I've been here."

His hands pressed against my sides, caging me in his arms, against the warmth of his body. "Come here," he said, lifting my chin.

I wrapped my arms around his neck, and he pressed his lips against mine. Being here with his family, miles away from Rosendell where we didn't have to hide, felt like a dream. As soon as my father was out of surgery and cleared and well, I vowed to make everything right. To tell them about Cade. Tell them about us. Tell them I was in love. "You're coming back to Rosendell, right?"

He nodded.

"Say it, then. I want to hear it. Tell me you're coming back for me." Anxiety was laced in every word that left my mouth.

"I'm coming back to Rosendell." His eyes blazed. "I'm coming back for you."

I framed his face with my hands, my fingers running against the stubble on his chin. "I love you. I want to be with you." I kissed him fiercely and firmly and with a passion that radiated in my chest.

He inhaled deeply, then pulled back, locking his eyes with mine. "I want you, too. Not just for a night. Not just for the next few months. I want you for years, for life, for forever."

CHAPTER 26

WE ARRIVED at my apartment at one o'clock in the morning and were both bone tired, but for some reason, Tene wanted to know every single detail about the Ryders, and I enjoyed giving her the lowdown. Jordan and his personal assistant had made sure that we had a private car waiting for us upon our arrival into the airport, which made our trip seamless.

We knew luxury. Tene and I had been born into luxury and had money. The difference was, where the Armstrong name was known in Rosendell and the few surrounding cities, CJW Investments was known on the world stage.

Private planes were not something we had access to. My father had chartered a plane a few times, but we had never owned our own. The Ryder brothers had money that only big boys played with.

I keyed into the condo and dropped my belongings on the floor. "Tene, we could get in a few hours before we head to the hospital." My mind was running like it was in a marathon, nonstop thoughts filtering through my head, but my body was so unbelievably exhausted I knew I was about to knock out standing up.

"Yeah, let's do that. Set your alarm and I'll set mine, too, just in case." She kicked off her shoes and readjusted her messy bun. "Crazy night, huh?"

"The craziest," I said. Every one of my muscles ached with fatigue from the long day.

She laughed to herself. "I can't believe Jordan Ryder is Cade's foster brother. What're the chances?"

I laughed and walked to my bedroom where she followed. "Yeah, well what were the chances that I'd leave Roland for a tattooed bartender?"

She brought her hands to her lips to stifle her laughter. "Things are just so unpredictable."

I slipped on a T-shirt and shorts and chucked some clothes in Tene's direction.

"Angie ... I think I may have a crush on Jordan." Her voice was like a schoolgirl's as she slipped on my clothes.

"Tene?" I lifted an eyebrow. "You've always stalked Jordan Ryder, so nothing has changed."

We headed to the bathroom and brushed our teeth in front of the double sinks. I didn't know if I should've been worried that Tene had extra toothbrushes in her purse. I knew she had quite a few sleepovers and didn't know if that was the reason, or if she always wanted to be prepared.

"He's much hotter in person."

"Yeah, he is," I agreed.

We both slipped into my bed, facing each other.

"His eyes," she sighed. "He has sex eyes."

Every single one of my bones wanted to go into deep slumber. "I can't believe you told him you didn't watch TV and pretended not to know who he was." I yawned.

We both laughed softly.

"That was pretty good, huh?"

"Yeah, it was."

We watched each other for a few seconds, then I yawned again, which was followed by her yawn.

Sleeping in one bed together reminded me of our teenage years when Tene would hop in my bed after a date and gush about her latest boy toy. Oh, how times had changed.

Her eyes fell shut and so did mine. Tiredness was taking us both under.

"Angie?"

"Mmm?"

"I've never seen you this in love," she said sincerely. "And I've known you all my life."

My eyes popped open to assess her face, but her eyes were still shut. Her words confirmed what reigned in my heart.

"I'm happy you're happy," she added. "You and Cade just ... fit. And it made me realize ..." she said, whisper soft, already dozing off. "You and Roland never did."

Her approval blanketed me in warmth, and I smiled, snuggling closer to my sissy. Then I fell asleep, dreaming that I was in Cade's arms.

Our alarms both sounded at 6 a.m., and we bolted from the bed, delirious from the lack of sleep and anxious to see Dad. We were silent as we approached Rosendell Central Hospital, both of us too preoccupied and worried to speak.

This high-risk surgery would open my father's heart today, unblock his arteries and fix him up, or ... I didn't like to think of the "or." I refused to think of the "or."

After his heart attack and multiple stents put in to unblock his arteries, this had to work. "Everything is going to be okay," I said as Tene drove like a maniac into the hospital parking lot and shifted my car into park.

"It will," she said.

Though neither of us had gusto in our voice. Our words were merely words without the strength behind them.

When we walked into the hospital, Tene reached for my fingers just as we did when we were younger, and she was ushering me to cross the street. This time was different. It felt like she needed my hand to comfort her, for the security that nothing would run us over.

I squeezed her fingers in return, and, before we entered his room, we put on our happy faces. This was what my father needed. He hated us worrying about him, and I didn't want to give him another thing to weigh him down right before he went into surgery.

Our smiles were big, but both of our palms were slick with sweat.

We walked in together and dropped our hands to see our mother and Nana sitting in the corner. Nana was holding her rosary, reciting Hail Marys that we could hear out loud.

Tene's smile was plastered on her face, but her step faltered, and my face fell. She had always been a better actress than me. I'd been prepared for him to be in bed. I'd been prepared to see both my mother and Nana in the room with him. What I hadn't been prepared to see was him hooked up to machines, an oxygen mask on his face and for my powerful father to look completely helpless.

A small cry escaped my mouth. "Dad!" There was no way I could disguise my worry as I rushed toward him and dropped to his chest. "Daddy."

My mom cowered, hugging herself as though she was two seconds away from falling apart. She was built like Tene, unable to show emotion, which made this so much worse. She turned around so we wouldn't be able to see her break down, but it was the light shake of her shoulders that told me she was far from okay.

I readjusted myself against his chest, making sure not to interfere with any tubes attached to him.

"Don't cry for me, Angelica." His voice mimicked the "Don't cry for me, Argentina" song.

It was meant to cheer me up, but it only increased the dread in every fiber of my being. "You're going to be fine," I said, trying to convince my own self. Maybe with repetition, I'd believe it.

"Of course, I am." His breaths came out in short puffs, as though he was using all his energy to speak. The gusto behind my father's normally powerful voice was absent, buried under the tubes that tied him up like a cobweb.

"Just save your energy because you'll need it after this surgery, and then I'm going to kick your butt in golf."

A chuckle escaped him and then a sigh, as though it hurt to laugh. "Where did you go, honey?"

I didn't answer because I didn't want to lie. I didn't want to tell the truth, either.

I swallowed. "Dad, I just want you to get well and not worry about me. I'm okay. I'll be fine."

I rested my head on his chest, afraid he'd be able to read the lie in my eyes.

"I always worry about you. And Tene, and, most especially, your mother." His hand tenderly stroked my hair, and I didn't want to move. "I'm so proud of you, little girl. For the person you've become. The way you've taken over the business."

I stifled a cry. "Dad ... You're not dying. Don't you dare talk like that."

"I know, but I feel like before I go into this surgery, I wanted to say that." I lifted my glistening eyes to him, and he brushed a tear from my cheek. "Don't cry, baby girl. I'm not leaving anytime soon. I'm going to walk you down the aisle, deliver you to Roland, and watch you get married and pop out those grandkids," he said with a weak grin.

"Dad ..." I squeezed his hand in mine, not wanting to let go when there was a knock at the door.

A nurse popped in. "Mr. Armstrong. The doctor will be in to talk to you and prep you for surgery." She offered him, then the rest of us, her cheery, professional smile before approaching him and tinkering with his cords and checking his vitals.

I wanted to hold up my hand and tell the world to take a time out. I wanted a few more seconds with my Dad, to speak to him, to bask in his company.

A knock on the door and the doctor stepping into the room had my heart beat racing. "Mr. Armstrong, how are you feeling today?"

"Ready as I'll ever be."

"Daddy, I love you."

"Why is it like you're the one saying goodbye?" he joked.

"I'm not." I squeezed his hands harder as my mother, Tene, and Nana approached his bed to give my father kisses.

We watched them wheel my dad, the patriarch of our family, out of the room and down the hall. And then we waited in the waiting room.

Minutes ticked by. Then hours. The surgery was supposed to last two hours, but time dragged, like watching ice melt or paint dry.

I sat, stood, stretched, and did everything possible not to stare at the clock that ticked molasses slow.

One cup of coffee. Two. Three. And still no word from the doctor.

I sat in silence between my mother and Tene. Nana was still heavily praying, her rosary in hand, her eyes shut tightly.

Five hours later, when the doctor walked through the door, we all stood automatically. The air thinned with our worry, our whole lives held by the news he had for us. At any moment, he could drop the atomic bomb or allow our airways to open and breathe again.

When he smiled brightly, we all seemed to take a breath together. "The surgery was successful," he said. "There were no complications, and he is in recovery now. Mr. Armstrong is going to be just fine."

There was a pause as if we needed to take it all in, then I was hugging my sister, my mom, kissing Nana's cheek. We were one big bubble of love.

My mother's arms were wrapped tightly around herself. "He's going to be okay?" Her fingers flew to her parted lips before she bowed her head and started to shake. "Thank God."

I was about to console her, do my job when Tene held up a hand for me to stop me in my spot with a tenderness in her eyes that wasn't usually there. She placed a gentle hand on our mom's shoulder, and, when my mother lifted her head, Tene wrapped her hands around her. "He's going to be okay, Mom."

For the first time in a very long time, my mom openly wept, in front of us, in front of the doctor, in front of everyone, and in Tene's arms.

CHAPTER 27

MY MOTHER OPENED the door and plopped down on the passenger side without permission or apology or restraint.

"Drive," she ordered me.

I gritted my teeth. Usually, I'd be scared of her. Not today. Today, I felt indignant. Determination crept up my back and straightened my shoulders. I already knew what she was going to say, and there was no way in hell I was going to let her change my mind.

This was my life.

"Drive," she repeated, annoyance now adding to the anger.

When I didn't move, she said, "Do you want that man to see the mother that loves your boyfriend in the car with you? Do you, Angelica?"

My nostrils flared, my internal temperature rising.

Not that I cared about him seeing her. He knew I was telling them, after all, just a bit sooner than I intended. And obviously softening the blow was out of the question at this point. But I could handle this, on my freaking own.

"When I came to your apartment, and Roland said you were here, I would've never guessed this." She laughed humorlessly, then shouted, "I said, drive!"

I gripped the steering wheel, keeping my cool as best as I could. I wanted to make sure this conversation was led on my terms, so I started the engine, pressed the gas, and said, "I left Roland, Mom."

I focused on the road ahead of me, and the air chilled with an eerie silence. My mother never stayed silent. Ever.

While she remained mute, I formulated every single word that I was going to say. With my mother, every word counted. I'd seen her twist Tene's words and use them against her. That was not happening to me.

I drove and drove. I didn't know where we were going, but I wasn't taking her back to my apartment or to Roland's where she would try to convince me I was making the biggest mistake of my life. I didn't know where I was going, but before I knew it, I was speeding down the road, windows down and wind blowing through her well-groomed hair.

The silence was deafening and almost too much to take. I broke the quiet first. "I'm not in love with Roland."

"I wouldn't be too sure of that," she said calmly.

Anger choked me, like hands around my neck, making it difficult to function, difficult to take my next breath. "You don't know how I feel. I'm tired of everyone telling me what to do, how to act, what to think." I slammed my hand against the steering wheel, so hard that my fingers tingled with pain.

"And you think that bartender is it? He's the guy for you?" Her voice was incredulous.

"Cade," I said through my teeth. "His name is Cade." I turned to face her as the cars slowed down in front of us at a red light. I spoke coolly, controlled. "Yes. Cade is it for me. I want to be with him."

"You think he's even a tiny bit serious about you, Angie?" She pointed a shaky finger in my direction. "That's exactly how I know you're such a child."

I pulled to the side of the road and jutted out my chin, my patience gone. "You need to tell me where to drop you off."

Her posture turned rigid. "I would've expected this from Tene. But this ... this shocks me. That you can easily fall for his advances."

"You don't know me at all. I didn't fall for his advances. I fell for *him*, Mother." My voice grew louder with each passing moment and conviction strengthened my resolve. "I love him because he believes in me. He lets me decide. He doesn't treat me like I'm a child, a wallflower. When I'm with him, I feel powerful and all woman and entirely in heaven because I'm so happy." I spoke with such truth, remembering how I felt this morning and every single time I'd been with him.

I added, my voice turning sad, "I haven't been this happy with Roland in ages. I don't remember a time where I wasn't taken for granted, Mom."

She looked at me, her mouth slackening. She regarded me for a second, and I begged her with my eyes to listen to me, her daughter. I had laid everything out on the table; I needed her to understand.

She seemed to come to some kind of resolution as she crossed her arms stubbornly over her chest. "You're not going to be with him," she said as if I were still a child and she was telling me I couldn't have a second cookie.

I gripped the steering wheel, my knuckles white from

the tension. "This is where I lead my own life. This is where I stop letting others dictate what my future holds."

She scowled. "And you think his future holds you in it? He's going to marry you?" Her laugh was cynical, crazy even. "He screwed a girl with a serious boyfriend. Yes, that's long-term material right there."

My cold eyes narrowed at her, and my breathing became ragged with impotent anger. I didn't have to explain our relationship to her. It wouldn't even matter that I'd broken up with Roland before anything physical had happened with Cade. She wouldn't be able to understand how we'd accidentally fallen in love with each other.

I met her stern gaze. If I wasn't absolutely sure about Cade, I would've backed down just by the look on her face. One look from my mother would burn a lesser person that wasn't as sure.

"He's it for me, Mother. I'm going to be with him with or without your approval."

Then her cool and calm façade faded, her eyes growing wide and her face reddened. "That's not what I wanted to hear, Angelica." Her tone was cold and lashing. "How much has Cade spent to set up here in Rosendell? I bet a fortune. I wouldn't want there to be any disruptions to his lease or anything like that."

I blinked at her. Was I really hearing her right now? Was she threatening his job, his restaurant? That's how I knew she was grasping for straws, at anything to use as leverage against me.

"He's signed a lease," I said evenly. "We're contracted for another five years."

She nodded furiously. "Yes, that may be so, but that doesn't mean we can't make it a little difficult for him."

I threw my hands up in the air. "Why are you doing this? Why?"

"Because I want to secure your happiness." Her voice, her posture, her demeanor was resolute.

"My happiness or your status?" I threw back at her.

"How dare you?" Her nostrils flared. "As a mother, I do everything for you. Everything. I live for this family, Angelica. For your father. For you and Tene. Think about this. He's on to his new location in a month or two or three. Are you going to do long distance? I know this is exciting for both of you. You've been in a relationship with Roland for so long, I understand this is like a shiny new toy. But exciting doesn't last. Exciting is temporary and what you're left with is love ... true love. Love that endures. Look at your father and me. I love him. The excitement is gone, but with his heart surgery and all he's been going through lately ..." She choked on her last words and averted her eyes, hiding her vulnerability.

For a brief moment, I wondered if she had done it on purpose, used Dad to manipulate me. I wouldn't think she'd stoop so low, but I wasn't sure I could put it past her at this point.

"Dad is going to be fine," I said softly. She'd hit a nerve. The one that connected to my emotions. My father.

"How do you think he's going to react to this, Angelica?" She dropped her lashes to hide the hurt in her eyes. "He adores Roland."

I looked away, knowing she was trying to guilt me into this decision. But she wouldn't change my mind. I wouldn't sacrifice my happiness just to fit into her mold of who she wanted me to be.

"He had trouble breathing today." Suddenly, her features were unguarded, and I knew she wasn't using this as a stunt to stop me. "He knows the whole family is on edge. He just doesn't want anybody to know."

Her head dropped to her hands, and all that was left were the raw sores of an aching heart. Automatically, I angled closer and placed a consoling hand on her shoulder. "Mom, what's wrong?" God, the world didn't revolve around me, and, as much as I was upset with her, my natural instinct to fix things and make it better pushed to the surface.

She glanced up, the hardness in her eyes gone. "They don't know if it's the meds that he's taking or if there is more blockage."

"What?" My heart pounded hard against my chest, like thunder booming in the sky. "What do you mean?"

She shook her head. "I don't know. They're running more tests tomorrow."

We sat there in silence, weighing what that meant. She peered up at me, and, with a sadness that I'd witnessed and seen before when it came to my father, she said, "Whatever you decide, you can't tell your father about you and Roland. He's in a fragile state right now." Her eyes begged me with an underlying desperation. "He worries about the two of you enough. He thinks he's dying tomorrow, so all he thinks about is you girls and of course ... me." The permanent lines etched on her forehead were evident. Long days of worrying about my father and Tene, and now I was added to her list.

I wanted to tell her I wasn't doing this to spite her and that I loved our family and upheld our values. That I hadn't meant for her to find out this way. But I wanted happiness for myself, and Cade Ryder made me happy.

"Mom." I tightened my hold on her hand. "He'll be okay." I wanted to believe my words, but there were never any guarantees. But still, I had to be strong enough for both of us.

She let out a long sigh, and the tension in her shoulders released. I watched the cars whiz past us as my car remained idle on the side of the road. Most people were heading to work, going on about their day, as though every-thing was right in the world while my life was in pure chaos.

Her eyes softened. "Please, Angie. Right now, you can't tell your father. He has a lot on his plate already. Please, just not now."

She was right. He'd eventually know, but not within the next few days. "Okay. But this is my decision, Mom, and I'm going to tell him eventually." I nodded once and squeezed her hand. "I want to go with you to the doctor's office."

I stepped into my condo, walked into the living area and dropped my purse on the table by the couch. My legs gave out, and I sat on the couch thinking of all that happened today.

The doctor's visit should've lightened my mood, knowing what was going on with my father, but it only made things worse.

My problems were nothing compared to what my father was going through. My problems weren't life or death.

The doctors deduced that it was the meds that he was on that was giving him shortness of breath. They had come to that conclusion after running multiple tests and deter-mining his meds were the only thing that changed from his day-to-day.

The ringing from my phone broke me from my trance.

It was my mother.

She was a barely composed, broken mess by the time we were done with the doctor's visit. She didn't cry nor shed a tear. She functioned like a robot, mechanical, unmoving, not even daring to peer up at my father. And I knew it was because she didn't want to break down.

"Angelica?"

"Hi, Mom." Our relationship was at a high stress level right now, but she needed me. I'd already told her where I stood with Cade. I'd be here for the family, but I wasn't sacrificing my happiness in the process.

"I want to set up a dinner tomorrow night for the whole family, to cheer up your dad."

"I think that's a great idea." That's exactly what my father needed—a normal day out with his wife and kids without feeling like a cripple. "Did you want me to make reservations?"

"No, I'll just pick a place and let you know where tomorrow. And, Angie?"

"Yeah?"

"Thank you for coming with me today." Her tone was soft, almost apologetic.

I let her words wash over me like a white flag being raised at the end of a war. "Of course, Mom."

We hung up, and I slouched on the couch, feeling all the weight of the day on my shoulders. And then I called Cade because I needed him the most.

CHAPTER 28

THAT NIGHT CADE had held me in his arms all night long, and everything in the air around me—the chaos, the worries—disappeared for just a moment. I snuggled in his arms and told him everything that had happened, from my mother to my father. By the time I was done, I fell asleep, emotionally exhausted. I hadn't slept so soundly in ages. I'd forgotten what it was to get a full night's rest. But the next morning, reality hit us both when we had to say our good-byes and head out to work. That our time together before he left was dwindling down, and soon, seeing him every day would cease, and our moments together would be interrupted by the distance between us.

I walked him to his car, trudging like I was being forced off a cliff because I never wanted to leave him, and, as crazy as it sounded, I wanted to be with him with each waking second and sleep next to him each night.

"What's the sad face for?" he joked, glancing at me with a devilish grin.

"Do you even have to ask?" I pouted like a six-year-old. I never did the pouting thing. That was Tene's MO, not mine.

He leaned against his car and tugged at my waist. "Come here." He lifted my chin and locked eyes with mine. "You've had a rough few days. How about we have dinner tonight, and you come over for a movie and then chill?"

"Sex," I added. "You're going to make my day better with sex." I lifted an eyebrow, "Movies and chill. And sex."

His deep chuckle warmed me from the inside out. "Now who has a dirty mind?" He pulled me in and pecked my lips. "But I'm all for that, too."

"Mmhmm," I sassed.

"Come in later tonight, right after the dinner rush, and we can do my version of movie and chill."

I almost groaned out loud. As good as that sounded, I couldn't. "I have dinner later tonight with the family. Can I just come in before that?"

"Just come?" He tilted his head and rubbed his thumb over his bottom lip. "That sounds oddly familiar. You've never had to ask before."

I laughed at his dirty joke, and he gathered me in his arms and kissed me more deeply this time, lips closed, but boy did I feel him everywhere.

He was the first to break our connection. "See you later, Angel." Then he readjusted himself, and I knew he'd felt me everywhere, too.

I laughed and half-skipped to my car.

Shutting myself in the car, I flipped open the overhead mirror and checked my color-filled cheeks. Who needed blush when I had Cade Ryder to force color into my cheeks?

I shut the mirror and put the key in the engine. When my phone pinged with a text, my smile widened. It was Cade.

Just so you know, if I meant sex, I would've asked you to come over and eat cake ;)

I giggled, my blush reddening as I remembered my birthday night.

What would I ever do with this man?

———

The day passed in a blur. I called my dad and ran errands, and before I knew it, it was the evening, and I was running to Allswell. My family and I were meeting at Chef Everest, an Italian restaurant right on Elgin Avenue, not too far from Allswell, so I had decided I'd spend time with Cade before I had to rush to dinner.

But it wasn't Cade's face that greeted me as I pushed into the doors of the restaurant—it was Tene's and Mom's and Dad's and Roland's parents and Roland, sitting in the same spot they'd sat in days ago for my horrible birthday party that had turned into a freak show.

Internally, my temperature rose twenty million notches as the hair on the back of my neck stood at attention like soldiers doing their drills.

For the love of God, what is going on?

Roland came charging toward me but stopped short at my scowl. I searched behind him for Cade, but he wasn't anywhere to be found.

"Everyone's here," I croaked.

He blinked at me, surprised that I didn't know. "Yes, your mom invited me, and I wanted—needed—to see you. You haven't been picking up my calls." There was an undertone to his voice, a disdain in his eyes.

Did he know? I shook my head. There was no way my

mother would betray me, not when she wanted me and Roland back together.

My sister's whole face twisted as though she had eaten something moldy. I had texted her to tell her I was stopping at Allswell before dinner. Why would she sabotage me like this? It was so unlike her. Of all people, she was the last person who would do this to me.

He intertwined our fingers, and I tore my hold from his as the nightmare played on repeat. I hugged Nana and my father and said my standard greetings to Roland's parents.

I need to talk to Cade.

That was my first initial reaction. Before he witnessed this chaos firsthand, I needed to speak to him. I searched for him at the bar, but he was nowhere to be found.

Tene rushed to my side. "I swear on everything that matters," she whispered, "I did not do this. I tried calling you when I knew we were coming here. Why weren't you picking up your phone?"

I groaned internally. My phone had died earlier, and I had it charging with my portable charger on silent in the bottom of my purse.

My sister's voice heightened with hysteria. "Mom planned this dinner. She changed the location and moved up the time from Chef Everest to here, and ... She knows, doesn't she?" Her face turned frantic. "Oh, my god."

"Angie." It was my mother, right behind us.

"You're bat shit crazy," Tene seethed, her eyes tight, hand balled up into fists by her side.

When my mother leaned in to drop my cheek against hers, I deflected and pulled back. "What's your game here?"

She smiled her fake smile—the one that she gave Tene when she pretended she wasn't upset but really was. "I'm not sure what you're talking about."

My chest tightened because I could read the malice in her features. How could she manipulate me like this? I'd seen my mother do some crazy things in my life, but this seemed to top them all.

I sat next to Tene, who rocked back and forth in her chair, her eyes flitting around the room. Her sweaty palm reached for mine under the table and gave me a squeeze. "I really think we need to commit her," she whispered in my ear.

I would've laughed if my stomach wasn't tied in triple Boy Scout knots. My mother wasn't crazy; she just always got whatever she wanted, whenever she thought she was right.

When I gripped Tene's hand in a tight vise for support, she stood and yanked us away from the table. "Angie and I are going to the potty room."

I didn't have a say in the matter as she dragged me down the hall into the bathroom and into the handicap stall.

"I swear I had no idea and I didn't know what she was up to."

"I know." My bottom lip quivered, the floor beneath me feeling as though it would swallow me whole. We said nothing, and she simply pulled me into her and continually rubbed my back. I basked in her embrace because that was all I needed—someone on my side.

"Why the hell did Mom insist on coming here today? What does she know?" Tene asked.

When I stiffened, Tene jerked back to assess my face. "How the hell did she find out?"

I nodded, feeling bile creep up my throat. "She saw us together."

Tene threw up her hands. "Angie. Four words. Just don't get caught." She paced the stall, talking out loud. "But you did, so now we need a solution. How are we going to get you out of this? We have to think."

I couldn't concentrate on anything other than the thoughts reigning in my head. Despair was gripping me. *What am I going to do?*

What I needed to do was find Cade first.

Determination firmed up my shoulders, and I straightened, ready to find Cade and warn him about my family being here. One thing I didn't want him to be was blindsided.

Tene continued to babble. "Yep, she knows, and that's why she pushed this dinner to show Cade that you're already taken. Maybe coming here once was a mistake, but twice ... yep ... not so much."

"Why would she do that?" I asked.

A slew of voices carried into the bathroom, indicating we were no longer alone.

Tene's voice went down a notch. "You don't know her as well as I do. Mother always will want to get her way. And she wants you with Roland. I want to secure your happiness, too, but the difference between her and me is I wouldn't sabotage your life to do it."

At that, Tene stormed out of the stall. Two women eyed us as we walked out together.

"Thanks, honey." Tene threw an arm over my shoulder and smiled. "I really didn't know how to stick that tampon in."

When we exited the bathroom, Tene pulled me closer. "You're not feeling well. I'm going to tell them I'm taking you home, okay? I'm getting you out of this."

I snuggled into her side, thankful that I could always count on her. I was leaving, but not before I did what I had to do. "I have to find Cade. He's expecting me, and I'd rather he sees me first than Roland and the whole family here."

When we walked in the room, Cade was at the bar. It was as though I felt him before I saw him because I could feel the blood pumping in my veins and the air in the room evaporate. I lifted my head to meet his eyes. The muscle in his jaw ticked, which made me want to rush toward the bar and wrap my arms around him, ending this torture—my torture.

His face was unreadable, but his eyes flew to behind me. When I turned around, his eyes locked, not with Roland's, but with my mother's.

Her face was stoic, and if her eyes could talk, she would be throwing him a slew of curse words. Sweat formed on the back of my neck as I witnessed a fury behind my mother's eyes directed at the man I was in love with. It was a war without words as her glances flickered between him and me.

I decided I'd had enough, and that I'd put us all through this misery. I turned to walk to the bar, but Tene gripped my forearm and whispered, "Not now." She tipped her head toward my father's direction who was talking to Roland's father. When our eyes met, he smiled.

Reluctantly, I sat down, promising myself that I'd explain this whole fiasco to Cade later and beg for his forgiveness. I needed to get this shit show over and done with.

My mother smiled my way before standing and lifting her wineglass, tapping her fork against it to get everyone's attention.

I doubted Cade could hear anything she had to say, but he could see her. She smiled big and spoke with such happiness that made my stomach churn because it was for Cade's non-benefit.

She lifted the wine glass. "I want to make a toast and thank everyone for getting together today. We all know this hasn't been the easiest week for us." My father shifted in his seat as all eyes glanced in his direction. "It's just so nice to get the family together to celebrate life and love." She motioned her glass toward Roland. "Thanks, Roland, for making reservations. But most of all for loving this family, and above all, for loving our daughter to pieces."

Everyone clinked their glasses together, and I gritted my teeth into a forced smile.

Tene gripped my thigh, her eyes feverish and darting around the room.

When Roland reached for my hand on the table, I flinched. What was his game? He knew we were over. When he bent down to kiss me in front of our families, I stiffened, shocked by the contact.

It was only a soft peck on my lips, feather light, but it felt like a gun in a mouth, locked and loaded. I couldn't move, couldn't speak, couldn't smile, couldn't turn around to see if Cade was watching because I knew he was.

For the show, I told myself. This is for the show. But I wanted this part of the movie—this scene—to end. I was ready to write the rest of my story, not have it written out for me.

I nonchalantly pulled away, placing a hand on his chest, keeping my eyes on everyone around me, simply ignoring Roland. Anger clouded my vision, warmth reaching the tips of my ears when Roland stood next to me and lifted his glass to follow my mother's speech.

"To Dad, we're praying for a swift and healthy recovery," he said, his gaze on my father. "It's good to get everyone together once in a while to celebrate life and love." When he shifted his gaze toward me, my whole body turned icy cold. Acid burned the back of my throat, making it difficult to swallow. "I love Angelica like she's my next breath. I fell in love with her when I was sixteen and to think how far we've come. We're basically family, and now ..."

Then he did the unthinkable. "I want to make it official." He dropped to one knee, and my whole body went rigid. My one hand flew to my throat, the other gripping the table to keep me steady.

This is not happening, this is not happening!

The ringing in my ears intensified to an unbearable volume, and I blinked, seeing black spots behind my eyelids. His mouth kept moving, yet I didn't hear a word. I was having an out of body experience as the people around me cheered without sound. As though the whole scene was on mute.

I glanced at everyone's faces around me—my mother's, who was standing right beside Roland—his mother, Tene in complete shock and disbelief. If anything, she understood me. After our talk, she knew if I said yes, I'd be making the biggest mistake of my life.

Everyone's eyes were on me. Not just my family's, but all of the patrons at the restaurant, the whole staff ... and Cade's. The people in our vicinity were elated, eyes wide, all smiling and staring at me with expectation, waiting for an answer.

Finally, I heard Roland say, "Angelica Armstrong, will you marry me?" His eyes were full of hope and happiness, and as surprised, panicked, and angry as I was, I almost felt sorry for him in the moment.

The glint of the ring caught my eye, but I stood shocked silent. He must've asked the question multiple times, but I had no words. The need to flee was overtaking me, yet I couldn't move.

I blinked through the fog. My father's face was full of uncontainable joy, a smile that lightened all his features, his first genuine smile of the night and guilt tore through me.

What he had said right before the doctors had wheeled him into surgery rang loudly in my ears: *Don't cry, baby girl. I'm not leaving anytime soon. I'm going to walk you down the aisle, watch you get married, deliver you to Roland and watch those grandkids pop out.*

His eyes were expectant and brimming with tears, causing a thickness to form in the back of my throat. I dropped my head to hide the shame.

The few seconds of silence and slight movement was broken up by a slew of actions that followed: my mother screaming congratulations, followed by Roland standing, then slipping the ring on my finger.

I couldn't breathe while I was passed around my family like a rag doll. Back and forth. Forth and back.

I wanted to scream at the top of my lungs for the commotion to stop.

I didn't say yes. I didn't agree to this.

It was the smile on my father's face and the pride in his eyes that had the word "no" choked in my throat.

And in that moment, I promised myself this was all for the show, for my loving father, and that this was temporary. I'd die before I walked down an aisle and committed myself to Roland. Everyone hooting and hollering and on their feet caused my stomach to roll, almost to the point of knocking me over.

I was engaged. An engaged woman, but completely empty and hollow inside.

My whole family continued to pass me around like a rag

doll, hugging me, telling me their congratulatory speeches. My mother hugged me the tightest, telling me that I was making the right decision.

For once in my life, I despised her. The woman who had given birth to me was dead to me from this day forward. She had started this fiasco, and she ended it with her screams of congratulations, which made everyone else's' follow.

When it was Tene's turn, she whispered over and over that she would help me get out of this mess. My *fiancé*—I never thought I'd loathe the word—wasn't by me. He was pouring himself another glass of wine, fire behind his eyes, but his stare was not directed my way. It was focused behind me.

I followed his line of sight, toward the bar, where I locked eyes with Cade, whose glazed look of despair began to take over his features.

Ice spread through my stomach, and I felt an overwhelming sense of loss.

When I glanced back at Roland, I noticed his eyes were laser focused on Cade, and every part of me wondered if he knew. But if he knew, he wouldn't have proposed, would he? Roland had too much pride.

Cade was oblivious to anyone else but me.

I'd never forget his look. I'd remember it until the day I died. His dark eyes held a hurt so strong, it made my knees buckle, and I was leaning my whole body on Tene's for support. Tears threatened to spill over.

When he turned away from me, my heart shattered like a glass vase thrown on the floor, the pieces scattering everywhere.

And I knew there was no way to put it back together.

CHAPTER 29

MY WHOLE BODY and face were numb like I had Novo-
cain running through my veins.

Roland had walked to the bar, paid the bill in cash,
thrown like garbage in front of Cade. I thought there would
be a full-on fight until Cade turned around, leaving the
money where it was, then charging through the kitchen
doors.

The image of Cade turning from Roland, muscles tense
and storming back through the kitchen, would give me
nightmares for an eternity.

An overwhelming sense of loss overtook me, my misery
so great that my chest ached with physical pain.

I shook and unwillingly followed Roland out of the bar
as a nauseating sinking of despair made my stomach roll.

The four-karat, internally-flawless diamond felt like a
two-ton weight that could sink me at any moment. I almost
wished it would. I'd rather die than marry someone who
didn't respect me.

After our families had gone their separate ways, I

flipped toward Roland, my face stern, my insides defeated. "We need to talk."

Without my family or his family, without the spectacle of a crowd, or the eyes of my ailing father on me, my backbone had grown back. This was not happening. Not now. Not ever.

And maybe he knew it, too, because his happy, cheery demeanor was replaced with a cold one. "Meet me back at the apartment." He dropped my hand like it was hot coal and clicked the unlock button of his beamer without a look back.

I debated on following him to our once-upon-a-time place, the residence I used to call home but decided I needed to speak my mind and clear the air. After parking in my usual spot, I followed Roland inside. We were silent on our way up the elevator to the penthouse floor.

When we entered the condo, he threw his keys on the counter, undid his tie, and slipped out of his suit jacket.

He was pissed. Pissed for what, though? He'd gotten what he wanted.

"Roland ..." I lay one strong hand on my hip and pointed to the door. "Back there, at the restaurant ... I don't know what that was. But I didn't say yes."

He turned to face me, his eyes blazing. The change in demeanor caught me off guard, jamming my next words in my throat.

"This is the next progression for us, Angelica. We're getting married." The finality in his tone had me wondering what he was smoking and the despair I felt moments ago turned into something—disgust.

Chin out, bitch face on. "No. We're not."

He ran one aggravated hand through his hair and

turned away, huffing as he stomped to the bar and poured himself a glass of scotch.

I clenched my fists, ready to fight this, fight with him. If this was what he wanted, I'd give it to him. I knew what would make him listen. What would get through his thick skull, through his pride, through his stubbornness?

"I slept with another man." I braced myself, waiting for his wrath, the backlash from my indiscretion.

He turned around, and his reaction was stoic because he already knew.

The shock of discovery hit me full force. "You knew, didn't you?" My heart thumped hard. "My mother told you." I staggered back a step, as though hearing the words from my mouth made them truer.

And like pieces of a puzzle falling together, everything that had happened today became so vividly clear. "The fact that we were at that restaurant was not a mistake, was it?" I gritted my teeth, my nails digging into my palms. "Nor was the fact that you proposed today." It hurt. Everything hurt. If I wasn't so riddled with anger, I'd curl up into a ball and start crying. My mother had tag-teamed with Roland to trap me, but this was going to backfire in their face.

"You didn't hear me," I said louder. "I slept with another man."

He had pride and dignity. There was no way he'd take me back.

"Your mom told me you were seeing him. Yes." His voice was cool and emotionless. "But I didn't assume anything." He tipped back his glass, taking a long swig of the scotch and poured himself some more of the copper-colored liquid.

"And now that you know? What? You don't care?" My tone came out loud, hysterics bubbling up my windpipe.

His jaw tightened, and he opened his mouth to speak, but no words came out at first.

I wanted to hurt him because I was hurt. But then he said, "I do care. And what matters now is that I forgive you."

I blinked, unsure I'd heard him correctly. How could a man take back a woman who'd slept with another man that quickly? Someone he supposedly loved and wanted to marry? None of this made any sense. "Forgive me? For what, exactly? We aren't together." My voice could've cut through glass.

When he didn't answer, I stomped my feet and threw both hands in the air. "For what? I want to *hear* what you forgive me for."

That lifted the fog of calm from his demeanor. He glared at me with burning reproachful eyes. "For fucking someone else when I've been faithful to you year after year." His temper flared, and anger reddened his face. "When I've been there for you through everything. That's what!" He shouted back, frustrated, but not hurt. There was no hurt behind his eyes.

I shook my head, the fight draining out of me. Clearly, I wasn't going to convince him of anything. "We were done when I was with Cade. I just want you to know that. And, yes, you may have never slept with anyone else, but there was always work in our relationship. You cheated on me for years with your crazy job."

"That's different, and you know it." He gripped my hand fiercely, the one that held the ten-ton anchor on my finger. "You're leaving him," he said with finality. "I'm not losing you to him."

I almost laughed. "Losing me?" What didn't he get? "You lost me many months ago."

I gritted my teeth, finally seeing the truth—his truth.

"This isn't about me anymore. This isn't about you wanting me because you think you can't live without me. This is about you winning." I tore my hand from his, my body shaking with my newfound realization.

My trembling fingers flew to my throat. It hurt to see Roland, the man I'd grown up loving for so long turn into someone I hardly recognized anymore. A man that didn't want to keep me because he loved me, but only because he wanted to win. He clearly stopped loving me long before we got to this point.

"It is, isn't it?" I asked, in a low tormented tone. "You just don't want to lose me to him or anyone. You don't want *to lose.*" My voice was small, barely audible as the realization set in. And the truth would set you free, they said. Above pride, above dignity, Roland didn't like to lose.

His laughter had an edge, cynical even. "You're crazy."

I placed both hands against my chest. "Crazy? Me? I just told you I slept with another man and here you are telling me you want me back in the blink of an eye and that you forgive me." He didn't even react, and I went on, my throat aching with desperation. "My mother found out about Cade and me a mere two days ago, and she tells you, and what do you do? You don't get mad. You try to trap me, but you know what, Roland? Like the billion times I've tried to tell you before—I'm done."

"You're wearing my ring," he said matter-of-factly.

I threw both hands up, unbelieving what I was hearing. "Not by choice. Everyone was there, and you backed me in a corner. You can't believe for a second that my silence meant yes."

"Stop acting crazy." His voice boomed with commanding authority.

This was pointless, the back and forth, the cunning cut downs.

I was done. Officially done with this conversation and endlessly done with Roland.

"You know what?" I said, turning to walk out of the room. "I am crazy. Crazy for another man." There it was, loud as a boom of fireworks in a silent night sky. My truth.

I placed the ring on the counter, walked out of the room, and out of his life for good.

CHAPTER 30

I JUMPED into my car and automatically reached for my cell. The phone rang and rang until it went to voice mail. And then I called again. When she didn't pick up, I called the house phone.

"Hello?" Her voice was pitched with panic as if her conniving behavior had been a figment of my imagination. "Angelica, is everything okay?"

I took a deep breath first so my voice would come out clear. "Is Dad with you? Are you in your room right now?" I debated on driving there and doing this face-to-face, but I wanted to save my father from heartache and stress. That had been the purpose of my idiotic silence at the restaurant, right? Why waste it now?

"Yes. Is everything okay?"

"Step out of the room, Mom." I was so done playing her games. It was time she listened.

She muffled something to my father, and I heard the rustle of the bed and a door shut before she got back on the phone.

"Angie, where are you?"

I breathed through my next words. "Did you tell Roland about Cade?" I knew she had, but I wanted her to admit it out loud.

"Angie ... I love you," she began, but I stopped her short before she tried to play on my emotions.

"It's over, Mom. With Roland, with you and your fantasies of getting to dictate what I want to do with my life. It's officially over." Tears nearly threatened to spill over, but I kept myself in check, kept my voice steady. There was no way I'd show her that she'd won, that she'd betrayed and hurt me in ways that were unforgivable, that her actions caused a permanent wedge between Cade and me.

"What did you do? Where's Roland?" Her tone was accusatory.

I blinked. Oh, my goodness. Did she think I offed him? Her voice was tinged with worry, which was not usually in my mother's vocabulary. "I told him we're not getting married."

She huffed, agitated, and aggravated. "You're making a big mistake, Angie. You have to think things through."

I pushed through my next words. "If you really loved me, Mom, you would've respected my decision, but you didn't." I had never once remembered raising my voice to my mother. That was Tene's job, but now I understood why. It was because I was the obedient one. I didn't break things, I fixed them. I could be controlled and Tene couldn't. And my mother couldn't handle things she couldn't control.

"Don't push this, Mother. Don't you dare push this any further, because if you don't accept my decisions in my life, then I don't want you in it."

I hung up before she got the last word in, then I took a deep breath and pushed my key in the ignition, driving to where my head and heart wanted to be—the restaurant.

I walked into the bar, my feet slow and deliberate. I shouldn't be here. Not so soon, anyways, yet nothing could keep me away from him. He was like a drug—addicting, exhilarating, and electrifying. Now that I'd had a taste of Cade, I couldn't go back to how I was, my life before him.

I stood by the door, fear and anxiety knotted my insides. I watched him wipe down the bar, worried out of my wits that I'd already lost him. Hours ago, I had been here, in front of another man down on one knee and pretending and lying to my family.

Guilt shook through me. It didn't matter that I was in front of my family and we had a slew of spectators watching us. I should've said no and not stand there, still silent. But I didn't. Because I was a coward.

I was just like Roland. My words said one thing, yet my actions spoke another.

I could only hope that by standing up to my mother and Roland tonight, things had changed. I just hoped I wasn't too late.

Beautiful tattoos highlighted his toned arms. I'd traced every one of them the other night with the tip of my fingers, now knowing what each one signified. God, what I'd give to run my hands over them now, to rewind time to just nights ago, when we'd made love.

I walked toward him, the sound of my heels clicking on the hardwood. As he turned around, my stomach plummeted to the floor and kept going.

The spark that had previously been in his eyes every time I entered the room was now gone, replaced with apprehension.

I waved my hand, dipping my chin as I approached.

"Hi." That's all I said because that's all I had. I had no words and sorry seemed overplayed. Roland had overused the word, and I'd been taking after him recently.

Cade rested both hands on the bar, his eyes dipping to the ground as though he didn't want to see me. *We are not ending*, I told myself. With my jaw clenched, I straightened my stance and moved forward, willing to fight for him—for us—because what we had was worth it.

The only thing that separated my body from his was the bar. "Please, look at me." My voice was shaky and fragile, just like my broken heart. I begged him to lift his head because I needed to see those hypnotic gray eyes, the eyes that drew me in like no others could.

And when he lifted his head, I saw the wariness had been replaced with war. The anger that I'd been waiting for, been expecting because anyone in his situation would have been livid at the predicament I'd put us in.

"What do you want?" His harsh tone made me jump, made me cower. I wrapped my hand around my middle, keeping myself together, keeping myself steady, straight.

I told him the truth. "I wanted to see you."

His nostrils flared as though I'd hit a nerve. He leaped over the bar, and I jumped back.

"See me? Why are you really here, Angel?" His head jerked up. "Or maybe you're not an angel, huh?" His voice seethed with mounting range. "Maybe you knew what you were doing all along. Playing me, my heartstrings and him like the player that you really are."

My eyes begged him to believe me. My tone was laced with heartbreaking regret. "It's not like that. I never said yes to Roland."

"Well you didn't say no, did you? I saw him put a ring on your finger."

His words were like a sucker punch in the gut, each word biting, hitting me, making me step back.

He kept on. "So, you get the boyfriend jealous, then he'll propose? Well, it fucking worked." His breath came out in loud, broken puffs and his features filled with a murderous rage, causing tears to well up behind my eyelids.

It took all my energy, all my might to keep them from falling, seeing that we had come to this. That our love—our passion—had come down to this hatred and knowing that this was my doing.

He stalked forward, and I retreated until the round table hit the back of my butt.

"I know what you want." He grabbed my forearms with such force and jerked me toward him.

He pushed his erection against my stomach. "Is this what you want?" His voice was distant, disconnected, disdainful. He tugged me forward again, the feel of his hard-on pushing through his jeans. "I know you came for this." He gripped my arms with such strength that the third time he pulled me in, tears fell, not from the impact, but from the unbearable hurt in my chest.

"Stop." My tone was whisper soft, broken like glass.

"Stop?" He laughed without humor, his voice incredulous, his eyes wide. "This is what you came for, right? I know this is what you want. Why you keep coming back."

He gripped my ass and shoved his length against my core, and I tensed, putting my hands up against his chest. "Stop." Tears cascaded down my face, the salt hitting my lips. Maybe, in the beginning, it had been the sex, but over the time we'd spent together, it had morphed into something more. Something special, and I was the only one to blame for its demise.

"P-please, Cade. Stop."

My words seemed to break him from the angry haze that controlled him.

He staggered back, releasing his grip. I peered up, and my tears blurred his figure. He ran one hand over the top of his black hair, and I cowered into myself, dropping my gaze to the floor and swiping desperately at my tears, hating how weak I felt in the moment. I had wanted to appear strong, win him back by fighting for him, and I was failing yet again.

With one step forward, he held both hands up. His chin lowered to his chest, his eyes defeated. "I'm sorry," he wheezed out, his voice cracking and thick with emotion. "I'd never hurt you—ever."

When I nodded, he closed the distance between us and cupped the side of my face, brushing the tears with his thumb as he leaned into me, his forehead against mine. "Never," he whispered.

He tapped his head against mine, so gentle. "I'm sorry." He tenderly kissed my head. "I'm so sorry." His lips trailed to my damp cheeks. "I want you all the time." His hard length pressed against my stomach again. "Even when I'm mad, even when I'm hurt."

He pushed into me. "I want this." He cupped the side of my face, his thumb gently brushing my cheek. "I want this." He kissed my lips, my cheek, my forehead, his touch light as a feather. "But I want this, too." He interlocked our fingers and placed them on my chest, over my heart. "I want this so badly because this—" He placed our hands on his heart now. "—is already yours."

The tears came down harder, faster, longer, and deep sobs racked my insides. "It's yours," I exclaimed with a mad desperation. "All of it."

"Last time I saw you, you were engaged." A small shudder ran through his body.

"I'm so sorry, Cade, it was for show, and I shouldn't have stayed silent and let that scene play out. I'm sorry," I gushed, emotional and anguished and wrecked. I shook my head fiercely and inhaled deeply through my nose. "My father was there, everyone was staring at me, and I cowardly gave in to the pressure when I knew that I wouldn't go through with it." I spoke with conviction and certainty and pure desperation. "I couldn't go through with it because he's not the man that I want to be with. Because I want to be with you."

He let out a huge unbelieving sigh and his eyebrows furrowed.

He's unsure about us. And I put that uncertainty there.

"I told Roland I wasn't going to marry him. I told my mother, too, because it's the truth. I know I've said a lot of things before, and my actions haven't always backed up my words, but before I came here tonight, I made things right. Made things right with them, so I could finally make things right with you."

My heart, my eyes, my soul were poured out for him to see. But when he tore his gaze from mine and stepped away, the spark of hope in me extinguished and a sensation of pure desolation swept over me. I was too late.

He dropped his hands, his arms limp at his sides. "I love you, Angel." He ran one shaky hand over his hair. "But ... but you were wearing *his* ring." He looked tortured as he drew in a deep breath. "And I just can't anymore. I can't do this back and forth." He pounded his chest with his fist, his eyes wary and defeated. "My heart is fucking breaking, and it's killing me. I ... I just can't."

Looking into the gray eyes that I loved so much, I knew

that nothing I said, nothing I could say, would matter because they were merely words, and my actions had failed him.

As he turned to walk away, tears blinded me and choked my voice. My heart shattered in a tiny million pieces at the finality in his eyes, at his words.

At the end of us.

CHAPTER 31

AFTER THE PITIFUL sorry-fest I had endured, the next day I picked myself up, went to work and drove straight to my parents' house right after, without apology, just how my mother had done in my car. My mom answered the door, but I was beyond pissed off to talk to her. I wasn't talking to her ever if I had a choice.

This was about owning up to my feelings, my life and living through actions, not words. So, as I straightened my back and stomped into my house, I knew without a doubt that I was going to tell my father that Roland and I were over. Cade or not.

I marched past her and to my father's favorite place in our whole house, the plush leather recliner in front of the television. His eyes were trained on the TV, and he hadn't noticed my arrival. He was slouched in his chair, looking a little frail, which made me stop midstep. For one brief nanosecond, I debated if I was doing the right thing, but then I shook my head and pushed forward.

"Angelica," my mother called out. "I'd like to talk to you

for a second." Her voice was soft, resigned, but I ignored her. I was done with her manipulation.

"I'm here for Dad," I said sternly without looking back.

My dad laughed, his whole belly shaking. "Is it me or did the temperature in the room just drop?"

I turned to my mother, jaw tense. "I want to talk to Dad *alone*."

"Honey ..." She stood at the living room archway, looking meek, but I wasn't falling for it.

I raised one hand to stop her. "Don't, Mom." Damn it. The back of my throat burned. My hands clenched, my nails biting into my palms. I was so angry, I was on the verge of tears. I tore my gaze away, not wanting her to witness my weakness. "Alone, please." I wished I was stronger. I wished I could've been a bitch, mouth off so I could hurt her, just like she hurt me, but I couldn't. Because it was taking every ounce of energy to simply shut her out.

"He knows, Angelica," she said finally. "Your father knows. I told him."

I blinked up at her, never more shocked in all my life. My gaze split between her unreadable face and my father's amused one.

He nodded, then his face softened before he took my hand. "Where is this handsome guy and when do I get to meet him?"

My head jerked back from the shock. Immediately I paced the room, my emotions a jumbled ball of havoc. She told him? He knows? And he's not even asking about Roland; he's asking about Cade.

My voice was hoarse and small. "Don't you want to know what happened with me and Roland? With Mom, with the night I got engaged?"

He sighed, his age-old wisdom showing on his face. "I

was there at your engagement, sweetheart, and I didn't see my happy Angie." He motioned me forward. "When Roland asked you to marry him, you know what you did?" He lowered his head and guilt rose to the surface of his brown irises. "You looked directly at me like it was my decision. Why would you look at me when Roland was asking you one very important question, especially when it wasn't my decision to make?" His forehead crinkled, and it took all my self-control not to reach over and smooth out the wrinkles. "I just want to ask you one thing. Does this man, this new guy ... does he make you happy?"

I nodded with a fierceness that was mirrored in my soul. "Completely, blissfully happy." I choked on my words, knowing that it didn't matter anymore because he was gone. He had made his decision. Cade wasn't mine anymore.

Dad smiled warmly, his eyes shining with emotion. "That's all that matters to me. Why would you think it wouldn't?" Then he gripped my hand, giving it a tight squeeze. "I love you, Angelica. All I ever want for you is happiness."

Big fat tears flowed down my cheeks like a river into a lake, and I bowed my head as tremors overtook me. My father pulled me closer with a tug. The gesture reminded me of those times when I was younger and had gotten hurt or a bad grade, and he'd been there to console me. "Angelica Michelle Armstrong, I know you're worried about me, but I want what you want, plain and simple."

He patted the back of my hair, taming the flyaways, soothing me.

"I ... I was scared," I choked out. "With your surgery, with his family being there ..." I sounded like a blubbering mess. "And with Mom. I had felt like I had no choice."

His voice lowered. "I already had a deep conversation with your mother."

"Angie ..." My mother began, but I held my hand up to stop her, wiping my tears which weren't for her to see.

"I don't want to hear it, Mom." I was tired. Tired of her and her games. I didn't care if she apologized a thousand times or if she got on her knees. Maybe our relationship would be repaired in the future, but I needed some space for a while.

She cupped one hand over her mouth while the other hand held her elbow. I could tell she wanted resolution. Well, I wanted to go back in time. We didn't always get what we wanted.

"One day you'll understand it," my father whispered to me. "The love you have for your child. The worry that never goes away. I'm definitely not saying what your mother did was right. It was wrong, and I think she realizes that."

A flash of grief tore through me, a huge, painful knot inside my chest.

"She only wants the best for you, and sometimes it leads her to be overbearing and controlling." His chest rumbled with a chuckle. "I know because she's the same way with me."

"Angie?" My mother's voice was even smaller.

I lifted my head, finally meeting her gaze.

"I ... I'm sorry." Her words whooshed out, as though she was afraid to say it. "I love you, but ... this time I took it too far."

I nodded, unable to form words, afraid again of crying further. Eventually, I'd forgive her, but it would take time to heal us.

"Look at me, Angie," he said, smiling. "I'm so proud of

you, little girl. For the person you've become. And I want to meet this person who makes you blissfully happy."

The soreness in my chest spread to my throat and lungs, constricting my airways. "It's too late." I sniffled. "He was there last night." Memories of last night, his reaction, him walking away ran through my head like a horrid nightmare. "He saw at the restaurant. Saw Roland down on one knee. Saw it all. He's left me." I swallowed a sob that failed to escape. "It's over. It's too late." Everything was out in the open. I no longer had anything to hide, yet it was all for nothing now.

With a firmness in his gaze and a tip of my father's chin, he said, "It's only too late if you've given up."

I blinked up at him, feeling like I was six years old.

He leaned in and lifted my chin up with the lightness of his fingertip. "So, Angelica, have you given up?"

CHAPTER 32

THE TIME on my car dashboard said 5:15. I was racing like my life depended on it, down the highway and through the streets to my destination—Allswell.

I parked in the first available spot and jetted out my car door, almost tripping in my four-inch work heels. I charged through the door and straight to the bar.

My chest heaved in and out, and I leaned on the counter for support. Super lucky for me, the first person that I ran into was none other than Kristy.

"Is Cade here?" I didn't have time to bullshit. My father's words had snapped me out of my fallen fog. I wasn't giving up on the love of my life without a hard fight.

She lifted her head for a brief second as she wiped up the bar and uttered the words that gutted me. "He's gone."

I ignored the way my heart clenched. It felt as though my breath had been cut off. "Do you know when he'll be back?"

She continued to wipe the bar without peering up. "He's not. He packed his stuff and went to Toline to finalize things at his new restaurant."

My shoulders dropped, and I pressed one hand to my abdomen. "Texas." My voice was barely above a whisper as a hopelessness spread through me.

The silence loomed between us like a heavy mist.

I closed my eyes and took a deep breath, and when I opened them, Kristy was staring directly at me. It must have been something in my voice, or maybe she read the sadness in my features because she asked, "Do you love him?"

I wasn't in the mood for her cut downs or her sly remarks. Of all days, not today. But her demeanor was without her normal rough edges.

I pressed both hands to my chest and spoke with such conviction and strength in my voice. "I love him so much." Because I did, I do.

Her eyes tightened. "You done with what's-his-face?"

My chin trembled, my body going limp against the bar. "I was never ever with him when Cade and I were together."

She cocked her head to one side as though to assess me, then said, "He's miserable. I've never seen him so fucking miserable. He left here like a sad lost puppy, and I know it's because of you." The rough tone in her voice was back, and her eyes narrowed.

Finally, I couldn't help but ask the question that had been burning in me since I met her. "Why do you hate me so much? What did I ever do to you?"

She rolled her eyes as if it stated the obvious. "You're not good enough for him."

Her words were like a cold shot of water in my face.

"Well, that's not your decision to make," I snapped. My back stiffened, my game face on and guard already up.

"But it's true, you're not," she went on casually. "Cade is a good guy wrapped in bad boy tattoos. He's got a heart of gold that you don't deserve, sweetheart." She shrugged.

"Cade is used to saving people. Redemption of sorts for Candice. Do you know I used to date him for a hot second? It didn't last too long. But he saved me, and a lot of us that grew up in Kritell."

My face must've registered confusion because she began to fill in the blanks. "Most of his managing staff and some of his cooking staff are from back home. He told everyone if people were willing to relocate and wanted to get away from the hood, then he'd help them get jobs."

I didn't think my heart could swell any bigger for the man I loved, but it did.

"So, yeah," She sucked in her cheeks, placed both palms against the bar and leaned in. "You're not good enough for him. But you're right, that's not up to me, is it?"

My voice hardened. "It's not."

She lifted an eyebrow, then jutted out her chin. "So, what are you still doing here, then?"

I blinked, a little shocked and a lot confused.

She huffed out a longsuffering sigh, then plucked out a small pad from her back pocket and scribbled down an address. "Get your ass moving," she said before pushing the piece of paper in my direction.

"Thank you." My voice was whisper soft, afraid the waterworks would start up again.

There was only one place I needed to be. And that was Toline.

━━━

After a crap load of money and booking a flight on the phone with the airlines, I landed in Toline, Texas with nothing other than my handbag, wallet, and phone. I inhaled the muggy scent of the humid air while my legs stuck to the leather seat of the cab.

When we passed by multiple bars, and the restaurants and high-end shops came closer in view, I knew we were close. My legs bounced with a jittery energy.

Then I saw it. I glanced at the paper in my hand, the one Kristy had slipped me. The address was on the door of the bar: Goodbar.

These men definitely had a theme going with their restaurants. Allswell, now Goodbar.

After I paid the cab driver and stepped out onto the sidewalk, I wiped my clammy hands on my shirt. I hoped that today, of all days, things would be in my favor.

I walked right in. Being a weeknight, the restaurant wasn't super packed, but still, a steady number of customers flowed in and out. Allswell was always busy, even during the weeknights. I had to believe that the grand opening hadn't taken place yet.

The decor was the same as Allswell. Circular tables in the middle of the floor, outlined by booths on the side. The lighting, the decor, the colors were all the same. If I closed my eyes, I could picture myself in Rosendell, at his bar. If I squeezed them tighter, I could feel the light touch of Cade's warm hands around me, the whiff of his cologne, and feel the hard span of his body against mine.

But we weren't in Rosendell, and Cade was no longer mine.

I straightened and took the biggest and longest heart-pumping breath of my life, then approached the bar, my eyes immediately seeking him. The bar was busy. Every seat was taken, and some patrons even standing around to be served.

And then I saw him. I stopped mid-step as I just stared

at him. Seeing him reminded me of the very first time we'd met.

God, was he beautiful. Simply breathtaking. It was the hard lines of his face and the darkness in his hair, the artistic line of every tattoo that had significance. He was beautiful, and, shit, I was going to win him back.

His head jerked up just as I took another step toward the bar. Then his eyes narrowed, deep steely gray met my brown ones. The emotions on his face flipped like the pages of a book—first surprise, then shock, then curiosity.

Actions over words, I silently told myself.

I walked toward him at a nervously slow pace, strong willed determination straightening my spine. I wished I could rewind to when he had jumped over the counter at Allswell that very first night we'd met, that very first time he'd asked me to dance.

With all of my heart, that's all I wanted—just to be close to him.

He leaned over the bar, and his eyebrows drew together in a cautious expression. "What are you doing here?"

I had to yell above the noise, above the music. "I need to talk to you." I bit my shaky bottom lip. "Please."

He scoured my face, seeming hesitant at first, then he raised a finger and pointed to the edge of the bar, where I walked around to meet him.

Cade stepped into me, his body overwhelmingly powerful and looming over my small frame. "What do you want?" His tone was tired, resigned.

I peered up into his eyes, and my initial instinct was to grab him, pull him down and kiss him with reckless abandon.

My mind was a jumbled mess like scattered Chinese characters, but I wanted him to hear me out. All I knew was that I wanted to start over, so I recited the words he'd said to me that first night. "Let's dance." That's all I had.

He studied me thoughtfully for a moment. "Angel, why are you here?"

I shook my head as full-blown emotions took over. "No," I said, wanting a do over. "This is where I start over. I say, 'Let's dance,' and you say, 'Okay'. Or you say, 'Let's dance,' and I say, 'Okay,' instead of 'I have a boyfriend.' I don't have a boyfriend, not anymore because he left me. Because I deserved it." I was talking about him, not Roland, as my words spilled out like a rapid fire. "Because I was stupid and couldn't stand up for myself because I was afraid, but I'm not afraid anymore. My parents know. They want to meet you. My father, especially. My mother has accepted this and ..."

His hands gripped mine and squeezed, stopping me mid-sentence. "Let's talk about this later."

"No, we're talking about this now." My voice heightened with hysteria. "Here. Or in the kitchen. But I'm not leaving until you hear what I have to say."

His face pinched, and his gaze dropped to the ground. "What makes now so different? Is it because I left? You only found the courage after I upped and left." His words flew out of his mouth with a bitter edge. "I figured it out. You just couldn't introduce the tattooed bartender to your parents when you had mister suit and tie at home. Tell the truth, Angel."

"That's not it!" I raised my voice, causing the people sitting on the stools to turn in my direction. "I'm sorry," I said, placing both hands on my chest. "I was afraid of my father's health. Afraid to cause a scene at that moment at Allswell. Just scared and I'm sorry. So, so sorry."

Our eyes locked in a silent tug-of-war, me wanting him

to forgive me, and his indecision that was causing both of us such anguish.

He let out one long shaky breath, and his gaze dropped to the ground. "I can't right now, Angel. Let's talk about this later."

And then my heart cracked, grief and despair shredding my insides because every single part of me knew I was going to lose him. I pushed back the tears and the emotions coursing through me. If I left here without him today, it would be for good. Final.

And I couldn't have that.

Every single customer in the bar and the surrounding tables was staring at me—the crazy person yelling in the bar and pouring out her emotions like she was on some soap opera.

Go big or go home.

I lifted my chin as the worst ever idea popped into my head, and I decided to do something so unlike me.

I hopped on the bar, butt first, then stood. I looked like a fool, felt like a fool, and I was a fool—a fool in love.

Everyone's eyes were on me, and this whole thing felt like a really bad rom com, super cheesy, but desperation rocked my core.

"I love you," I shouted, fixing my stare directly on Cade. "So much. I've been in love before, but never like this. Never like this because it wasn't you." Both of my hands flew to my chest. Then I directed my attention to everyone in the room. "I love that man, tattoos and all." I pointed to Cade, then cupped both hands to my chest. "I wasn't able to tell my family before because I was scared." Adrenaline and fear shook my body. The fear of losing him, but I pushed through, courage straightening my spine. Because I needed to win him back.

My eyes met his, glossed over with tears. "But they know now, and I want the whole world to know that I love Cade Ryder. I want to shout it from the rooftops. I. Love. Cade. Ryder!" I yelled, looking and sounding crazy, my arms spread wide.

I felt vulnerable and open as everyone witnessed my declaration. "It's not only his good looks but his unbelievable good heart. I love him so much it hurts when I'm not with him. He's all I think about, all I dream about, all I want." But I swallowed back a choked sob. "But I messed things up, and ... and I just hope to God I'm not too late. Am I ... am I too late?"

My voice quivered, and I stood in front of him, on top of the bar, both hands on my chest, waiting for his response. He held my world in his one answer. The answer that could unlock my happiness.

I could read the swirl of emotions running rampant through his irises. Irises that were a deep, steely hypnotic gray.

"Take her back," Someone said, breaking the silence. Then the chants of 'take her back' began.

Mere seconds staring into his eyes seemed like a lifetime.

"Fuck it." Suddenly a broad-shouldered male sitting at the bar stood up. "I'll take you, beautiful lady."

That seemed to break Cade from his trance because he stepped forward. "Sorry, sir, you can't." His eyes met mine, gray, powerful and unwavering. Then he extended his hand. "Because she's already taken. She's mine."

Tears nearly burst through when I peered down to see the devotion, the longing, but mostly love through his eyes.

My hands met his, and I bent down to get off the bar, but not before he swooped me up in his arms.

The crowd's cheers became a deafening roar around us, and he smiled, the crooked smile, the smile I loved.

I wrapped my arms around his neck and snuggled closer. "I'm sorry. So sorry."

The heart rending tenderness of his gaze was over-whelming. "No more 'I'm sorries' in this relationship. Only 'I love yous' from now on," he whispered. The nearness of him made my head spin. "He may have been your first love..." His burning eyes held me still. "But I'm your last. Forever love."

I angled closer, pecked his lips, and whispered, "Forever and ever, amen."

Then he met my lips in the most soul crushing, body melting, panty dropping kiss—a kiss that scorched my insides and one that touched the inner most part of my heart.

Our kiss deepened, in front of the crowd. When he pulled back, his breathing was labored, so was mine.

He motioned with one hand and lifted his head to someone behind me. "A round for everyone, on the house. I'll be right back."

Hoots and hollers echoed throughout the room.

He deepened his kiss and bit my bottom lip. "I've missed you," he said, carrying me away from the noise, the crowd, the chaos, and through the doors that led to the back. "I'm about to show you how much."

My stomach did non-stop flips, but that was nothing to the pounding of my happy, love-filled heart because he was mine.

EPILOGUE

IT HAD BEEN two weeks since Cade and I had reunited in his office at Goodbar. We had texted and talked on the phone constantly. He said he'd been busy with work, setting up in Toline, and a big part of me believed I was repeating my past.

But just when those thoughts filtered through my mind, I'd take a step back and remind myself that Cade was not Roland and that I was not the same person I used to be.

I would no longer take shit. So, I took the time to get all my work in order, to make sure all my tenants were happy, their rents were collected, and everything was fixed at the properties. I also took the two weeks to put all my Roland memories into boxes.

I was pushing boxes into my closet when I heard a knock on the door. I frowned. The doorman didn't call. I wasn't expecting anyone.

My feet padded across the bedroom carpet and onto the hardwood floors that led to the front door.

I glanced through the peephole, but someone was covering it.

"Hello, who's there?"

"Are you going to make me stand here all day, or are you going to come and open this door, so I can kiss you?"

Cade.

I pulled open the door and jumped into his arms, squealing with delight. His wide eyes showed me I had caught him by surprise, and then I saw that he was carrying a bag of groceries in one hand. But he easily held that bag tight while also anchoring me against his hip, cradling my butt as he carried me inside my apartment.

My hands were in his hair, my chest against his, my legs wrapped around his waist and my lips were connected to his.

"I missed you," I said, with a flick of my tongue against his lips.

"I can tell," he chuckled.

He dropped the brown paper bag on the floor. "I've missed you, too."

And all of a sudden, it was like fire melting ice.

The air blasting in the room was no comparison to the heat coursing through my body.

"Show me how much you've missed me," I whispered against his lips, anchoring my body against him.

He pressed his hardness against my center, and I gasped at the contact, at the strength of him, at the sizzle of spice between us. He pushed us against the wall, his strong thighs holding me up. With one hand, he pulled down my shorts and slipped a finger inside me. His lips trailed a path of blazing kisses from my ear down to my neck, his finger working its magic, making me slick.

I missed this man, my man. Oh God, how I missed him.

"Is this how you want me to show you?"

I moaned from the sensual friction he was creating

and the burning desire inside me heightened. "Yes." My voice was hoarse, and my body was horny and hungry for him.

I pushed at his chest, and he flinched, which stopped me. I assessed his face and stepped back, but in the next beat, he said, "Come here." He unbuttoned his jeans, shoved them down to the floor, followed by his boxers, and grabbed my waist.

Our eyes locked and that was all it took for him to anchor me against the wall and enter me all at once.

My eyes fluttered shut at the impact, at the fullness of him, at the heat of him inside of me. He gripped my hips and rammed into me, his lips falling to the crook of my neck. All I could hear was the panting of our breaths, all I could feel was the sensation of his body against mine, all I could smell was the aroma of our heat.

His eyes were at half mast, his movements erratic. He wasn't going to last long, but neither was I.

I loved the feel of him inside of me, balls deep inside of me, ravenous as though he couldn't get enough.

"You feel so good, Angel," he said, pounding into me with fiery fervor like I was his first breath and his last.

I shifted until he hit that certain spot and my moans heightened. His head dropped to the crook of my neck, his movements faster, harder, sweeter. Then my orgasm rippled through my body. One after the other, a never-ending tidal wave of pure, exhilarating ecstasy.

He came undone when I did, and with one final groan and last thrust, he slowed until he stilled in me. Our chests heaved from exhaustion, and our hearts raced against each other, beating as one.

When our pulses returned to a normal rate, he lifted his head and kissed me with a passion I'd only ever experienced with him. "Hello," he said when he pulled back. "I don't think we said hello yet."

"Yes, we did." I laughed, nipping at his bottom lip. "That was the hottest hello ever. I think we should greet each other like that all the time."

He caressed my cheek with his fingers and scoured my face like it was the first time he was seeing me. He dipped his head so he could lock his eyes with mine so I could know the sincerity, the truth, the impact of his words. "I love you so much, Angel. So much."

His words filled me with such happiness, the kind that you couldn't contain. My insides soared because he made me feel like the most beautiful person in the whole entire world and I just knew with all my heart and soul that we were it for each other.

I smiled. "You just love me because your Angel is no longer an angel. You've officially corrupted her."

A deep chuckle rumbled from his chest, and I felt it everywhere. "That, too." He gently placed me on my feet, and it took me a couple of seconds to not feel like the earth was shaking. "And just so you know, you'll always be *my* Angel. Mine."

I didn't miss the emphasis on the word.

After he pulled up his pants, he took my hand and pulled me into him. "I've missed you."

"I think that was already established."

He kissed the top of my head and moved my hair from my forehead. "How's your dad?"

"He has to do therapy for a couple of months, but otherwise he's like his old self again."

He kissed my cheek, then my lips. "That's good."

I peered to the side to see the brown bag that Cade had dropped on the floor. "What did you bring me?"

"Condoms." He wiggled his eyebrows, chuckling. "But I think it's a little too late for that now."

"Rude." I slapped his chest, and he closed his eyes, wincing. "What's the matter?" Instantly, I grabbed his face, forcing him to look at me.

"Tat-Tattoo," he uttered, gritting his teeth.

"Oh, I'm so sorry, babe." I stepped back, and he lifted his shirt to show me a section of white gauze covering his upper left pec. "I had to get it retouched because it wasn't perfect."

"What is it?"

When he lifted the gauze from his skin, my stomach flipped. One hand flew to my mouth, while I took in the beautiful figurine outline of an angel. It wasn't her face that was exquisite, it was the strength and span and mightiness of her wings, the colors a beautiful array of blues and greens and yellows.

"It's beautiful." I inched closer, getting a better look.

"You're beautiful." His eyes were shining with an inner glow. "Years down the road, when I think back to this year and what has had an impact on me the most, it would have been you, Angel. I'm more selfish now, but a lot happier now that you're in my life."

I knew exactly what he meant. I had to admit I was more selfish now, too. We were no longer living for other people but living for ourselves. And that wasn't a bad thing because I'd never been happier.

He added, "And that bag has eggs, cocoa, flour and a bunch of other baking stuff."

I quirked an eyebrow, curious.

"Since birthday cakes signify new beginnings for you." His gaze dropped to the ground, seeming a little sheepish. "I figured we could start our new beginning with cake, anniversary cakes."

I sucked in my bottom lip and nuzzled closer against my man, loving his sentiment and knowing there would be many more anniversary cakes in our future.

"I love it. And after we bake cake, maybe we can *eat* cake," I said, lifting one sexy eyebrow.

He didn't miss the way my voice dropped seductively.

"We'll add that to our annual tradition," he said, kissing me one more time.

And then we baked a cake. And ate it, too.

THE END

Loved this story? Want to know when Jordan's book releases? Sign up for my newsletter. Plus you never know when these characters may pop on by.

You can sign up at *www.authormiakayla.com*.

ABOUT THE AUTHOR

Mia Kayla is a New Adult and Contemporary Romance writer who lives in Illinois. She is the wife to the husband of the year and mommy to three unbelievable cute little girls who have multiplied her grey hairs.

In her free time she loves reading romance novels, jamming to boy bands, catching up on celebrity gossip and designing flowers for weddings.

Most of the time, she can be caught on the train with her nose in a book sporting a cheeky grin because the main characters finally get their happily-ever-after at the end.

She loves reading about happy endings but has more fun writing them.

ACKNOWLEDGMENTS

Whooo weee! The first book in the The Ryder Brothers is done.

Like always, it took any army and I'm forever grateful to everyone that has encouraged me and in some way, shape or form contributed to making this book the best it can possibly be.

Once again, I thank God for that creative side of me that can't keep quiet, the crazy characters that can't shut up and for my fingers so I can continue to tip-tap-typing away these crazy stories.

To the hubs and my kids—Thanks for letting mommy disappear sometimes in the car outside karate, or inside my room, when I'm on a deadline. I hope my journey teaches you that you can have it all— a family, a successful career and all your dreams brought to life.

To my super-awesome-to-the-max editing team—Gwen, Megan, Mitzi and Marisa. Thank you so much for helping me dig deeper to bring out the best in these characters and keeping me in check with punctuation and making sure my words make sense.

To my writer friends that keep me accountable and listen to me vent day in and day out— To Michelle, I don't know what I'd do without you, truly. I heart you big time, writer wife. To Tracey, goodness gracious, thanks for listening to me vent and being just a really good friend throughout this whole process.

To my great author friends in Indie Chicks, Do Not Disturb and Alpha & Fairytales—thank you so much. Only writers understand the struggles and insecurities of this journey and I appreciate each and every one of you. You guys keep me sane and truly understand that the struggle is real.

To my PA—Emily, you keep me organized and sane and happy. Love you long time.

To Jessica—Thank you for your constant lifting words, your non-stop encouragement and reading the very first drafts of this book. I heart you like no other. You truly have a gift for what you do.

To my friend Jenn—Thanks for helping me out through the whole stress of release. I know I can always count on you and your constant support of the Indie Chicks.

To Kristy—Thanks for being truthful about everything —from the book to the cover. Your opinion and friendship means the world.

To my PR team from Sassy Savy Fabulous—Kristi, thank you so much for helping me market this book and keeping me organized as it relates to releasing. Ena from Enticing—Thank you so much for taking this new-to-you author on and pimping out this book.

To my cover designer—Sommer, thank you for putting your magic touch on my covers. To Wander—I love my book cover and it wouldn't be perfect without the picture on it.

To Daniella—I love my teasers. You truly have a gift of integrating the perfect picture with my words.

To my beta readers—Amy, Alyssa, Emily, Elizabeth, Jenn, Kris and Michelle—I appreciate your feedback and also your friendship. I know you guys were super busy but you still took time out of your day to help me tighten this story. Without you, this book wouldn't be what it is now.

To the bloggers that have consistently supported me from my very first book to now. I heart you! Obsessed with Romance, Divas Book Lounge, Sarah Reads— thank you for following me on this journey.

Last but not least to my readers— From those who have followed me from my very first book and to the new readers, thank you! thank you! thank you! I write for you.

ALSO BY MIA KAYLA

The Torn Duet
Torn Between Two - Book 1
Choosing Forever - Book 2

The Forever After Series
Marry Me for Money - Forever After Book 1
Love After Marriage - Forever After Book 2
The Scheme - Brian's book -Forever After Book 3
Naughty Not Nice - Forever After Book 4

Stand Alone
Everything Has Changed